DADDY'S DIRTY LITTLE SECRET

AN AGE GAP, SECRET PREGNANCY,
WORKPLACE ROMANCE

SOFIA T SUMMERS

Copyright © 2025 by Sofia T Summers
All rights reserved.

The following story contains mature themes, strong language and sexual situations. It is intended for mature readers.

No part of this book may be reproduced in any form or by any electronic or mechanical means, including information storage and retrieval systems, without written permission from the author, except for the use of brief quotations in a book review.

OTHER BOOKS BY SOFIA T SUMMERS

Billionaire Baby Daddies
Knocked Up by the Silver Fox | Silver Fox's Twin Babies | Daddy's Double Surprise | Daddy's Dirty Little Secret

Forbidden Fantasies
My Irish Billionaires | Toy for the Teachers | Three Grumpy Bosses | Feasting on Her Curves | 4 SEAL Daddies | Ice Cold Hearts | Nanny for the Bratva Daddies | The Professors' Plaything | Age Gap Academy | Snowbound with the Santas | The Naughty Elf | Pucked and Pregnant | Power Play with My Brother's Irish Friends | The SEALs' Single Mom Baby Surprise | Campus Daddies

Forbidden Doctors
Doctor's Surprise Twins | Written in the Charts | Rendezvous with My Resident | The Doctor's Twin Secrets | My Ex Boyfriend's Dad | Secret Baby for Dr. Dreamy | The Doctor's Secret | Baby Bump | Doctor Baby Daddy | Wi-Fi Wifey | Dirty, Bossy Doctor | Code Blue | Doctor Daddy Dilemma | Doctor's Orders | Dr. Wrong | Grumpy Doctor's Holiday Twins | Dr. Scandal Claus

Forbidden Temptations

Daddy's Best Friend | My Best Friend's Daddy | Daddy's Business Partner | Doctor Daddy | Secret Baby with Daddy's Best Friend | Knocked Up by Daddy's Best Friend | Pretend Wife to Daddy's Best Friend | SEAL Daddy | Fake Married to My Best Friend's Daddy | Accidental Daddy | The Grump's Girl Friday | The Vegas Accident | My Beastly Boss | My Millionaire Marine | The Wedding Dare | The Summer Getaway | The Love Edit | The Husband Lottery | Christmas in the Cabin | A Very Naughty Christmas | Make Me Whole | Take a Chance

Forbidden Promises

Maid Without Honour | The Wedding Witness | Honeymoon Hoax

Join Sofia's mailing list here to get notified of her new releases, exclusive bonus content, and other updates.

OTHER BOOKS BY SOFIA T SUMMERS

Billionaire Baby Daddies
Knocked Up by the Silver Fox | Silver Fox's Twin Babies | Daddy's Double Surprise | Daddy's Dirty Little Secret

Forbidden Fantasies
My Irish Billionaires | Toy for the Teachers | Three Grumpy Bosses | Feasting on Her Curves | 4 SEAL Daddies | Ice Cold Hearts | Nanny for the Bratva Daddies | The Professors' Plaything | Age Gap Academy | Snowbound with the Santas | The Naughty Elf | Pucked and Pregnant | Power Play with My Brother's Irish Friends | The SEALs' Single Mom Baby Surprise | Campus Daddies

Forbidden Doctors
Doctor's Surprise Twins | Written in the Charts | Rendezvous with My Resident | The Doctor's Twin Secrets | My Ex Boyfriend's Dad | Secret Baby for Dr. Dreamy | The Doctor's Secret | Baby Bump | Doctor Baby Daddy | Wi-Fi Wifey | Dirty, Bossy Doctor | Code Blue | Doctor Daddy Dilemma | Doctor's Orders | Dr. Wrong | Grumpy Doctor's Holiday Twins | Dr. Scandal Claus

Forbidden Temptations
Daddy's Best Friend | My Best Friend's Daddy | Daddy's Business Partner | Doctor Daddy | Secret Baby with Daddy's Best Friend | Knocked Up by Daddy's Best Friend | Pretend Wife to Daddy's Best Friend | SEAL Daddy | Fake Married to My Best Friend's Daddy | Accidental Daddy | The Grump's Girl Friday | The Vegas Accident | My Beastly Boss | My Millionaire Marine | The Wedding Dare | The Summer Getaway | The Love Edit | The Husband Lottery | Christmas in the Cabin | A Very Naughty Christmas | Make Me Whole | Take a Chance

Forbidden Promises
Maid Without Honour | The Wedding Witness | Honeymoon Hoax

Join Sofia's mailing list here to get notified of her new releases, exclusive bonus content, and other updates.

DESCRIPTION

I slept with my boss.
My dad's best friend.
The billionaire who bought out our company... then bent me over his desk and made me forget my own name.

Xander Blackwell is forty-one, ruthless, and dangerously off-limits.
He signs my paychecks.
He owns my body.
And now—without knowing it—he's the father of my baby.

It was supposed to be one night.
A drunk mistake.
Just his rough hands, filthy promises, and no strings attached.

But then I saw two pink lines.
And I ran.
I quit. Disappeared. Left behind an empty desk and a trail of silence.

Now, I am not just running from my mistakes.

My dad owes **Victor Hayes**—a loan shark who doesn't take no for an answer.
And now... he's watching me, circling like a predator.

I'm hiding in a run-down motel, clutching my belly and my secret, when my phone lights up.

Unknown Number: *Found you, sweetheart. Time to come home.*
My blood turns to ice.

Because I don't know who's coming for me—
Xander Blackwell... or the man who wants to use me as payment for Daddy's sins.

1

XANDER

Applause vibrated the room after my comment, and I raised my glass to silence the team. Forty-two developers, ten program managers, nearly twenty project managers, analysts, office staff, you name it; and all of them attended our New Year's Eve bash, where I stood at the microphone giving my obligatory speech.

"Thank you ..." My voice was barely audible as their cheers died down, but they graciously grew quiet to allow me to continue. "The final quarter of last year was the best we've seen as a company since I took over." I nodded at Laurence, my former partner, who made his appearance tonight despite protesting my invitation. He had his arm around his daughter's waist, chuckling with her about something.

Both of them had eyes that sparkled with drink, though the tap hadn't shut off all evening so I was sure they weren't the only ones slightly inebriated. I myself felt the buzz of alcohol as vibrantly as the buzz of excitement. This year would be the turning point for the company started by Laurence and passed on to me after our brief partnership. I felt it in my bones.

"And thank you for your hard work and dedication to our goals." More applause went up, which I couldn't help but wonder if the cause was more to do with the event than the hard-fought success of our final quarter. "We will double our profit sharing by midyear, and triple it by this time next year if we stick together and work hard."

Laurence nodded and clapped his hands as Amelia slipped out of his grasp. At twenty-six, she was already an integral part of this team. She'd been that way before I even bought Laurence out, and I kept her on when I learned she knew our clients and accounts better than anyone. Eighteen months ago, I hardly knew her, but today she had proven herself to be essential to the function of this business—just not while she was as tipsy as she was this evening.

"And thank you for your continued effort to make Next Gen the biggest development firm in the country. To all of you—for your hard work, sacrifice, and dedication." Raising my glass in the air, I signified that my speech was done, and the team erupted into more cheers and applause. I heard glasses clinking together across the room as I stepped to the side and down the stairs. I wanted to catch up with Laurence before he left for the evening, and with the number of people here, I hadn't been able to say hello yet.

I weaved through the crowd decked out in their most formal attire. Women wore heels and gowns, dripping in jewelry, and men wore their best suits. It wasn't often our gang of nerdy backroom coders got to gussy themselves up, so tonight felt like a treat, even to me. I hadn't worn this old tuxedo in years, though my strict office dress code for myself always included a suit and tie.

Still, it was nice to see everyone enjoying themselves, and I didn't mind the expense. When I bought Next Gen from Laurence it was booming. We went through a small slump, which we were still digging out of thanks to Amelia's help, and I felt we were finally on our way skyward again.

I passed Amelia on her way toward the drink table and she grinned at me. I could've sworn she winked too, but that wasn't unlike her. She had a bit of a bubbly personality I'd grown to tolerate. It brought a beam of sunshine into the stodgy work environment, though at times I had to ask her to tone it down for my own sanity.

She seemed to be enjoying herself as I strutted up to her father and accepted a drink from a nearby waitress.

"What a turnout," Laurence said, whistling through his teeth. He had his own glass of champagne, sipping from the flute in his hand. "I don't think we had a single celebration or team meeting for that matter that was as well attended." His eyes raked over the mass of moving bodies. More than one hundred employees now, grown from the seventy-five he had when I took over.

"It is a good turnout," I agreed, matching his pose. "The team gets along well. I'm proud to call them my staff."

Laurence and I had a bit of a colorful past. When it was time to hand over the reins, he had a hard time doing so. It was his baby, something he built from scratch with Amelia's help, so I couldn't blame him for having a difficult time letting go. But we were still thriving, doing well. It was the reason I invited the former owner, my former partner, to come to the company New Year's party.

"You're doing well, Xander. I'm proud of where you're taking things." His hand gripped my bicep and he squeezed, then nodded at a passing analyst. She made eyes at me, batting her eyelashes. Clearly, she'd had too much to drink.

I ignored it, but Laurence whistled under his breath and elbowed me gently. "Seems like the ladies still enjoy the eye candy." His chuckle made me smile and join him. But a sigh cleared the air between us.

"I'm not dipping my toes into that water, Larry. You know I'm too much of a player to do it. It'd screw with company dynamics." My eyes unconsciously wandered the room, searching for the one person who always got my attention, the one person I knew was completely off-limits to me.

And I found her moving in my direction, chestnut hair swaying, hazel eyes darting around the room working the crowd. Those thick curves never ceased to amaze me, though I'd tempered my reaction to her appearance so well over the years that I could finally interact in a professional way without letting my lust for her fog my brain.

"Boss," she chirped, grinning as she stopped in front of her father.

"It's a great party." I could see the glossy film of alcohol over her eyes and knew she was feeling good, maybe not wasted, but definitely tipsy.

"I'm glad you're enjoying it." My eyes stayed on her face, though if Laurence weren't here, I'd let them glide down over her curves and enjoy the view. "Thank you for coming, Amelia, and thanks for making sure the old man came too." I winked at her father and nudged him with my elbow, which was his signature move.

Laurence downed his drink and nodded at me as he handed me the empty glass. "This 'old man' has to go home. It's past midnight now. I've kissed the beautiful lady." He grinned at Amelia and continued, "And I am ready for bed."

"Oh, Dad," Amelia whined playfully. She loved him so much; it was evident every time I watched them interact. I knew life hadn't been easy for her at times, losing her mother so young, and she had a bond with her father like no other. They were often seen doing menial things like banking and grocery shopping, just to keep each other company. I adored it, on top of her pragmatic and practical business sense.

She wasn't just an employee; she was like family now. She had been for a while, which made her all the more off-limits—but try telling that to my dick. When she was around, I was on high alert, tripping over my words, drooling and admiring how attractive she was. It was no surprise to me that she had a power over Laurence to make him give her everything she wanted. I'd have laid down across broken glass and let her walk across my back.

"I don't want to go yet. The party is still going strong." Amelia grabbed his hand and tugged on it. "Stay a bit longer …"

Laurence sighed and checked his watch. I knew it was late for a guy his age. He had a few years on me yet, but at forty-one, midnight was pushing it for me too. That catnap in my car on the way here was the only reason I was still bopping around.

"I am too tired, Mimi." Laurence's pet name was sweet, but it didn't dissuade her.

"I don't want to pay an Uber. It'll take ages to get one this time of night on New Year's, and it'll cost me half a month's rent. You can just sleep in the car. I'll sober up and drive home." Her pleading wasn't moving him this time. I could see the way his eyes creased in the corner and remembered all too well his mannerisms when he wasn't happy, so I cut in.

"I'll bring her home, Larry. Go on. Get some rest." With a flick of the wrist, it settled the tension between them, and Amelia squealed and pecked her father on the cheek.

"Thanks, Xander. I'm gonna get another drink. Love you, Dad. Be safe," she called, and then she was gone, and both of us were watching her saunter across the room. But I knew for a fact Laurence wasn't thinking what I was thinking. Those thighs would feel great wrapped around my face.

"Thanks, Xander. I'll owe you one." Laurence rubbed his forehead and jerked a thumb over his shoulder. "I'm heading out. Just don't let her drink too much. She's twenty-six, but she has no clue how to handle her liquor."

I chuckled as he walked off and then turned to look for her again, but she was gone, vanished into the crowd of bodies dancing to the music, celebrating the new year. I hadn't intended for the evening to go this way, but I wasn't complaining. Amelia wanted to enjoy the party, so I made it my job to ensure she did, even if my mind was thinking wildly inappropriate things about her. After all, I was just helping a friend out, right?

2

AMELIA

The music crept upward in volume the later the night went, and I was only mildly annoyed by Godwin's sniffles and coughing, which kept him sidelined on a stool rather than the middle of the dance floor where I wanted to be.

"Gosh, I hate that you feel sick," I told him, unable to keep my hips from swaying and my tits from bouncing. The beat was infectious. Whoever Xander hired to do the music seemed to understand the minute the older crowd started heading home for the night meant it was time to crank up the volume and spice up the dance tunes.

"I'm sorry, babe. You go dance." He fanned his hand at me, but I wasn't leaving him to sit here alone. Godwin was my best friend and not well received by most of our coworkers. His body was under the weather but that didn't mean I had to desert him.

"Are you crazy? You're the best dancer here. I'm not leaving you to sit here alone." I laced my fingers through his and kept moving my hips as he smiled at me weakly. Our friendship had no boundaries. When he ate, I ate. When he drank, I drank. When he got sick, I got sick too. We shared everything. And though the night was winding down and he'd be going home soon, I kind of wanted the distraction.

"If you don't let me go, I'm going to throw up on you." Godwin's playful warning was enough to make me shy away.

"The alcohol?" I asked, wincing as I lowered my body onto a chair.

"I think I'm really coming down with something." He sighed and rubbed his temples. "I think I'm gonna head home. I have to make a clinic appointment or something." He stood and I frowned at him, pushing my bottom lip out in an exaggerated manner. "Don't give me that. You've been makin' eyes at the boss man all night anyway. Bet you can't wait to get a ride home."

Godwin smirked at me as he grabbed his jacket and slung it around his shoulders. He'd been privy to more than one of my naughty-girl venting sessions where I'd divulged my secret crush on our boss. Except, he wasn't supposed to mention it out loud, nor was he supposed to tease me about it.

"Just stop," I said as I pinched his arm. "You're not allowed to pick on me about that." My body thrummed with extra energy, and I wondered why they said alcohol was a downer. I was most certainly not down at all. I was loose and uninhibited, and really quite horny too. "It's not my fault liquor gets me all worked up."

"No, but you could've gone home with your pops, and you made a show of wanting a ride home right in front of him. Would you just seal the deal already?" he gushed and slid his arms into his jacket before picking up his coat. "And give me all the marvelously juicy details."

I just imagined Godwin picturing some really raunchy things, and it made me laugh so hard I snorted. "That's not going to happen —ever," I protested, but if Xander Blackwell even so much as looked in my direction, my panties would be in his pocket. There was never mistaking that.

"Good luck with that, honey," Godwin said, pressing a kiss to my cheek. "I'll see you Monday. And you call me when you get home to let me know you're safe."

I caught Xander watching me say goodbye, but I couldn't help the way I looked at him. He studied me, and I swore there was a hint of jealousy in his eyes, but he had nothing to be jealous of. Godwin was as gay as a rainbow and had it bad for someone in accounting. And maybe I was seeing things, imagining Xander had the same lusty crush on me I had on him.

"I'll call," I said, but I was distracted, my attention torn away by the smoldering way Xander looked at me.

When Godwin sauntered off, I looked around the room. The place was starting to empty out; there were only about ten people left, all beginning to clean up. The music was still loud, but it was obvious the party was over now. A tinge of disappointment threatened to soil my mood until I remembered Xander was giving me a ride home, and I always loved time alone with him, though it didn't happen that often.

My eyes traced back to the spot he'd been standing moments ago, but he was gone, moving around the room now, speaking to people, probably saying his goodbyes. Not quite ready for the night to be over, I grabbed my sweater and slurped the rest of my drink before heading in the general direction I'd seen Xander vanish.

Balloons on the floor kicked up as I walked; the streamers in the doorway brushed my tousled hair and I swatted at them. The oversized conference room had been transformed into a party hall for the evening, but I saw the cleaning crew pushing their wheeled garbage cans up the hall to transform it back to the normal work environment.

I tracked up the hallway toward Xander's office, passing mine along the way. My coat was still draped over my chair, my office light still on. I had shown Dad my new digs compliments of Mr. Blackwell, who had taken the past several months to entirely redesign the office space up front to be more aesthetically pleasing to clients coming in. After one too many meetings being crammed into the old, much smaller conference room he had tripled the size of it too.

His light was on in his office, calling for me to come closer. My head spun a little from the alcohol, but not too badly. I wasn't the speech-slurring, blackout drunk sort of buzzed. I just wanted to rip my clothes off and turn the music up to have more fun. But that wasn't necessarily okay either, especially since I was going to be in close quarters with Xander, alone—and I'd been admiring his good looks and commanding personality for forever.

"Hey," he said as I swayed into his office. I hated that my body wasn't under my full control to some extent, so I sat down in the chair by his door to look a bit less obviously drunk. I also loved that the pulse of arousal warmed my body to a feverish degree, making me fan myself when he smiled at me. "You feeling okay?"

"Just had a bit to drink," I said, snickering. I hiccupped and covered my mouth, hoping he didn't hear it. It felt like my body temperature rose another thirty degrees instantly; my cheeks were probably bright red. I thought of how many times I'd checked him out tonight, how the rush of arousal when he agreed to bring me home had soaked my panties. I thought of every time I saw him looking at me and wondered what he was thinking, and my eyes rose up to meet his.

"I'd say ... It's a good thing you have a sober driver," he commented, then continued. "You look nice this evening. It's not often I see the crew dressed to the nines." His eyes raked over me, lingering on my chest for a moment. I was not mistaken at all—he was noticing me.

"You always look good," I said awkwardly, followed by: "Like James Bond in that black tux." I couldn't believe how silly I sounded, but the compliment seemed to work. In my head it seemed so much sexier, but when I said it, the words sounded juvenile. Xander smirked at me and picked up his phone, sliding it into his suit pocket before picking up his outer jacket.

"You ready for that ride?" he asked, moving toward me, but my mind was in a very dirty place by that point.

"I'd ride you home." I stood slowly, using the wall for support as he passed by. He didn't see me wobble a little, and I tugged the hem of the fitted dress lower, which only made the collar dip lower, exposing more cleavage, which wasn't the point. It did, however, catch his attention when he turned to wait for me to leave his office.

"Amelia," he commented, pausing a second. I thought he was

going to question my flirting, but he held out his hand waiting. I took a few stutter steps toward my office, and he shut and locked his office door, then followed me toward mine. I purposefully swayed my hips a little extra, though I wasn't sure what had gotten into me. Maybe it was Godwin's comment about Xander or maybe it was the alcohol.

Everyone in this office knew Xander was a bit of a playboy. He'd never made a move on anyone who worked for him, but he was known to have a different woman around every few months. I thought about flirting with him on more than one occasion, but my better judgment always silenced that inner urge. He was my boss and my dad's good friend, and he was so far out of my league they'd need a space shuttle to get me close enough to orbit him.

"Forget something?" he asked as I stepped into my office to grab my coat, phone tucked into the pocket.

"Yeah, I forgot how hot you are before I drank so much." My muttered reply, followed by my drunk snickering, made the space between us crackle with electricity. Xander fought a grin as I shrugged into my coat and walked toward him. His eyes narrowed on me and he dipped his head, taking a step back into the hallway to give me space to shut my office door, then his eyes narrowed.

"You seem to be pretty cozy with Mr. Tharmor. Do you think he'd be okay with you flirting with me like this?" He stood in my path, so close to me I could see the fuzz on his coat, which I plucked off with my manicured fingers and patted his shoulder.

"Are you jealous of Godwin?" I hadn't expected him to stand so close, focus on me so intently. I almost lost my nerve, in spite of the swirl of alcohol pushing endorphins toward my groin. The way he got under my skin all day, every day had culminated in a potential tryst right before my eyes. I should've drunk too much a long time ago.

"Not jealous, just not wanting to step on anyone's toes," Xander said thoughtfully, and a surge of hormones made my body overheat.

"Now, how could you step on his toes?" My hand lingered on his shoulder, sliding across his chest to his tie where I wrapped my fingers around it and let my hand slide down the front of his body, across his abs, pausing above his belt.

"I think we should get you home before you say something you might regret." I could've sworn I heard him mumble, "Or I do something I regret." He took my hand and started walking, and I followed leisurely.

My heels clicked on the floor; my body begged for more liquor. As it was, the night had exhausted me, but I knew if I had any more to drink, I'd be pass-out drunk, and I was enjoying the flirty banter too much to do that.

"We don't get to spend too much time alone, do we?" Xander pushed the door open, and a burst of chilly air rushed in. A car pulled up outside as I stepped into the crisp January air, and Xander followed behind me.

"It would be highly inappropriate for us to spend alone time in your office, don't you think?" I turned, walking backward carefully as he advanced on me. I saw it now—the desire in his eyes. The same desire I'd seen multiple times before when he looked at me, including tonight a few times.

"Then I think we should make the most of our time alone." Xander's voice dropped an octave, a course whisper, almost a growl. I thought he was reaching for my hip, fingers reaching toward my curve to caress it, but he reached right past, grasping the door handle. He stood very close for a moment, almost pinning me to the side of the car. "Don't you?"

I watched his eyes drop to my lips then rise back slowly to capture my gaze again, and I waited for my heart to stop throwing itself against my rib cage. Squirming a few inches to the side, I gave him space to open the door, and when he did, I turned and climbed in.

The limo wasn't a full stretch limo, but it had a mini fridge and a bench seat. The leather seat chilled the backs of my thighs as Xander stood outside the limo speaking to someone, maybe his driver? And I took the moment to fluff my hair and tug the hem of my dress up, pushing my tits out. It was warm in here, the divider between the driver's cabin and ours shut, and I turned to watch Xander slide into the seat next to me and shut the door.

At the very same moment, I began to feel ashamed of myself. I flirted with him, made a few too many suggestive comments, and probably looked like a drunk floozy who had no self-control. It wasn't good for my reputation at work, and it wasn't like this was going anywhere. Shrinking back into the seat, I was ready to apologize and tell him I was out of line when he turned to face me and loosened his tie. His eyes were still filled with a lusty desire.

"You are making it very difficult to keep my professional distance this evening, and I'm normally pretty good at it." His hand splayed on the leather next to my bare leg, fingertips only millimeters from touching me. His other arm rests casually on the armrest on the door, and his body angles to face mine.

"You're normally good at it? You mean you have to try to keep your professional distance other times?" The electric charge in the air seems to make my core throb harder, in time with my heart rate. I was ready to back off, but now he was giving chase. I couldn't say I hated it.

"I never knew you had a bold side. It's sort of irresistible ..." Xander's hand moved from the armrest, reaching toward my leg where his fingers warmed the inside of my thigh. "Are you sure this isn't just the alcohol? Cause I'm not one of those guys, Amelia."

I swallowed hard. The way he touched me had my body inching forward, wishing his hand would slide a little higher up my leg.

"And you think I'm one of those girls?" I wasn't offended at all; he was taking his time to obtain consent, which I wholeheartedly gave him. "I have a hard time keeping myself professional around you too." I wanted to call him by name, but the idea of calling him boss, begging him to order me to be bad to him, had my heart racing.

"You're playing a dangerous game." His hand inched higher until his fingertips brushed the outside of my panties, and I almost lost it. "I like it."

"This isn't a game, Mr. Blackwell." I finally found my inner vixen again, the one who got lost in the excitement of flirting in his office, and I turned her loose. My body bumped on the seat as the car hit a pothole, and I scooted forward until his fingers jammed against my core. "And I'm not playing." I locked eyes with him as he stared me down and felt when his fingers slid the elastic of my panties aside.

"God you're wet. You really do want this ... With me?" Again, the consent thing? I almost groaned audibly but managed to contain my frustration. Instead, I leaned in, brushed my lips against his ear and whispered my next words.

"If you don't stop talking and just make me come, I'm going to spontaneously combust."

The car seemed to grow hotter, and I could feel every movement as he shifted on the plush leather seat. His finger slid inside me, and I could've sworn he whispered my name into my ear as I arched into his touch. The world spun away from us as his finger stroked inside me, hitting that spot again and again that had my toes curling in my shoes. Xander's other free hand went to the base of my neck, palm curved around the nape, angling my mouth upward toward his.

"Do you know how many times I've thought about doing this to you?" My breath caught at his confession, but the shocking part heated me even more. "You have no idea how badly I want to fuck you senseless right now."

"Then do it," I taunted.

His finger worked inside me, thumb pressing into my clit, and I whimpered as I pawed at his coat, wishing I could feel his skin under my palms. His lips claimed mine, opening my mouth so his tongue could search me. I kissed him back as I managed to open a few buttons on his shirt and feel the heat of his chest muscles on my fingertips.

"Such a wet little pussy," he purred, but his fingers pulled out. I felt him curl them around the crotch of my panties, and then he tugged hard. The waistband scraped over my hips; I thought the material would rip so I lifted my hips, and he had my panties around my knees with one strong pull.

"God," I hissed, feeling his eyes burning into me. He slid my panties down my legs and carefully removed them, leaving my heels in place. After shoving them in his pocket, he hooked two fingers around the back of my left knee and tugged, and I knew what he wanted.

"I think your dick got a little swollen, Boss," I mewled as I settled onto his lap. The bulge was unmistakable; he was rock-hard. His hands left my legs and worked the fly of his tux pants. He was fumbling with his belt, hands shaking slightly in excitement he couldn't mask. I felt the same way as I watched him.

"You want to be a bad girl for me, Amelia? Want your boss to tie you up and make you work hard?" Xander's hand thrust into his slacks then reappeared wrapped around his hard dick. He was huge, and precum already dripped from the tip. I had no idea that I had gotten him that worked up already, and it only made my arousal for him stronger.

"Yes, sir. I want to do everything you tell me." The way his hand stroked his length made my mouth water. My pussy throbbed, making a mess on his lap, and I rubbed my own clit in anticipation.

"Good girl," Xander purred, nuzzling my neck. His other hand inched up my dress, seeking out my swollen clit, and my nipples tightened as his magic fingers found the right spot to stroke me. I slid forward and leaned down to kiss him again, covering his mouth with mine. He rubbed his length up and down my slit until my hips were rocking involuntarily. "I don't have a condom," he warned, but I wasn't even thinking clearly.

I blurted out, "I'm on the pill," and arched my hips to meet him.

The first inch of his dick inside me made me shudder, and when the car hit a bump and he slid all the way in I gasped. His dick rammed into my cervix hard; I clenched around him and he groaned.

"God, you feel good." His hands cupped my hips, guiding me down as he rocked upward into me. My dress rode up to just above my waist and Xander's fingers dug into my thighs as he assisted me. "You're so hot, my God."

"Oh Christ, it's so deep!" Every nerve ending was screaming in pleasure, especially when his thumb pressed into my clit and started swirling. He yanked one side of my dress down and grabbed my breast, closing his mouth on it and sucking my nipple. Then he pulled me down so he could speak right into my ear.

"Say my name," he growled, nipping at my earlobe and sending waves of sensations through my body; tingles in my lower extremities and heady swirls of pleasure in my chest and core.

"Oh my God, Xander," I managed to whimper through gritted teeth. He was so long, every thrust hit my cervix and made me clench around him. My hands groped for something to hold onto, finding his lapels, squeezing them in iron fists.

"Say it again," he demanded softly. His breath feathered over my cheek, hand still massaging my clit, and I whimpered. The coil was tightening down, stretching me thin, pushing me to the edge. It was incredible.

"Like that, Xander. Right there ... yes ... don't stop." My hips rocked in time with his thrusts, and I felt the tension building. I was a pressure cooker ready to explode, and when he bit my ear again, I almost lost it. But I held on, waiting for his words to push me over the edge.

"Say it again. Beg for me, Amelia. Beg me to let you come."

I whimpered, grinding on him, desperate for release, and knew he felt the pending orgasm building in me as he hammered his cock into me. "Please, Xander, oh my God. Please, make me come, please ..."

"Louder!"

"Oh God, Xander let me come!" I pleaded, arching my head back.

He hit a place deep inside me that made my vision go white. His hand worked me to orgasm, pistoning in and out as I grunted and spasmed. I saw stars and draped myself over his shoulder. Xander continued to thrust, rubbing my clit, and I felt his heat flood me. My body jolted and twitched; his hand slid from my breast and rested on my hip, and both of us heaved for breath.

For a moment, we were frozen in time, him buried in me, my body dripping moisture onto his pants, soiling them. Xander's hand retreated from my core, and I felt him tugging the hem of my dress lower across my hips. I slid backward and he pulled out, his cock springing up to slap his belly and glisten in the light of the streetlamp outside that lit up the back seat. We were stopped outside my building, and I was so tired and delirious from post-orgasmic endorphins.

"Wow," I breathed, not sure what to say. I had just had sex with my boss in the back seat of his car, and I was still very drunk.

"Yeah, wow," he repeated. His hand worked to tuck my tit back into my dress, and he didn't even cover his own dick yet.

"So I should, uh …" I swallowed hard and shoved the hair out of my face. Things just went from steamy to awkward in a split second.

"Or you could stay," he suggested, raising his eyebrows, tipping his head. It was a bad idea. One I wanted to indulge in very badly, but one I knew would end in regret. As if I didn't already feel that gnawing at my conscience.

"Thank you for the ride," I said, suddenly feeling overheated with my coat on. I reached for the door handle, and Xander continued to shimmy my dress down over my hips as I opened the door and leaned out. If not for him, I might have walked up to my apartment with my dress around my waist and no panties.

"Should I walk you?" he asked, and I turned to lean back into the car. He was tucking himself away, buckling up his pants.

"Nah, I've got this," I slurred. The effects of that last glass of alcohol I slurped down right before Godwin left were finally kicking in.

"Are we good?" Xander asked, but I couldn't read his expression. I was still very much aroused and feeling flirty, and after that romp, my inhibitions would forever be gone around him.

"Depends what you mean by good? Your dick is magic, Mr. Blackwell," I said lewdly, "and if you ever want to bend me over your desk and spank me, all you have to do is order me to do it." I hiccupped again and snickered, but the look on his face wasn't humorous. It was arousal. "Good night, Boss."

Stepping away, I wiggled my fingers at him and then turned to sway into the building. I heard the car door shut, but I never heard it pull away from the curb. When I got inside, the doorman held the door for me as I glanced over my shoulder to see the limo gone. It took every bit of my concentration to find my way to my apartment, and I crashed on my couch the minute I had locked up.

I just threw myself at my boss the way Godwin joked with me to. I never expected it to go down quite like that, but now that it was done, I wasn't sure how to react. This week was going to be interesting. I just had to sleep off this buzz and think about how to act when I got to work Monday morning.

3

XANDER

I rode home with my shirt untucked and my dick still tingling from that release. Amelia was drunk, but not so bad she couldn't consent, and I reeled over how bold she was. The dumb grin on my face wouldn't go away, even when I stopped to consider how this might affect us at work.

Amelia was a model employee—never late to work, always met her deadlines, never caused work drama. She had even helped in ways most of my staff couldn't, by helping me gain insight into our clients and their lives. Having been Laurence's right-hand woman for a while in the beginning, she knew more about the company than anyone else on staff.

She was smart as a whip and apparently just as bold. I rubbed my face and still couldn't shake the giddy feeling. Never in my life had a woman come onto me so strongly, and I enjoyed it very much.

But the nagging feeling of guilt that started low in my gut and snaked its way up into my chest and higher into my thoughts was pervasive. She was one of the most integral people on my team. She was the marketing manager, and with our need to boost sales, I couldn't afford to screw up the team dynamic with something like this. It was a poor move on my part, giving in to my selfish desire, but how often is it that a woman throws herself at you? I had desires and needs, but I should've met them in a more ethical way.

David pulled the car around front at my place, and I slunk out. When I gave him Amelia's address before leaving the office, I informed him to take his time, and he knew what that meant. He wasn't ignorant of my ways, of which I was ashamed. *"Always a playboy, never a partner,"* my father would chide, but I didn't really have time to get wrapped up in another dead-end relationship. I had my needs met in healthy ways with no desire to go through what I'd seen my father go through.

I'd heard his lectures about finding a woman to settle down with, but it wasn't a realistic thing to hope for. Dad couldn't even find a woman to stick around longer than a few months. Why should I try?

"Goodnight, sir," David said as he rounded the car to shut the back door I climbed out of.

I nodded at him, ignoring the mess of my untucked shirt and sex-stained pants. I wondered what went through his head as he drove me home from wherever I was with whomever accompanied me in the back seat of my limo. It'd been ages since I entertained a woman, but tonight wasn't an anomaly. Not something I was horribly proud of, but better than having my heart torn out.

As I stripped off and dove into bed, I thought about what to say to Amelia on Monday morning. I couldn't let this go very long. If we said nothing it would develop into something awkward where we couldn't look each other in the eye at work. Eventually, she would want to talk about her feelings, and I'd be the horrible monster who had no regard for her heart. It was better to nip it in the bud immediately before she put too much thought into it.

Life was easier when emotions stayed contained, so that was my goal. I would tell her first thing Monday morning that while I very much enjoyed the rush of excitement preceding what was probably the best orgasm I'd had in years, we had to be nothing more than boss and employee. And I hoped she took it easily.

~

THE OFFICE WAS QUIET, save for the low hum of the air conditioning and the occasional click of my keyboard as I tapped aimlessly on the keys. I wasn't really typing anything productive. My mind was too occupied with the events of Saturday night. No matter how hard I tried to focus on the stack of papers in front of me, all I could think about was her. Amelia. Her flushed skin, her intoxicating scent, and how she felt pressed against me in the back of my car. It was reckless. It was stupid. But in that moment, it was everything.

Steam rose from the tiny hole in the plastic lid on my to-go coffee. I sat behind my desk with a stack of files in front of me of potential clients' names collected from a local business fair. It was one of Amelia and Godwin's ideas to have the team set up a booth and attend the two-day event for businesses in San Jose, but since it was last-minute and we were ill-prepared, all we had were a few outdated forms used by Laurence's team for booth visitors to fill out. It meant me poring over paperwork when I should've been able to put an algorithm to work for me.

A tap on my door perked me up and I sat straighter, fixing my crooked tie as I called, "Yes?"

"Sir," I heard before I saw Charity's hazel eyes and warm complexion. She poked her head in and glanced at my phone. "Your intercom is muted again ..." She bit her lip. "I have Ms. Johnson. She's not on your calendar but she insisted you told her to come to your office." Charity was a great secretary but a little ditzy. Sometimes she missed the obvious and behaved more like a bouncer at a club than a personal aide.

"Let her in, thank you," I said, gesturing. It was sweet that she wanted to protect my time while I was in my office, but sometimes it felt like she was nosy or overbearing.

The door creaked open, and I blinked, pushing aside the thoughts that threatened to consume me. Charity stepped in first, her usual cheerfulness a little subdued, before gesturing Amelia inside. She looked different today. A little more composed maybe, but there was something in her eyes—a slight unease—that made my stomach twist. She stepped in cautiously, her usual confident stride replaced by something a little more hesitant.

"Xander," she greeted, voice soft, but there was an edge to it that said she wasn't quite sure what to expect from this meeting.

"Amelia." I stood from behind my desk, folding my arms across my chest, trying to maintain some semblance of control. It was difficult to keep a straight face as Charity stepped out. All I could think about was the minx who wormed her way into my pants. It made my dick pulse with desire for her. "Please, have a seat."

She did as I asked, smoothing the front of her blouse nervously before sitting down. There was a moment of silence as I watched her, noticing how she fidgeted slightly in the chair, how her hands rested on her lap, and how her gaze kept flickering to the floor, avoiding mine.

"I just ... I wanted to say I'm sorry," she started, her voice tight with tension. "I was out of line Saturday night. I've thought about it all weekend, and I realize it was completely inappropriate. I shouldn't have let things go as far as they did." Her cheeks flushed a deeper shade of red as she continued, eyes fixed firmly on the ground. "It won't happen again. I swear."

I felt a pang of guilt deep inside me, but I pushed it down. This was the right thing to do. I had to keep my distance from her, especially now that I knew how I felt. It wasn't just about the rules of being her boss—it was about the way I'd felt the night we'd ... crossed that line. I couldn't allow myself to be consumed by it.

"Amelia," I said, my voice steady, though I couldn't hide the undercurrent of regret. "Thank you for being honest. And thank you for keeping it between us. I'm grateful for that." I paused, making sure she heard the sincerity in my words. "Look, we're both adults here. I don't want you to feel ashamed. You were drunk; I was drunk ... We both made a mistake."

She nodded quickly, her blush deepening as her eyes met mine, but this time they weren't avoiding my gaze. They were searching, uncertain. "I just ... I didn't mean to make you uncomfortable," she whispered. "I don't want you to think less of me."

The way she looked at me, vulnerable and remorseful, made something inside me stir. It wasn't just the guilt of what we'd done, but something else ... something much harder to ignore. It was the way she seemed to be fighting back tears, and how she couldn't seem to sit still. Her body language screamed that she was still shaken by the whole thing. I noticed the way her fingers played with the hem of her blouse and how her lips parted slightly as if she wanted to say something else but couldn't find the right words.

I couldn't lie to myself. I wanted her. And I wanted to take that guilt, that desire, and turn it into something real. But the impropriety of the whole thing gnawed at my insides. She was my employee, and knowing what I knew about relationships and how abruptly they were prone to ending, it was better to draw the line in the sand here.

"Don't worry, Amelia," I said, my voice softer now. "This doesn't change anything between us. We're fine. Just ... let's keep things professional moving forward. For both of us."

Her lips parted as if she wanted to say something more, but then she bit down on them, her eyes flicking to the door as if she were considering making a hasty exit. I could practically feel the heat radiating off her, but I knew she was trying her hardest to pull back, to put a wall between us. She was trying to do the right thing, and I had to respect that. I had to do the same thing.

But God, she was still so beautiful. Her cheeks were flushed from embarrassment, but she still looked like an angel to me. I couldn't help it—I studied her, lingering on the way her blouse clung to her curves, the way her hair framed her face. Every part of her seemed to beg for my attention, and for a moment, I couldn't pull my eyes away. She looked ... exquisite.

"I appreciate you coming to speak with me," I said, trying to give her the space to leave. "You can go. I think we've said what needed to be said."

She stood up slowly, her movements slightly stiff. She was still flustered, and as she turned toward the door, I caught sight of the way her hips swayed slightly with each step. The heat in my chest flared again. My mind raced with thoughts of her pressed up against my desk, bending over for me. The image was vivid—too vivid. Her parting words, about me ordering her to bend over my desk seemed lodged in my brain in a way I couldn't shake. Why had she said that?

I stood frozen, staring at her, but before I could collect myself, she turned back to face me. "Thank you for being understanding," she said, her voice barely a whisper.

I nodded, but the words that nearly escaped my lips were completely inappropriate. I bit down on them—that urge to ask her if she meant it—feeling the moment pass. "You're welcome, Amelia."

As she walked out, I sat back in my chair, trying to force the image of her bent over my desk from my mind. I scrubbed my hands over my face, but the arousal in my body was proof that I'd have a very difficult time following my own instructions. I didn't want to put that night out of my thoughts; I wanted to see her again, experience her body in the throes of ecstasy again.

My phone rang, however, pulling me out of the gutter and back into my office. I reached into my desk drawer and pulled it out to see Laurence's name on my caller ID, and just like that, the shame I felt over lusting after his daughter consumed me. Desire vanished and my swelling dick deflated like a flat tire.

"Hey, buddy, what's up?" The forced pleasantry felt like deceit. If he knew I had sex with Amelia, I doubted he'd be so cordial with me.

"Xander, I just wanted to thank you again for inviting me to the party. And thank you for bringing Mimi home. She had a great time. She told me all about how you were a perfect gentleman and offered to walk her to her door ..." His words trailed off, painting a picture of a happy daughter whose whole world was alight thanks to my chivalry. If he only knew the nasty things I wished I could do to that young woman he called his little girl.

Yes, cutting that off immediately was the best decision. I was already in too deep.

4

AMELIA

The room felt a bit colder to me than what the thermostat said, but January was always a cold month. I hugged my sweater around my body tighter as I sat down on the couch next to Godwin and sipped my hot tea. We had documents spread out on the coffee table, both of our laptops open with glowing screens revealing the hard work we'd been doing for the new project.

"I think the blue graphics are better, but the yellow ones really pop too." He fanned his hand at the screens side by side, displaying the choices the development team laid out for the customer's review. It was our job to take whatever they decided and create an entire marketing push for it when final choices were made.

"I think I'm tired and I'm sick of working late hours." I sniffled and hugged my mug with my hands, willing it to warm me up as Godwin let out a hard cough.

"It's totally my fault, Meals. I am so sorry for missing almost the whole week." His hand splayed on his chest in dramatic fashion, he pushed his lip out in a pout and sighed hard, which brought on some more coughing. "But at least I'm not contagious."

He was right. Had he been at work during the day, we wouldn't be spending our Friday night on my sofa going over things we should've had decided by Tuesday. Bronchitis hit him hard, and now with my body feeling chilly and my sinuses beginning to drain, I worried I might be coming down with it too.

"You can't say I didn't warn you," I chided playfully, "but you were sick. Don't beat yourself up. Just help me get this crap done so I can go to bed. I'm not feeling too hot."

Godwin chuckled and picked up a stack of papers, one of which had a tea ring from his mug centered over our company logo. It made me think of Xander and what happened after the party. He'd been out of town for a few days on a business trip, and today in the office we had passed like ghosts in the night. Gearing up for a difficult first quarter after a slump in sales had the entire marketing department in crunch mode. I hadn't had time to look up, let alone stop and think about that chat Monday morning.

"What?" Godwin asked, shooting a cheeky grin at me. His eyes scrutinized my expression as my cheeks warmed. I couldn't very well tell him about what happened because I'd given Xander my word that I'd keep it confidential. Godwin was my best friend and he could keep a secret, but I was a woman of my word. I wouldn't even put those thoughts into the universe for fear that a bird would carry them back to Xander's ears and he'd be upset.

"Nothing," I mumbled, feeling embarrassed that he'd caught me off my game. I was his manager and we were working right now, but the relaxed setting and the fact that he was my best friend made it easy to slip in and out of personal and professional modes.

"You have that look—the one where you're daydreaming about something steamy. Come on, honey, dish. You know I want the details." He inched closer, picking up his mug and sipping from it. By now his tea was cold and wasn't soothing the ache in his throat from coughing, but he grinned over the rim anyway, like a gossip queen waiting for juicy tidbits.

"You're such a pain," I said, snickering.

"Am not, besides, you know how long it's been since I got any drama from you. Honey, your love life is as boring as a librarian filing card catalogues." Godwin's lips pursed and he snickered at his own dumb joke while I rolled my eyes and set my mug down on a coaster so it didn't leave a ring on my wooden coffee table.

"My love life is null and void. I don't have one. You know that." This conversation always got me in trouble. Godwin insisted that he knew a million hot guys, most of whom were gay but still, and he'd set me up. I just wasn't interested in playing the field and getting my emotions jerked around a million times before finding *the one*.

"It seems like you are thinking about a certain someone? I guess it didn't pan out after the party last weekend?" Forever he'd been trying to get me to do what I'd done with Xander. Everything inside me screamed to gush with all the details—details I was sure Godwin would eat up like jam on toast. But I couldn't, and it was killing me.

"He's my boss, Godwin."

"Meals—" he whined but I cut him off.

"Oh my God!" I snipped, then snickered. I hated that nickname, and he insisted on using it just to annoy me sometimes. "Stop calling me that, you brat." I swatted at him and he laughed as he downed the rest of his mug of tea.

"Fine, but I'm going to set you up. I know this guy—five two, pretty cute, but man, does he need platforms. And he's a banker. You'll like him." Godwin stood, but I was already protesting with a head shake.

"No, absolutely not. The last short banker you set me up with was gayer than you!" I gave his hip a playful push as he walked past, and he turned around with his hand on his hip, overemphasizing his actions in every way.

"I'll have you know, no one is gayer than me, honey." With eyebrows up and pinky out, he clicked his tongue, and I laughed as he walked toward the kitchen to put his mug in the sink.

"I don't want a setup. I just want to be invisible for a while," I mused, but as I did I slumped back against the couch and sighed. Invisible to everyone but Xander Blackwell—who was very much not interested in anything real, at least that was what I gathered after that conversation on Monday.

"Gonna hit the head, honey. I'll be right back." He passed through the kitchen and set his mug down then went on to the bathroom.

I sat up straighter, staring at the blues and yellows, wondering how to push this new project management software our team was developing. Normally, I could take one look at something our team did and know exactly how to present it to potential customers. This time, however, I had no clue. I felt stuck in old ideas and patterns, and I needed something to shake me out of it. Maybe it was Xander and feeling slightly miffed at the rejection, or maybe I was just in a slump.

My phone rang, offering me the perfect way to procrastinate a few moments longer, so I swiped to answer the call from my dad.

"Hey, old guy, what's up?" Dad and I had a good relationship, probably closer than most father-daughter duos. When Mom died, we were all each other had, and it forced us to really dig in and take care of each other. We fought through a few years of heavy mourning, but building Next Gen was really what helped heal us and bond us together.

"Amelia, I need you to pick me up. I've had a bit of car trouble and I'm not going to be able to drive my car home tonight." Dad's voice was tense; he sounded irritated or on edge. I glanced at the clock, which showed me it was past eight thirty. Dad lived on the other side of town, and by the time I got him picked up and home, then got back here, it could be as late as ten. Far too long to make Godwin wait for me.

"Where at?" I said, sighing. I hated to make him feel like a bother, but I was already in my pajama pants and ready to close my laptop and relax for the night. I had no interest in heading out.

"The Farmer Jack's grocery on Eleventh street. Look, I'm sorry, Amelia. If you want, I can just get a cab." Dad never wanted to be a bother, and I felt horrible for making him feel like I was put out.

"No, I'll be there. Give me a few minutes though. Godwin is over and I have to get dressed; I'm wearing my pajamas." I stood, stalking toward my bedroom as I said my goodbyes, and Dad sent his well wishes to Godwin, whom he'd known for years now.

I was dressed in my jeans and sneakers, ready with my purse on my shoulder when Godwin finally walked out of my bathroom. He was yawning, covering his mouth as his eyes scanned up and down my body.

"Who's throwing the party?"

"Dad's having car trouble. I have to run." I clenched my hand around my purse strap as I slid my phone in the outer pocket and snagged my car keys. "We'll have to finish up tomorrow. We can just leave things here if you want?"

"Sure, honey, I'm getting sleepy anyway." Godwin offered a hug, and we made plans for him to return in the morning. We locked our computers and he grabbed his jacket, then I walked him to his car and headed toward the grocery to pick up Dad.

Before I even got a few blocks away, I smelled the stench of smoke. Traffic was backed up a few blocks, and it took me a while to get through the series of traffic lights. As I rounded the corner, I saw the flashing lights of a fire truck and a few police cars. But it was the ambulance lights that made my heart try to escape my rib cage by way of my throat. It looked like the scene of an accident.

I had to park all the way at the back of the lot and walk toward the scene; the whole time I had my phone out trying to call my dad. He didn't pick up, and a million terrifying thoughts flooded through my mind. I'd been telling him to get his starter fixed for months. The dang thing would crap out on him and he'd wrestle with it for twenty minutes trying to start it. It needed to be repaired.

When I saw the horrifying sight—Dad's car burnt to a crisp next to two other cars that had major damage, I freaked out. "Dad!" My eyes scanned the crowd as I pushed into the mass of bodies trying to gawk at what was happening. The stench of alcohol wafted up at me, and I realized a lot of these people standing out here probably came from the bar across the street. "Dad!"

"Amelia," I heard, and my heart started beating again.

"Dad?" Pushing past a few more gawkers, I came to a police barricade and tried to climb over it. An officer walked up to me and pressed his hand on my shoulder.

"Ma'am, I can't let you in here." The flames were out, but his eyes still burned with determination.

"That's my dad's car. That's my dad!" I pointed at the back of the ambulance where Dad sat with two EMTs and a bandaged hand. The officer glanced that direction and saw Dad waving, and he turned back to me.

"Alright, but go straight to the ambulance, nowhere else."

Before he'd even finished, I was over the barricade and racing over to the back of the ambulance. Dad winced as one of the EMTs touched his hand and waved them away as I walked up. He wrapped his arms around me, squeezing tightly, and I could smell the stench of smoke in his hair and on his clothing.

"A little car trouble?" I asked, shaking as I clung to him.

"You were right. The starter was bad." He patted my back and then let me pull away. I was shaking like a leaf as one of the EMTs stood.

"I'll let you talk," she said, backing away. I took her spot on the cold metal bumper and clutched my purse to my chest as I stared at Dad in disbelief.

"You think the starter did this?" I shook my head, not believing anything I saw. Did cars really just spontaneously combust?

"I think so. I'll have to turn it in to the insurance company." Dad massaged the bridge of his nose. His hand was covered in soot, thick black swaths across his fingers.

"You're hurt?" I asked, taking his wrist and turning his hand over.

"He has second-degree burns," the other EMT said as he carefully took Dad's arm back from my grasp. "But he'll be fine."

"I'm sorry, sweetheart. I should've listened to you before and had a mechanic take a look at that." His eyes glistened with emotion, but it looked more like fear than concern. I was just glad he was okay.

"Dad—" I started, but I watched him puff his chest out, shoulders going stiff. His eyes were trained over my shoulder to something behind me. I glanced that direction and saw the mass of bodies hovering, watching. But behind them, two men wearing dark suits stood staring at the scene. They were out of place, not random strangers on a Friday night who wandered out of a grocery store or bar to be nosy.

"Dad?" I asked, turning back to face him. He was pale, eyes blinking rapidly. "What's going on? Are you sure it was the starter?" I got the feeling he wasn't telling me something, but why? He blinked back into focus and turned to me.

"It's the starter. I'll report it to the insurance company. I'll get a payout, okay, honey?" He gripped my hand, and when I started to look back over my shoulder, he pulled my arm and said, "Hey, it's just an accident. We'll get me fixed up and you can take me home."

My body felt on edge, goose bumps appearing on my arms and the back of my neck. Dad was hiding something—something he didn't want me to know about. I didn't think this "accident" had anything to do with a starter going out, but I wasn't an expert. And right now, I had to be thankful he was healthy and fine, nothing more than a small burn. When I finally did turn to look over my shoulder at where those men had stood, they were gone, and I was glad.

I wanted to take Dad home and pour myself a drink.

5

XANDER

The nine iron felt good in my grip and the swing was smooth, but the ball sailed right into a slice, taking it to the far right of the fairway. I let the club slide through my grip until the head settled on my curled fingers, and I stepped back from the tee.

"Not horrible," Dad said, which was his way of telling me the stroke was bad. He was like that—backward compliments that were actually aimed at correcting my behavior. I was sure he had developed the habit sometime after Mom split, a coping mechanism aimed at shutting down his negative nature to preserve whatever relationship was left between the two of us.

"Yeah, well let's see how you do. That wind didn't help." I walked toward the cart to stash my club and passed Gerard Millet, a potential client I'd invited to my early morning tee off with Dad.

"Don't let it get to you, Xander," he said, patting my arm. "This course is a tough one."

Dad and I opted for Pebble Beach when we could, though the ninety-minute drive prevented too many midweek tee offs. It was one of the tougher courses in the state, but nicer to play than any of the nine local courses around San Jose, and the ocean breeze was always stiff, though that had little relevance to why I sliced so badly. My mind was elsewhere.

"Look at that," Dad purred, shielding his eyes to the rising sun on the horizon as he watched his ball sail straight down the middle. "Perfect shot, boys. Try to beat that."

Gerard chuckled as he carried his club, ball, and tee to the teeing ground. "If only life worked so smoothly," he said, and I turned my back to the chatter. I was tense, overly so, wishing I had some way to escape the stress of work for a while. My mind had been tangled up in thoughts of Amelia and that romp in my back seat for almost two weeks now.

"You look troubled, son," Dad said as he slid his club into his bag. "How's work?" He took off his glove, used it to wipe sweat from his forehead. It wasn't that warm yet, but he was a big man, conjured a good sweat easily.

"I'm fine," I told him, because the last thing I was going to discuss with my father was relationship status. He had zero good advice, never had a woman who stayed around long enough to call a true relationship after Mom.

"You should go to dinner with me and Candy. Maybe you'd like her daughter." He fiddled with his golf bag, zipping and unzipping pockets with no real purpose. The way he brought up his new mistresses so casually made me cringe. I might've had different sexual partners often—always with protection and consent—but I never purported to call them girlfriends, and I never introduced them to my father.

"What kind of a name is that? And how long is this one gonna stick around?" My cynical view on true love never ceased to annoy him. He scowled and climbed onto the cart, both of us ignoring Mr. Millet's two-hundred-yard drive. He joined us at the cart, cutting off our conversation and climbed in, still holding his driver on his lap.

"Let's go, boys, I have a feeling today is going to be a good day." He grinned and I slid onto the back seat as he pressed down the gas pedal. "It's a beautiful morning for golf."

"Yes it is, and a beautiful morning to talk business. So what sort of app does your team need?" Dad was schmoozing better than me, but he'd been along for the ride since I bought Next Gen off Laurence. Dad was never a self-made man, having inherited his money from his father. I was raised with a silver spoon, but I worked hard for everything I had now. After Mom took more than half of Dad's fortune, he'd toned down his lavish lifestyle. Now that I was making my own millions, he had become a staple in my social calendar to supplement things he no longer wished to spend his own money on.

I didn't mind. It meant his business acumen was at my disposal in instances like this, and he had a knack for knowing how to land a tricky client like Gerard.

"It's a dating app to help pair people with their perfect match. I'm not going into specifics—confidentiality and all that—but if Next Gen presents a package I like, I may just bite." Gerard turned the golf cart toward the fairway and accelerated. I'd already given him my personal pitch about timelines and budgets, how my team excelled in meeting every client's expectations. We hadn't gotten into specifics, but Gerard seemed to be the type to be more hush-hush.

"Yes, I understand confidentiality. Something my former wife clearly never caught on to." Dad chuckled while I pinched the bridge of my nose. Bringing his past and present relationship statuses into this conversation was inevitable. He thought comparing business deals to relationships was the best way to nail a client, and for the most part he wasn't wrong. I just hated how he bragged about playing the field. At his age, he should've been more mature.

"Ah, marriage and partnership ..." Gerard hummed for a second. "They have a lot in common, don't they?"

"Yes," Dad replied, pointing out my ball almost fringing on the rough only a few meters away from where Gerard stopped the cart. "And they can be tricky to navigate. You have to trust your partner without question in both circumstances, which was the mistake I made."

"Ah, yes. When emotions get twisted up in things it gets messy." Gerard stepped out of the cart, and I winced as I realized where this was going.

"Pardon me," I said, sliding off the seat. I took my pitching wedge and walked out across the fairway to take my next stroke, grateful for the escape from what was sure to be Dad rehashing how my mother just decided to leave one day. She packed her things, kissed my forehead, and left. Only when she had to fight for the millions she believed Dad owed her did she come back, and it was hell on earth to a child.

My chest was tight as their conversation faded behind me. Getting emotions tangled up in things had been something I cautiously avoided, though I did find myself lonely. As I lined up my club to make the next stroke, I allowed that sense of loneliness and isolation to weigh me down.

I judged my father harshly at times for dating so many women, calling them his girlfriend, giving them whatever they wanted, then letting them dump him for someone younger. Most times the women were my age or younger than me, often out for his money. He had his heart broken repeatedly, and in my opinion, he was too soft at times.

But regardless of how many times I'd watched that happen to him, and how carefully I guarded my own heart to not allow any of my flings to hook into my heart, I still felt like I was missing something. I wasn't in the market for a girlfriend or any serious relationship at all, for that matter, but I did wish there was something more, something deeper than random casual sex with different women.

The rest of the game, I made sure to focus my attention on the app Mr. Millet wanted built and the game of golf. Dad attempted to throw in his two cents every now and then, but I managed to work out what the client might need and promised him to develop a plan he could be proud of, to present it to him when he met with me and the team next week. Then I dropped Dad at home to have brunch with Candy and headed into the office.

The office was busy, most of my staff with their heads down working. I passed by Amelia's office, but she wasn't at her desk, and when I stepped into my office, she was hovering over my desk with a stack of files and a pen in hand. Her eyes popped up to take me in, and I could see right away she looked horrible.

"Oh, Mr. Blackwell, good," she sighed, dropping the pen. Her other hand clutched around a wadded-up tissue, puffy nose and red rimmed eyes showing her misery. "I have that marketing packet ready for your approval. Godwin and I worked all weekend, but my God I feel like death warmed over." She moved away from my desk and gestured.

"You look like crap," I said, chuckling, though I meant it in the kindest way. Even obviously sick, Amelia was striking. She always had been. Her thick curves, the way her chestnut hair framed her face—I'd never been able to think of her any other way than beautiful and brilliant, though even as short as three weeks ago, I'd have thought she would nail down a handsome young bachelor.

Now those thoughts had shifted, and I wished she'd nail me down, or let me nail her—over my desk. I swept past her, but her floral perfume tickled my senses, made me remember how her body writhed against mine in the back seat of my limo. How she came apart around me, grunted my name, begged me to do bad things to her.

"Thank you for this. You don't feel well? I asked, remembering how a member of her team she was very close with had been out most of last week. They were sharing germs, which was discouraged by strict sick-day policies, but inevitable.

"Yeah, I think I caught Godwin's bronchitis. I need to make an appointment at the clinic." She sniffled and shook her head, and I sank into my desk chair.

"Take the rest of the week off. It'll give me time to go over this." I picked up the top file and saw the name Assure scrawled on the top in some fancy font. Probably the final style decisions from the design team.

"Thank you, sir." Amelia turned to head toward the door, and I watched her hips sway. I had a bad habit of allowing myself to do that now, ever since that night. And a random thought popped into my head about her, about how calm and collected she was since we screwed in my back seat. She hadn't been awkward or flirty, hadn't brought it up with me. She was professional and did her job, exactly the way I would expect her to be.

"Amelia?" I called, and she stopped and turned toward me.

"Yes sir?" Her eyebrows were high, but her demeanor was professional. I almost felt bad preparing to make this personal.

"Have you told anyone ... about that night?" I studied her carefully, watched as her tongue flicked over her lip, and she shook her head.

"Of course not, sir. You asked me to keep it private and I have." She tucked a strand of hair behind her ear and looked down, avoiding my gaze. The cheeky minx who threw herself at me in that car hid below the surface, though the tint in her cheeks betrayed her. She was flustered.

"Have you thought about it?" I asked, sitting forward in my seat.

"Absolutely not," she said. Her head popped back up, face determined. "I'd never breach your trust." I admired her fire.

"I mean, have you thought about what we did?" I asked again, this time with clarification. She wrung her hands and then crossed her arms over her chest defiantly, but she wasn't defying me. She was wrestling internally, the same way I had been for almost two weeks now.

"Of course I have." Simple and honest. I liked that.

"Have you thought about doing it again?" I was pushing the limit. At any point I could back off and pretend this conversation hadn't happened, but I didn't want to. Seeing her squirm, her cheeks grow darker, her eyes cloud over with lust—it excited me. The whole atmosphere of my office shifted, felt more like the back seat of my car again, supercharged with attraction and chemistry.

"Yes, sir, I have." Her shoulders tensed, her toes turning inward. I saw the way she chewed the inside of her lip as if I couldn't see her doing it. If I wasn't mistaken, I'd have sworn she would have done just about anything I asked right then and there—and not because I was her boss.

"That's all, Amelia. You may go."

She nodded, turning on her heel and walking out the door

quickly, and I sat back in my chair reveling in the sensation of excitement and arousal pulsing through my body. We weren't that different, me and Amelia. Flings like that weren't abnormal; people had them all the time. And with her ability to keep quiet and stay emotionally level, she was the exact sort of woman who could handle a no-strings-attached sort of relationship.

Plus, her generation was light years ahead of mine when it came to sexual freedom and maturity. She probably had NSA sex with other men before, though what I was thinking of wouldn't be off tap. There would be rules for it—if I could convince her it was a good idea. If …

But I walked a fine line. If I presented the idea and it didn't land well, I'd have a sexual harassment lawsuit on my hands. It was touchy, but I might just be willing to take the risk if it meant having what I craved—a sexual partner who could help take care of my growing needs while remaining emotionally aloof and relaxed. Amelia might just be what the doctor ordered.

6

AMELIA

After three days of being bedridden, I was starting to feel better. The doctor scolded me—as did my father—for procrastinating for so long in making the appointment. He said I'd been suffering with bronchitis for at least four days before I broke down and called him. He put me on the strongest antibiotics, which lay in Dad's hand as he hovered over me with a glass of water and a frustrated expression.

"Stop scrolling that phone of yours. You're going to make your eyes go crossways." He scowled, though I knew he only lectured because he cared. He had been here for a few days now to care for me while I was holed up in my bed.

"I'd roll my eyes and say 'thanks Dad,' except you really are my dad and that would sound too snarky." I took the medication, thankful that my head was no longer throbbing from the fever. It broke sometime last night, and I was on the mend.

"I'll stay a few more days. You know ... take care of you." He bustled around picking up my used tissues and tossing them in my trash can. Then he came to collect the water glass and attempted to steal my phone.

"I need this. It's work." I had been scrolling social media for a few hours, seeing how the ads for our new software were performing. I wasn't able to log in to the company servers to check metrics, but the ad looked good at least.

"Hmm ..." Dad mumbled. "How's that going? Is Blackwell treating you well?" He seemed to hover near my dresser, rearranging things and wiping dust away with his fingertips.

"He's a good boss," I said, sitting up. "Why?" Dad wasn't ever very interested in my work life. At times, I felt like he was sad he sold the company to Xander, jealous of its success. He had a decent profit-sharing dispersal every December that allowed him to live comfortably, probably would for the rest of his life, but he seemed bored at times, and lonely.

"Oh, no reason. I just want to make sure you're doing well, that you're taken care of. He turned and walked back to me, sitting on the edge of the bed, sitting near my feet. After a few days of his doting and carrying on, I was ready for him to go home, but it seemed like he was comfortable here. He had never moved on after Mom died, and sometimes I felt like he needed to. He was too preoccupied with my life.

"You know, when I sold the company, I had no idea what an amazing job Xander would do with it." Dad had a faraway look in his eye as he went on about Next Gen and how his dreams for it were coming true.

I, however, zoned out. My thoughts about Next Gen were entirely different than Dad's. The last conversation I had on company property was with Xander about the night in his limo, and I wasn't sure what to make of it. I left his office feeling sick as a dog but flustered. It was like he got off on making me squirm, watching my reaction to his questions. I didn't feel uncomfortable by it, just aroused and conflicted.

Xander had told me not to talk about it again, not to bring it up. I promised to keep it confidential, so when he asked me if I'd done that, it was easy. Of course, I'd kept my promise, and I would continue to do so. But when he asked if I'd thought about having sex with him again, I also had to be honest. I had. A lot.

"As much as you do for him, you'd think he'd pay you better. I ought to ask him for a raise for you." Dad patted my leg and I shook my head. It was the last thing I needed—my Dad going to bat for me and trying to talk my boss into giving me a raise. It didn't matter that they were good friends, probably best friends if adult men could be considered that.

"No, Dad. Xander pays me well. I have more than enough. Besides, when I nail this marketing campaign he'll see my value. If he believes I need a raise, I trust him to offer one." Scooting up on the bed, I leaned on my headboard and heard the doorbell ring. "That must be Godwin."

Dad's scowl returned. It felt like his conversation was going somewhere in his mind and it had been derailed. He stood, but he grumbled, "You should never have been that close to him when you knew he was sick." It wasn't the first rebuke about Godwin I'd gotten from him, but I understood his heart. He hated seeing me suffer, and in his mind, Godwin shared the germs that made me feel the way I'd been feeling.

I locked my phone and plugged it in on my nightstand and listened as Dad greeted my best friend. For a moment, I thought Dad was going to ask about how I enjoyed working with Xander, not for him. There were a few tense moments in the beginning, when Dad caught on that I thought Xander was handsome. He warned me early on that Xander was a player, not to get too close to him, but at that point, there was never any chance something would happen between us.

Now, when Godwin walked into my bedroom carrying his laptop and Dad followed on his heels, not giving me a moment of a breather, I wondered if Dad would freak out if he knew I'd slept with Xander. Godwin didn't know, but if anyone in this world could read my mind and figure it out, it would be one of the two of them.

"Got the numbers," Godwin announced, holding his laptop high. "And the boss can't believe it. He's so extra, Meals. He actually told the whole team how amazing you are, and he didn't say your work. He said *you*." He plopped onto the foot of my bed as my body flushed, and Dad eyed me. He suspected something, or maybe I was overthinking things.

I had just been thinking of sex with my boss while Dad talked about his fond memories of the company, after all. "Highest praise, huh?" Dad hummed, narrowing his eyes. "I guess that raise will be coming then." He slid his hands into his pockets and I sighed, avoiding eye contact with him.

"We should work a little. Dad, do you mind?" I glanced at the door, and he scowled.

"Of course not. I'll just start collecting my things." His tone was slightly manipulative, but I didn't respond as he slunk out.

If I didn't know any better, I'd have said something was going on with him, but with the launch of our new software looming and the marketing going strong, I didn't have time to stop and suss it out. He was a grown adult, and if he had a bone to pick, he had to say something. And if I didn't want to answer, it was my prerogative.

7

XANDER

My chest burned a little, coughing fits taking me for a run every few hours, but I wasn't the sort to call in sick or go running to the ER for help due to a little cough. Amelia had been under the weather for days now following Mr. Tharmor's absence. It was probably the bronchitis they passed around, but I had to grit my teeth and work through it. With the new marketing push going on I had no time to sit back and play hooky, even for something like this.

I tossed a soiled tissue into the trash and willed my eyes to focus on the reports. Our lead generation had gone through the roof thanks to Amelia and her team's brilliant marketing. They'd chosen a red and blue color scheme that really popped off the computer screen, which I was certain was the real reason for the ad's success. Our sales were skyrocketing over this, and while it wasn't the sort of work we were used to doing, it was helping generate revenue we'd been losing for the past few months.

The phone buzzed across my desk like it had a mind of its own, dragging me out of my numbers haze. I saw the name on the screen —Gerard Millet—and immediately felt a pinch in my chest that had nothing to do with the cough still dragging through me like barbed wire.

I cleared my throat and answered. "Mr. Millet. Just reviewing the projections. I've got you down for a demo next week—"

"Yeah, listen, Xander." His tone was apologetic, which meant nothing good ever followed. "You've been great, and the tech is solid, but we're moving forward with another partner."

I leaned back in my chair, silent for a beat too long. "Another partner?"

"Tacticon," he said, not bothering to pad it. "They threw in a six-month integration package and cut their licensing fee in half. I mean, your platform looks cleaner, but theirs ... you know how it is. Upper management likes the spreadsheet with fewer zeros."

I let out a breath through my nose, jaw tight. "You said after the golf meeting the contract was nearly finalized."

"I know," he said quickly. "I meant it at the time. But I don't make these decisions alone. My CFO and legal team flagged the cost margin and started pulling comparisons. Tacticon came back fast with sweeteners."

"Sweeteners," I repeated, standing up and walking to the window, needing the movement. "And stability doesn't matter anymore? We've been in the space two years longer than they have. Our platform doesn't glitch out in the middle of team syncs."

"It's not personal," he said, his voice quieter now. "You're still ahead, tech-wise. But you know how procurement is. Dollars speak."

I said nothing for a moment, eyes scanning the skyline like it might offer answers.

"This decision's going to bite you in six months," I muttered, half to myself.

"I hope not," he replied. "But listen, I still believe in what you're building. If anything changes with Tacticon, I'll be back on the line. And I meant it when I said we should keep in touch."

I ended the call without another word, letting the phone fall back to the desk with a dull thud.

ProForge, Tacticon—it didn't matter. Every one of these firms was circling like vultures, nipping at our ankles while we were mid-sprint. They didn't have to be better, just cheaper. And right now, I was bleeding patience.

I stood there, chewing over the loss, until the familiar tension settled in between my shoulders. That call could wait. Langston, Millet—it was a pattern now.

I picked up my phone again and scrolled to Amelia's name.

She answered on the second ring. "Hey. What's up?"

"Need you in my office. Now." I didn't wait for confirmation before hanging up.

I stayed standing, phone still in my hand, staring at the city beyond the glass.

It didn't matter how sharp our product was or how solid the pitch. I couldn't seem to close these deals—not like he had. Laurence had a way with people. Clients trusted him. Believed in him. Half of them were still here because of promises he made before I bought the company.

I'd thought I could take what he built and scale it. Make it better. Sleeker. Smarter.

But the trust he carried into every room didn't come with the sale.

I glanced at the screen again—engagement was up, leads were pouring in. Amelia was killing it. The whole team was delivering. But conversions? Still slipping through my fingers.

I didn't build this company. And sometimes, it felt like the clients knew it.

A quiet knock broke the thought before Amelia slipped inside, a soft rustle of her cardigan brushing against the doorframe. Her cheeks were still a little flushed from whatever was left of the fever, and her nose was pink from the cold meds or tissues, or both. But her eyes were clear now, focused. Sharp.

"Hey," she said, stepping in fully, a portfolio under her arm and her phone in her hand. "You sounded murdery on the phone."

I didn't respond. Just turned the monitor slightly toward her as I sank back into my chair.

She circled around behind me without asking—she never asked

—and leaned over my shoulder to get a better look at the dashboard. The scent of her hit me like a punch: warm vanilla and citrus and something uniquely her. Her hair brushed my temple as she pointed at a section of the heatmap.

"We're getting the most traction on the side-scroll version of the landing page," she said, sniffing softly. "That weird decision we made to test vertical versus horizontal layouts? It worked. Horizontal won, hands down. Sixty percent increase in engagement from mobile users alone."

I barely heard her. I mean, I heard her. The words were there. But her body was close—too close. Her arm was braced on the desk beside mine, her breath warm against my cheek. And the way she leaned, bent slightly at the waist, chest pressing softly against my shoulder ...

It was like gravity stopped working properly. All my focus tunneled.

I turned my head slightly, glancing up at her, and before I could stop myself, the words slipped out.

"You do realize you look incredibly sexy right now."

Her head snapped toward me, brows lifted, surprised—but not offended. Not exactly. Her gaze flicked around my face, but she didn't pull away.

"I'm going over engagement metrics," she said, her voice dry, amused. "Not pole dancing on your desk."

"You're the one who leaned in like that." And my Lord did I want her to lean closer. Her tits brushing over my shoulder was horribly distracting when I was so stressed out. I should've been thrilled with the marketing success, but not landing clients ate at me. She was the remedy I wanted.

"Sorry," she said quickly, standing, tugging the edge of her cardigan closed over her top—not that it helped. Those perfect fleshy globes were imprinted on my thoughts. "I'll make sure to dress more professionally next time."

I looked up at her and let the silence stretch for a beat, then said, evenly, "That's not what I meant."

She blinked. "No?"

"No," I said, my voice low. "I'd rather see you in less."

There was a pause—one second, maybe two—where I saw her cheeks darken, saw her throat work as she swallowed. She didn't move away. Just held my gaze like she wasn't sure whether to laugh or slap me. Or both.

And I had no idea which reaction would wreck me more.

"You mentioned you'd thought about doing it again ... What we did in my car." I stole a glance at the door, shut but not locked, and then I turned my swiveling computer chair to face her.

"I did," she said, her finger curling around the pendant dangling by the thin chain around her neck.

"What would you say to an arrangement?" I paused for emphasis before continuing. "No strings attached, no love, no relationship—just hot sex when either of us wants it." I'd been mulling it over, and I hadn't specifically planned to ask her, but the way she made me feel every time she walked into my office, I knew it would come up.

"Sir, I—"

A hand covered her lips, her eyebrows high. I had her right where I wanted her, shocked and caught off guard, and it made my dick harden as I thought of bending her over my desk right now. What I wouldn't do ...

8

AMELIA

I took a step back, and Xander rose from his chair, looming over me. When I came rushing in here, I wasn't expecting him to proposition me, not that I hadn't daydreamed it a few times in the past few weeks. But he was my boss, and while we had managed to sail through the last indiscretion easily, I wasn't sure it would be so fluid if it happened again.

"Xander," I breathed, fighting my own urges. Godwin had been poking at me for months about my crush on the boss, and the sex in his car was so hot I had dreams about it still.

"Amelia, I've been around a long time, and I'm sick of playing games. I know what I want, and that's you, bent over my desk with your skirt up around your waist, and don't lie to yourself and say you don't want it too." His hand shot out to grasp my wrist as he took the portfolio tucked under my arm and laid it down on the corner of his desk. He wasn't wrong.

I'd spent the better part of my week holed up in bed with a fever wishing my dad would leave the apartment so I could quench the burning ache between my thighs. Xander had no clue what us having sex had done to me. I was a flustered wreck, shocked my work was any good at all. All I could think about was him, and it took every ounce of my emotional energy not to vomit all the details of our encounter at Godwin every time he teased me.

"I'll even draw up a contract if you want." His fingers reached up and curled some hair around my ear. He was so gentle, so charismatic. I found myself melting and he wasn't even touching me yet. But here? In his office? Anyone could walk in. I glanced at the door and bit my lip.

"I don't think that's necessary," I said, and I had every intention of backing away and telling him it was a bad idea—for so many reasons. But his hand slid from my cheek down my arm then rested on my hip.

"I can't keep my mind off of you, Amelia. You are quite possibly the sexiest woman I've ever laid eyes on. You made me feel incredible before and I'm jonesing ..." Xander pulled me toward him, and I dropped my cell phone. It clattered on the floor by our feet, but I didn't look down at it.

"I, uh ..." I swallowed hard and tried to breathe. His cologne was intoxicating. "I can be professional. No need for a contract." What was I saying? How could I agree to this? My heart was going to get beat up so bad. I didn't just have a sex crush on this man, I liked him. I really liked him. And I knew him. He wasn't the sort to get emotionally involved, and I wasn't the sort to be able to keep my feelings out of it.

"So we're good?" He stalked closer, pressing me backward. He was already hard, which only proved how badly he wanted me.

I couldn't believe this was happening. For months, I'd been fighting my urges because I knew there was no way I'd ever end up with him. If Godwin were here, he'd tell me to go for it, because being close to someone I was crushing on was better than watching from far away, pining over him. But my better judgment was screaming for me to stop. I was going to get hurt. It might be good sex for a while, but in the end, my heart would be the casualty.

"Any deal breakers?" he asked. "Things that would make you get cold feet?"

It was here I had every chance to end this and walk away with my heart intact, but my mouth fell under the power of my lustful fantasy, and I said, "The only deal breaker is a man who can't get me off."

I didn't even get a chance to breathe before his lips were on mine.

His hand slid up my leg, lifting my skirt, and his other palm cupped my breast. The bud of my nipple was already hard, and I moaned into his mouth as I wrapped my arms around his neck. He was hot, muscular, and more importantly, highly aroused. And I knew deep down that Amelia the Rule Breaker was about to take over, and I wasn't sure I cared anymore. I was sick of being the good girl and following all the rules. I felt selfish and hungry and powerful, and I lifted my leg and wrapped it around his waist in full rebellion against the little voice inside my head telling me to stop.

"I'll take that as an invitation," Xander growled against my neck, and with one fluid motion, he turned us and lifted me up onto his desk. His hands left no inch of my skin untouched, groping me, undoing the buttons of my shirt. His palms were hot against my chest, baring my breasts to the room before stooping to suck one into his mouth. Electricity shot straight down my spine, and I threw my head back with a moan. I couldn't remember the last time I felt so alive, so free, as if the world spun just for me and pleasure, and at this moment, it did.

Tugging his shirt up out of his waistband, I sucked his earlobe and nipped at it. He continued to suckle my nipple while his hands inched my skirt up my thighs, and I reached for his belt buckle. A quickie on his desk wasn't my favorite idea, but we were too far gone to stop now.

Xander's hands went for my panties, pulling them down to my ankles and over my heels, and I gasped again when his fingers dipped inside my wet folds, spreading me. My mind reeled with need, something so carnal and base I didn't even recognize myself anymore. "Xander," I gasped, arching into his touch. Heat pooled low in my belly and I squirmed, aching for more of him. Hungry for every part of him.

"That's sir to you, Ms. Johnson," he growled as he pushed his finger into my slick entrance.

"God," I hissed, my head lolling as he added a second finger. I clenched and he clicked his tongue.

"Take those pretty manicured fingers of yours and touch your clit." His voice was commanding, but he kept his volume low. I raised my eyebrows but obeyed him, reaching for my clit to rub it. "God you're so sexy when you take orders." He stepped back, and I moved my fingers only to draw a scowl. "Did I say stop?"

"No, sir," I purred, realizing what he wanted. "Sorry, sir."

"Good girl," he purred, pulling his cock out. He stood stroking me while I rubbed myself. His tongue flicked over his bottom lip, and he jerked his chin up at me.

"Spread your legs farther, let me see that slick pussy." His thrusts were hard and quick; he used a thumb to hook around his boxers' elastic waistband and hold it low away from his balls. I spread my legs farther, resting one on the arm of his chair and letting my knees fall apart. It drove him wild; his eyes were hooded with desire.

"Mmm, look at you, milking your clit for me," he groaned. His voice was an octave lower—deeper than I'd ever heard it before, and my insides liquefied. He palmed the length of his engorged erection as his knees bent, his body dropping to the floor. "Move those fingers and let me taste you," he ordered, and I complied. My God did I want this.

I was breathing erratically before he even released a hot breath on my core, but when his tongue touched my sensitive flesh, I whimpered and jolted. I closed my eyes, unsure if I could handle the way he looked at me while he lapped at my core. His grip on my ankle tightened as he started to go faster, circling my clit with his tongue until I was squirming and moaning. When his fingers slid into me again, I came undone.

My body pulsed and jerked. I gripped the edge of the desk hard and rode out the waves of orgasm, careful to grit my teeth and not allow myself to make a peep. He groaned against my entrance, lapping up every drop of moisture my body produced, and I made him look up, my eyes begging for more. Gripping his tie, I pulled him up and he obliged, groping my breasts and pinching my nipples as he ran his length against my core.

"Do we need protection?" he asked before kissing me hard. We hadn't used it last time, but I'd been on the pill for a few years. I never had a thought in my mind about it until he said something.

"No, I'm on the pill ..." My taste on his mouth was intoxicating. "And I'm clean," I added, biting his lower lip. I felt his cock press against me and whimpered when he inched in.

"Tight." He groaned, his eyes rolling with pleasure. "You feel so tight." He pulled back a fraction before sliding in again.

I moaned, biting my lower lip as he hit me in all the right places. Every thrust eliciting a moan or a wordless sound of pleasure that seemed to spur him on. "You like that?" he growled, slamming me harder against the desk. He held my hips tightly as if he were afraid I would slip away, and I felt the second orgasm riding high in my belly.

"Harder, Xander!" I whimpered, and my eyes flew open. He was looking at me, through me, as if he could see all my secrets and dirty little fantasies. I couldn't hold the eye contact, too into it to focus, so I shut my eyes and arched into his thrusts. "Oh God, yes, just like that."

"God you're so dirty for me. A bad girl, on my desk, begging me for more ..."

His filthy talk and dominant touches fueled me on. I was close again, the sensitive nerves in my core tingling as he pistoned in and out of me. His thumb found my clit again, rubbing and circling until I grunted into the bend of his neck. My body tensed around him, and he growled against my skin. He bit down on my neck, and I felt his heat flood me while I pulsed around his length.

His thrusts slowed, and he kissed my collarbone softly before pulling out. I felt the sex drain from my body onto the desk and watched it drop to the floor. Xander backed away, tucking his moist dick into his boxers as he reached for a tissue and wiped up the mess —from the desk first, and then from my core. It was erotic and intimate, and I had to remind myself this was NSA. I should not be feeling what I was feeling.

"Holy shit," I breathed, still reeling from how good it felt.

He tossed the tissue in the trash and locked up his pants again before offering me a hand.

"Language, Ms. Johnson," he winked. "Someone might think we're having fun."

I didn't try to hide my grin as I slid off his desk, careful to avoid the mess on the carpet, and reached for my panties on the floor.

"Ah ah ..." He wagged a finger at me. "Those are mine now. I'm collecting them."

"But," I protested, realizing he was serious. I had to work the rest of my day with no underwear and his sex dripping down my thigh?

"And I'll send you my cell number. Text me so I'll know it's you and you've got it. Any time, day or night ..." He tucked his shirt in as he spoke, making sure his gig line was straight. "I trust I've satisfied you so we won't have a problem?"

It felt a bit distant and cold, like he was ushering me out of the room so quickly, but if he wanted NSA then I had to give it to him. At least I was getting something out of this arrangement.

"Yes, we're, uh ... It's fine," I mumbled, feeling stupid. I bent and picked up my phone then took the portfolio off his desk, amazed it hadn't taken a topple too. And I turned to go.

"Remember, no kissing and telling," he said, and I waved a hand at him. I knew if I looked back, he was going to see the stupid grin on my face, and I was certain that wasn't supposed to happen.

"Got it, Boss," I called, already feeling the swell of giddiness. There was no way I could keep this from Godwin, but why would I want to? He was good at keeping secrets, and if I didn't tell someone, I was going to burst.

Halfway back to my office, my phone started to ring. I didn't recognize the number, but it wasn't unusual for me to get calls on my personal number. I swiped to answer, and got the shock of my life.

"Hello?"

"Ms. Johnson, this is Sergeant William Pratt from the San Jose Police Department. We're at your father's house. We'd like you to come over and sit with him. There was a home invasion and your father was assaulted."

"Oh my God," I gasped. My heart sank so fast it felt like someone burst a balloon inside me. "Is he okay?"

"He's fine, just a knock to the head, but he will need someone to help him."

"Oh my God, I'm on my way." I hung up in a panic, then felt stupid for doing it, and turned toward Xander's office, deciding not to tell him. Dad would hate me dragging him into this, and it wasn't my place.

Instead, I shot a text to my team saying I was out for the rest of the afternoon and stopped by my office to grab my keys. Something was going on in Dad's life, and I felt like he didn't want me to know about it. First the car fire, now this? It just didn't sit right. I had to get to the bottom of it, and man, was I glad Xander had gotten me loosened up.

I needed it for what I was about to walk into.

9

XANDER

The day had been long and grating after Amelia left yesterday so abruptly. I wondered if it had anything to do with the proposition I gave her, the way I claimed her body like a piece of land. This morning, however, she came into work like nothing had happened, acted just as professional as always. As I walked past her desk on my way out, her head popped up and she nodded at me with a knowing look in her eye.

I had absolutely no problem with this arrangement, and if she never asked me once to hook up, or simply didn't respond to my call for her to tend to my needs, I would get the point. It was just sex to me, but I felt guarded. I'd never had an arrangement like this with a woman, not officially anyway, and I felt wary about how she would take it.

"Heading out for the evening, if you need anything." My tone carried the heavy insinuation that she was welcome to call me if the mood struck.

"Of course. You have that meeting with the new client, remember? And don't forget to check the new numbers. I'm excited to see what you think." Her eyebrows rose with anticipation, fingers clicking away at the keyboard while she still spoke. A master at multitasking, she had no clue that her ability to set aside the emotional pull a sexual relationship could have on a person and do her job professionally turned me on. It was like a drug watching her work, knowing she was a genius at what she did and she was doing it for me.

"Of course ... but you know you're not my secretary?" I narrowed my eyes at her in a fun expression and she rolled her eyes.

"Yeah, well I'm not working my butt off to land these cold contacts for you to forget about the initial contact. Just doing my due diligence, sorry if it seems like I'm nagging." The matter-of-fact way she spoke made me chuckle.

"Good night, Amelia. My phone will be turned on all evening." I wasn't sure I wanted to push send on a message yet, considering we just had sex on my desk yesterday. Not only did I not want her to think I was a sex-crazed lunatic, but I also wanted to test if she was really into this agreement.

"Sure thing." Her mumbled reply came as she refocused on her computer screen.

I pushed off her door frame and turned toward the elevators. The new potential client, whose name sounded an awful lot like an alias, was supposed to meet me at the Italian bistro down the block. John Smith was just too plain, too *white noise* to be his real name, but sometimes a man liked to feel out a situation before he jumped in. I could appreciate that.

I headed out to the restaurant, opting to walk the block in the brisk January air rather than having my driver usher me a few hundred yards to drop me at the door. San Jose was beautiful most days out of the year, and today, despite the winter chill, I was glad it wasn't raining. And there was a bit of foot traffic too, reminded me of my younger years when I'd get out and pound the pavement hunting down a good idea to expand on.

Next Gen had been a godsend for me. Buying the company from Laurence had paved a way forward for me, set me on a path to success I otherwise wouldn't have found. Oh, I'd have adored spending my father's fast-dwindling money, probably ended up landing on something else to make my fortune, but the tech firm was solid gold. I knew that the minute he asked me to partner with him.

Now, however, I felt like I was grasping at straws for ways to keep the thing booming. If my track record for scoring new clients held, this man, like the few before him, would walk away and end up not biting. Maybe I was wrong and I just had a few bad apples, but I was beginning to think it was something I was doing.

The host seated me and I ordered a bottle of wine. The menu was in Italian, making it difficult to understand the items, but I chose a simple lasagna, which was one word I could read easily. When the client approached, I folded the menu and set it to the side, standing to shake his hand.

"Mr. Smith," I said, gripping his hand firmly.

"Mr. Blackwell, it's good to meet you." Smith was dressed well, a tailored suit and dark blue tie, cuff links that cost as much as some men's used cars, and his hair was slicked back and to the side. Judging by the crow's-feet around his eyes, I'd have said he was in his fifties, but it was the storm in his eyes that caught me off guard, like he wasn't just here to talk business, or maybe he'd just left a stressful encounter.

"Sit," I said, gesturing. "I ordered us a glass of wine, and the waiter will be around to take our food order."

Unbuttoning my suit jacket, I sat and smoothed my tie against my chest. I'd done several dozen of these meet and greets with potential clients before. Most times they wanted to jump right into the action, talk about their project, what Next Gen could do for them. But Smith picked up his glass of wine and sipped it, giving me a once-over to end them all.

"How is business?" he asked casually, like he was asking about the weather, but his eyes never left mine.

I gave a small nod, letting the wine sit on my tongue a second longer before swallowing. "Strong. A few hiccups lately—normal stuff, nothing concerning. We've onboarded two new clients in the last quarter, and revenue is up 12 percent. I'm not exactly losing sleep."

Smith tilted his glass, watching the deep red swirl before taking another slow sip. Still didn't say much, just raised an eyebrow like he was waiting for more.

"You know how it is," I continued, setting my glass down. "The market's always changing. Tech moves faster than most industries. One day you're ahead of the curve, the next you're playing catch-up. That's why I'm selective with who we work with. Partnerships have to make sense."

He finally set his glass down, resting his hands on the table. "And you believe Next Gen is still ahead of that curve?"

I didn't hesitate. "Absolutely. We've got the infrastructure, the team, and the foresight. What we do best is pivot. That's what saved us when a few of our early projects lost steam—when other firms would've folded or floundered, we adjusted. We don't bet everything on one horse. Diversification keeps us agile."

Smith didn't nod or smile. He just stared like he was trying to read my heartbeat through my damn forehead. It wasn't uncomfortable exactly, but it wasn't pleasant either. I was used to being the one in control in these meetings. This guy? He felt like someone who'd done a lot of sitting across tables, sizing people up.

The waiter approached, polite smile in place, pad in hand. I glanced at Smith, waiting for him to give his order first, but he shook his head without even looking up. He had planned it this way, maybe a power move?

"Not hungry," he said.

The waiter's smile twitched but he turned to me. I gave a small shrug.

"I'm good too," I said. No point in eating if this wasn't going to be that kind of meeting. It unnerved me, but I tried to think about what Laurence would have done and not let myself get ahead of the curve.

The waiter nodded and disappeared. I brought my glass to my lips again, but didn't drink. Just held it there. Something about the way Smith kept watching me like I was the presentation made me want to step outside of myself for a second and recalibrate.

"You mind if I hit the restroom?" I asked, already pushing my chair back.

"Of course," he said, barely moving.

I stood and walked off without saying more. The hallway to the back was dimmer than the rest of the place. Clean, quiet, and just far enough from the dining room that I could exhale. I wasn't rattled exactly, but I needed a moment to clear my head. I splashed water on my face, took a deep breath, and stared at myself in the mirror for a beat longer than necessary.

When I came back into the dining room, Smith was exactly where I left him, except now his posture was just a touch too casual. Elbow on the table, fingers still resting near my wine glass. My phone, which I'd left beside it, was sitting half an inch closer to him than before. Screen on.

He didn't look up right away.

I crossed the space between us slow, deliberate. Slid back into my seat and glanced down at the phone. No notifications. No shift in the angle. But I knew. There wasn't anything overly sensitive on the phone, everything that was needed a password to access, but the idea that he felt comfortable enough to peruse my personal information irked me.

He met my eyes then, as if nothing had happened. "Everything all right?" he asked, voice smooth.

"Yeah," I said, forcing a slight smile. "Clean mirror. Good lighting. Got a second opinion on the tie."

He smirked, but didn't comment. Just lifted his glass again, sipped.

I let the moment sit. Let the silence stretch long enough to make it clear I noticed the shift. He didn't flinch. That told me what I needed to know—he wasn't sorry. If anything, he wanted me to notice.

I picked up my glass, gave it a slow turn between my fingers. If he wanted me to react, he'd be disappointed. I wasn't going to hand him that much power, but chances were, I would not be doing business with this gentleman.

"So," I said, voice even, "you said you like to know what you're walking into. What exactly are you looking for from a firm like mine?"

Smith relaxed back into his chair, like we'd hit a checkpoint he was waiting for.

"Consistency," he said. "Clarity. I've dealt with enough flash-in-the-pan companies to know how easy it is to get distracted by the next big thing. But I'm interested in something sustainable. Scalable."

I nodded. "We don't chase trends. We set our own direction. That's why we're still here."

That earned the faintest raise of his brows, like he approved but didn't want to make a show of it.

The conversation moved from there, threading through expected checkpoints—project lifespans, internal teams, client retention, our cloud architecture. All the stuff he probably already knew but needed to hear me say out loud. I gave him straight answers, kept my voice level, didn't oversell. The wine helped smooth the edges.

By the time we wrapped up, the bottle was mostly gone and the sky outside the restaurant had deepened into that post-sunset blue that blurred the city lights. Smith stood first, offering his hand.

"Pleasure," he said, voice as unreadable as ever.

"Likewise."

He walked out without looking back. I watched him go, waited until he was halfway down the block before I pulled my phone back in front of me and woke the screen.

A single text waited.

Amelia 6:28 PM: *M4S?*

The corner of my mouth pulled into a crooked smile. I didn't need to think twice.

I knew exactly what it meant. And it was just what I needed after such a strange interaction.

10

AMELIA

Dad insisted I take him to his place to pick up a few things, which I was adamantly opposed to, but how was I supposed to tell my father no? The night I went to sit with him at his house, it was hard seeing the way the vandals broke down his door to get at his stuff. But in the daylight, it was awful. I didn't even live there and I felt violated, like someone had crossed a line that made me feel vulnerable.

Dad was at my place now while I walked up the driveway at Xander's massive house. The sun was off duty, and the lights on the front of his house made it seem larger than I knew it was. I rang the bell, and he opened the door almost instantly, like he'd been waiting.

Of course he was waiting; I asked him to meet for sex.

"Come in," he said, glancing around outside before backing away and opening the door inward.

I passed by him, shuffling into his living room awkwardly. It was a mutual agreement, one where we both had equal say in when it happened or how frequently. That didn't make me feel any less out of place or tense as the reason for me showing up sank in.

Back when I saw the front of Dad's house boarded up, caution tape still pinned in place while the home awaited repairs, I felt so tense I could throw up. Dad would be staying with me for a while again, this time so that I could care for him. I'd gotten my fill of his parenting when I was sick, which was why I sent him home, but now I felt like he'd be safer at my place.

"Nice digs," I said stiffly as my eyes scanned over the oversized leather furniture. The hearth had a crackling fire, though it wasn't wood burning. The perfect flicker of gas logs created a good aesthetic, but the glass kept the heat locked away.

"Thanks. I hired a designer, barely spend any time here." He chuckled as he walked past me, leading me deeper into the cavernous space. I could see straight through his entire house to his well-lit backyard where a pool stretched past a cement patio. The kitchen lights were off, but the glow of a smart refrigerator made me choke back a sound of awe.

"Wow," I breathed, and he heard me, chuckling again as he stepped up to a polished liquor cabinet.

"Glad you approve." Xander pulled out two tumblers and a bottle of amber-colored liquid. After the past twenty-four hours of dealing with Dad's denial that the car fire and the break in may be related, I could've used a lot more than a stiff drink. I wanted to be held, to have my hair played with and my emotions validated. But if a quickie was all I'd get, I had to be okay with that. It was the arrangement we had come to.

I meandered over toward the fireplace where I saw a few pictures in silver frames. A few of them looked like the images that came with the frames. But one of them stood out—a picture of a teenage boy that looked a lot like Xander next to a middle-aged man who could be his father. It was a sweet image, but there was no woman in the picture.

"Ah, don't pay any attention to those," he said, setting a glass of whiskey down on the mantle in front of me. I felt his hand on my hip slide around to my belly and his palm splayed on my shirt as he pulled me back against his chest. I took the glass, downed it, and turned in his arms to find his lips ready to devour mine.

I wanted to ask about the portrait, where his mother was, but he consumed me entirely. His hand slipped the glass out of my grasp, and I didn't even know where he set it. The next thing I knew he was moving me, guiding me away from the fireplace. I kept my eyes shut, instinctively following his lead as I devoured his hungry kisses.

"I am so glad you texted. I was going to call you." Xander's words came between heavy breaths and contact between our mouths. I gripped the sides of his shirt and pulled it upward out of the waistband of his slacks.

"Dinner didn't go well?" My concern wasn't about work. It was about him. He must've needed me the way I felt I needed him. The release of endorphins too great of a relief to ignore my body's call for it.

"Let's just say I'm having you for dinner." Xander backed me against a door and reached for the knob. When it gave way, I stumbled into a dark room. My hands reached for my blouse's buttons, working them quickly as he flicked on the light and undid his belt. "I've been fantasizing about you all day."

I didn't bother asking if it was his bedroom; I knew it was. The scent of his cologne, a mixture of earthy tones and leather, wafted through the room. My vision zeroed in on the four-poster bed and satin sheets. I couldn't wait to be straddling him, riding him until we both called out each other's names in release.

"Well, you're welcome to help yourself," I purred as my blouse parted ways with my body, landing in a pool at my feet. My lace bra and matching panties complemented the fire I felt between my legs as I slid my pants down my thighs and kicked them aside. His eyes raked up and down my semi-naked body, lust in their depths. "Or would you rather I help myself to you?"

Xander growled as he pulled his dress shirt up over his head and tossed it, a sound that came from deep in his chest. He hurtled himself toward me, and his hands cupped my breasts, kneading them through the lace. My moan elicited a smile from him as he broke away.

"You're definitely the main course tonight, gorgeous. And I've been starving for you." His lips trailed along my collarbone as he pushed me toward the bed. My back hit the cool satin sheets, and Xander leaned over me, his weight pinning my wrists above my head.

His chest was cut and bronzed, my eyes raking over every ridge of muscle and flesh. I hadn't seen him naked entirely yet, but I had a feeling I was about to.

His eyes were slanted and dark with hunger as he ducked his head and moved my bra to the side with his chin, worshiped each of my nipples, then dipped lower to my stomach. He lavished adoration on the curve of my hip before sliding my panties to the side and pressing a finger between my thighs. "So wet already." His voice was husky with lust as he brought his wet digit to my lips. "Sample yourself?" His hands loosed my wrists then and he smirked.

I didn't question him. I parted my lips and flicked my tongue against the digit, lapping up every drop of my own arousal and the taste of me on his skin. His groan of approval spurred me on to suck his finger deeper into my mouth, tonguing it in arcs. My hips twisted against the mattress as arousal flooded through me, Xander watching with hooded eyes and a cocked eyebrow as if he knew what I wanted even before I did.

"Christ, Amelia," he breathed, and then he was devouring my mouth again.

A moan escaped me as he slid two fingers inside me, his tongue matching the demanding rhythm of his hand. I felt like liquid heat, molten under his touch and I arched my back, pushing against his hand and the steely length of his erection pressed against my thigh. I wanted his flesh, not his pants in the way.

"Xander," I whimpered, "I need you."

He chuckled low in his throat, a sound so wicked and foreign coming from him it made my blood sing. I hated how he backed away, but I loved how he took my panties with him. As I lay there watching him smell them, I pulled off my bra. He shoved them into his pocket, and then stripped the rest of the way as I watched. His body was exquisite—rock-hard abs, his cock thick and ready for me. I blushed but didn't cover myself as he locked his lust-filled eyes on mine and crawled back up the bed.

"God I'm going to enjoy this." His voice came out raw as he looked at me. The anticipation was almost too much to bear. "You're so beautiful." He breathed in between kisses along the line of my jaw and down my neck, descending until his lips met their target. I arched into him, needing this release.

My heart beat faster as Xander's hot breath tickled my sensitive folds. He reached for his nightstand, stubble grinding on my core, and pulled out a bottle of whiskey. I knew what he intended, but it didn't prepare me for the feeling when the liquid made contact with my already sensitive flesh. It burned slightly, then cooled, and his tongue lapped at it and sucked me.

"Xander," I whimpered as he started to lick, his chin damp against my pussy, his tongue circling my swollen clit. My hips rocked back and forth, seeking more contact, more friction. A moan escaped me as I felt him slide a finger inside me, then another, and I was so close already before he poured more of the fiery liquid across my mound.

"Mmm, messy and delicious," he growled, and I began to shudder.

He continued to tease me, his tongue flicking at my core, licking up the alcohol, until I was arching off the bed, clawing at the sheets as my orgasm crashed through me. I jolted and shook, squeezing his head between my thighs, and he growled in pleasure as my hips arching off the bed took him for a ride.

His aggressiveness only made me want him more, and as soon as my trembles subsided, I pulled his hair, urging him closer to me. I wanted the taste of my juices on his mouth, the flavor of the whiskey to drink down. He obliged, his lips crashing against mine hungrily, his tongue demanding entrance, and I gave it to him without hesitation. He was hard, throbbing against my thigh, and I reached down to guide him to my center.

I could feel every vein on his cock as I stroked down his shaft, aroused by my own wanton behavior. I'd never been this woman before, but with Xander, I felt like an animal. His eyes were dark with lust and need as he braced himself over me, our chests heaving in unison.

"Tell me you want it hard," he growled, and I arched my hips against him in response, effectively silencing any words that might have come out. He growled again, this time with my moan of approval, and then he was inside me, thick and hot and oh so deep. I wrapped my legs around him, pulling myself closer, my nails sinking into his back as he thrust hard and fast.

"Like that, don't you?" he gasped, his eyes locked onto mine, and I could only moan in response, my head thrown back against the pillow as he continued to pound into me relentlessly. I scratched against his back harder, my nail digging into the sweat-slicked skin as my orgasm built again.

"God, you're tight," he groaned, his grip on my hips tightening as he slammed into me even harder. I clenched around him, hoping to increase his pleasure, and he gritted his teeth before crushing his lips against mine again. My coil was tight, and my body was ready to tip over the edge. The way his dick stroked my insides was electric.

"Come for me, Amelia," he growled into my ear, and lost to the ecstasy of the moment, I obeyed him.

My body contracted around him, hands clawing at his sides, and I felt him flood me, cock pulsing against my convulsions. He bit down on my shoulder and groaned out my name, his hips still jerking against mine.

As our breathing returned to normal, he collapsed on top of me, hands planted on either side of my shoulders as he panted. I could feel his dick still inside me, softening but not yet ready to fully withdraw. "That was ..." he trailed off, his eyes filled with something I couldn't yet decipher. Afraid of the answer, I bit my lower lip and averted my gaze.

"Yeah," I mumbled. He had no clue what that was to me, but I couldn't tell him.

Xander rolled to the side, sprawled out on the comforter. The sex drained from my body, mingling with the whiskey spilled on the bed, and I wondered what I was supposed to do now. The stress was slowly evaporating, just like it was supposed to, but my heart ached to be held. I turned on my side, ready to get up and get dressed when Xander took my wrist.

"So you had a bad day? What happened? Why the booty call?"

I lingered, legs draped over the side of the bed with my back to him. "No one says booty call anymore." I chuckled and he groaned.

"And people really say M4S? It was always a hookup to me."

I sighed again, feeling the weight creeping back into my shoulders. "Dad's house got broken into so he needs a place to stay until the crew fixes the front door. It's stressful having him around." My white lie allowed some of the steam to vent off of me, but I didn't want Xander fully involved. Dad would be angry if I told Xander the whole story, and I didn't want a pity party.

"Wow, yeah. I'm sorry. Does he need help?"

"Christ no," I hissed, turning over my shoulder. "You can't tell him I told you. He's ... prideful." I winced as I accused my very vulnerable father of something he most certainly was. But it was a family thing. Still, Xander was his close friend, and I appreciated that he wanted to help if need be. "Thanks though."

"Yeah, well, thank you. I needed that." He scrubbed a hand down his face, but I sat there feeling like a lump. When he opened his eyes he reached out to touch my thigh. "It happens, Amelia. I'm sure the police will sort it out. Man, that guy has had a string of bad luck; first the car, now this."

"Yeah," I mumbled, thinking about it with fear needling my conscience—that Dad might have gotten in with the wrong crowd—but I wouldn't tell Xander that. God knows I'd never hear the end of it from Dad. "I should go ... He's going to expect me, and if I'm not on time, he'll freak out."

I stood to grab my clothing, now acutely aware that Xander had too many pairs of my panties stashed away somewhere. He watched as I dressed, lying on his side unashamed. When I finished buttoning up and found my shoes, I stood by the door, wondering if I was supposed to kiss him goodbye or how this worked.

"So, see you at work?" I asked, now feeling awkward. If this was a real relationship, I'd stay. We'd hold each other. He'd make me breakfast in bed in the morning.

"Yeah, see ya." He didn't even get up. He just lay there watching me slink away with my hollow shell of a heart that was already regretting this decision. Godwin was wrong. NSA sex was not amazing; it was torture. I needed arms around me, not orgasms—though those were amazing.

I was a fool for thinking I could do this, but I didn't want to back out now. And cut myself off from him entirely when I really liked him? No, I had to stay and let my dumb heart get attached only to be shredded later on. Which was what was going to happen.

On the drive home, between bouts of frustration and heaviness, I thought about what Xander said. I was sure the police would try to get to the bottom of things, but my gut told me there were things Dad wasn't telling people. Things I needed to know. And if he wouldn't talk about it, I had to look into it myself. The fool was too prideful to know his own limits, so someone had to watch out for him.

I just prayed it wasn't something dangerous. Sometimes he made really bad decisions.

11

XANDER

The head of the table was the perfect vantage point to observe every member of the marketing team. Amelia and Godwin were sitting side by side, their chairs practically touching. Their quiet chatter during our meeting was like a persistent buzz in my ear, pulling my focus away from the task at hand. I had noticed them buddying up before, exchanging whispers and leaning in closer than professional decorum would typically allow. It reminded me of high school days when passing notes and stifling giggles was a daily routine. I wanted to dismiss it, to brush off the nagging feeling, but something inside me stirred, uneasy at how Amelia leaned in, her shoulder almost overlapping his.

"And the new app for Touchstone?" I asked Meredith, the head of our sales department. She stood by the whiteboard, ready to present this month's numbers. Her fingers deftly handled the laser pointer as she directed our attention to the screen.

"Excellent, sir," Meredith replied with a nod. The pointer's red dot circled a series of charts. "You'll see the team has done a fantastic job with the build. Donahue is pleased with the work." Her voice was steady, a rhythmic background to the visuals, but a flicker of movement to my right stole my attention. I found myself glancing at

Amelia again. She was smiling at Godwin, her eyes sparkling with a warmth that seemed more personal than professional.

I had known from the start when I arranged our no-strings-attached relationship that Amelia and Godwin shared a close bond. They seemed inseparable, often seen whispering and laughing together in the office corridors or sharing lunch at the tiny café across the street. When I first joined Laurence's company years ago, Amelia was the sole powerhouse of the marketing department, tirelessly crafting campaigns and juggling multiple projects.

During the final stretch of her degree, she convinced her father to hire Godwin, passionately arguing that he was "magic with marketing." True to her word, Godwin had consistently delivered impressive results, boosting our client numbers and enhancing our brand's image.

Yet, despite understanding all this, a knot of jealousy twisted in my stomach, a feeling I couldn't easily dismiss. Amelia was undeniably single and stunning, with her dark curls and confident stride turning heads wherever she went. I had no legitimate claim over her personal life—or her body, for that matter. As long as she maintained her professionalism at work and satisfied my desires when I felt the need for connection, I had no grounds to complain. Despite their shared moments and the whispers that sometimes reached my ears, I had no reason to be jealous or act possessive, regardless of the dynamic between them.

"After the Valentine's Day launch, they went full scale," Meredith explains, snapping my wandering focus back to her presentation. She stands confidently in front of the conference room, her slides glowing on the screen behind her. It was the last presentation for this meeting, and I was eager to return to my desk and dive back into my tasks. "Touchstone has grown by 30 percent, with their user numbers steadily climbing. If this momentum continues, they'll see their revenue double by April."

The room erupted into applause at the announcement. Our team knew that one of our biggest clients' apps had become a massive success, translating into a significant boost in revenue for us. These were the high-stakes projects we aimed to secure and absolutely excel at. Except, I continued to fall short in discovery meetings, and clients didn't seem to want to feast on what I presented to them.

"Excellent work today, team." I stood, splaying one hand across my chest as I slid the other into my pocket. "Thank you for having your presentations finished on time." I focused my eyes on Amelia and remembered that shade of lipstick well, the same shade that stained my dick three days ago when she was on her knees in my office—not in the mood for the full thing, but willing to take care of me in my time of need.

"I'll see you all next month for our team meeting unless I see you sooner."

One by one, they stood to leave, Godwin trailing behind Amelia, who was one of the first to pop out of her seat. I wasn't sure why I expected things to change. It'd been three and a half weeks since I presented that offer to her—sex whenever either of us wanted it without any change in our professional interactions. We'd gone at it like horny teens at least four times a week now, and to her credit, she really hadn't missed a beat.

Amelia arrived on time for work, never clocked out late. She carried herself in every professional way she had previous to that first time in my car, especially when we were alone, which amazed me. It was everything I was looking for, so why was I upset that she was doing it so well?

"Okay, sir?" Meredith hovered by the doorway of the conference room with her portfolio clutched in her hand, and I nodded once at her. So lost in thought that other employees could see the distraction was what I expected out of Amelia, not something I thought I'd be doing.

"I'm good, thank you." After dismissing Meredith, I cracked my neck and loosened my tie, then headed down the hall toward my office.

The way she smiled at him still nagged at me though. It was intimate, the way you see happily married couples. She and Godwin had a bond so close they could do that, something so open between them they could offer a simple expression without words and know what the other was thinking. I'd never had that with anyone, never felt the need. But for some reason it really bothered me that she had it—and with someone other than me.

My office door pushed open easily, not latched the way I remembered leaving it. When I strolled in, I saw Laurence standing by the windows, staring out over San Jose's city skyline with his hands tucked in his slacks pockets. He turned to smile at me as I stalked toward my desk. I wanted time to think, and I'd gotten thrust into another meeting, except I didn't know this one was on the books.

"Larry, what brings you in?" I strutted to my chair, tightening my tie back up, and sat down, gesturing to the leather-and-wood chairs parked opposite the overly large desk. He turned and seemingly glided across the faded blue Berber to one of the chairs to sit down, unbuttoning his suit jacket as he sat. It was a hideous tan number, but the man didn't need to dress well when he knew how to finesse a client like a race car driver on the back roads.

"Just checking in. I've got lunch with Amelia planned, thought I'd pop in." He relaxed in the seat, stretched one leg over the other. "How are things going around here?"

He acted casual and nonchalant, but Laurence never came around asking how things were going. I'd owned the company for two years, hadn't had him on payroll for over a year now. He got his profit share every year in the fourth quarter and knew that things were on track. His visit seemed suspect, but after Amelia's venting session about how his home had been broken into a few weeks ago, how repairs were taking longer than planned, I felt bad for him. He was hiding things from me as a friend, but it was due to his own pride. He could've asked me and I'd have paid the insurance claim myself—gotten his house fixed up already.

"Things are good," I told him while pulling out my phone. I shot a text to Amelia quickly, rather than calling to have her paged down here. I didn't want Laurence to think I wanted him gone, but I did. It annoyed me more than I expected to see Amelia next to Godwin like that.

"Good, good …" He nodded his head absently, scanned the room over once. "Sales are good? Marketing is going well?"

When he mentioned Amelia's department, I came to the natural conclusion that he was here on her behalf, with or without her knowing it. I understood it. He was a doting father, worried about his daughter after selling off his company where she was employed. I relaxed back into my chair as I decided he was probably checking to make sure she was being taken care of and paid well. I didn't blame him.

"I think you might have more problems than me right now. Amelia told me you're staying with her? Your house was broken into?" The springs on my chair bounced as I rocked in it, waiting for Amelia to show up and drag her father out of my office so I could stew and obsess in peace.

"Well, I wish she wouldn't have said anything. No need to worry you." As an old friend, I did worry about him at times. After he sold off the company, he got quiet, went to some dark places sometimes. But he always rebounded, so I never said much. "Just a random break-in, but boy did I get a knock to the head." He rubbed the back of his as he chuckled.

"She didn't mention that, but you were right for defending your home." I leaned forward as I heard the rhythmic click of high heels on the hallway floor. "You know, if you need anything you can call me. I might be able to help."

"Actually, maybe you can—"

"I'm so glad you texted," I heard, cutting Laurence off, and my eyes popped up to see Amelia looking down at her blouse, fingers on the third button from the top. She stopped three strides into my office and looked up at me as Laurence slowly turned over his shoulder.

Amelia's jaw dropped, and her face went white as a sheet. "Oh God," she mumbled before turning on her heel and walking back out the door. I laughed it off, but Laurence narrowed his eyes in confusion.

"Wrong office maybe?" I chuckled, but I knew I was the one to ask her to come down. I should have assumed she would take that text as a sign I wanted her, though we'd gotten used to using the term *M4S* lately. It was her way of talking, and though I was much older than her, I tried to talk her language.

"Now, what's gotten into her?" He stood, staring at the door.

"Don't let me keep you. Go on and have your lunch. I'll be around if you want to chat when you're done." I wasn't trying to rush him out, but I was glad to see him go. If Amelia came running the instant I texted her, then the Godwin issue must not have been a problem.

"Sure, I'll catch you later," he said, seeming frustrated or worried.

Laurence let himself out, but instead of stewing and obsessing, I found fresh energy. Call it an ego boost, but her rushing to my beck and call was kind of hot. I liked that a lot, and I planned to tap into that more. Maybe she'd forget Godwin Tharmor existed, and I wouldn't have to sit through any more meetings like that ever again.

12

AMELIA

I rushed out of that office faster than the blood rushed to my cheeks, buttoning up my shirt to hide my shame. The heat crept up the back of my neck to my ears too, making them burn, and when I heard Dad in the hallway behind me—the telltale squeak of his Doc Martins on the ground—I reeled around and stood with my shoulders squared.

"What are you doing here?" I hissed, not meaning to come across as angry or as flustered as I was. Here I thought that text was Xander asking me to come relieve some stress, which we'd gotten very efficient at this week, and I walked in to see Dad seated in the very chair Xander bent me over only two days ago.

"I came for lunch," he said, narrowing his eyes defensively. "Can't I just have a quick catch-up with an old friend before my date with my daughter for lunch?" His hands splayed out, in defense, palms upward.

My first instinct upon seeing him seated there was to feel mortified that my father had seen me in a state of undress while entering my boss's office. It was only a few buttons, but it was enough to make a fast assumption. But seeing the defensiveness in his expression made me stop and try to rethink things on the fly. Had he even looked up at me before I turned and ran out? Maybe he never saw my shirt unbuttoned at all.

"I just meant—" I huffed and tried to calm myself. "I'm sorry. I wasn't expecting you, and I thought Xander needed me for something important." I inwardly winced as my brain subconsciously reordered my father's visit to a lower priority than a booty call with my boss. It wasn't how I wanted to feel, but apparently it was the depth of my true emotion. Reason number one why I shouldn't have been screwing Xander in the first place.

"Are you ready for lunch? If not, I can hang out with Xander a while longer." He pointed his thumb over his shoulder, and I tossed my hair, willing the blood to drain from my cheeks so I could breathe again. I was sweating too, palms so wet they felt like I just got out of a pool.

"Yes, now is good. I'll just grab my purse ..." Turning, I led him toward my office, door standing open after leaving in a hurry. I was excited to get that text. After Godwin teased me the entire meeting about how flustered I was over Xander, my body was worked up. I had told Godwin in a moment of weakness that some *things* were happening, though I didn't give explicit detail, and ever since he'd been playing devil's advocate.

After snatching my purse, I let Dad escort me downstairs and across the street to the little café. When he owned Next Gen, we had lunch a few times a week—whenever he wasn't in meetings with clients or potential clients. It had been a fond habit, one I missed. So when he invited me to dine with him today, I couldn't pass up the opportunity. He'd been staying with me since the break-in, and it appeared he'd be around a while longer. The insurance company was butting heads with contractors, and Dad was stuck in the middle of a financial battle over how much it would cost. I pitied him, which was the only reason I didn't offer to put him up in a hotel.

The café was busy but not packed, the kind of midday lull that made the clinking of forks and the soft murmur of conversation feel more intimate than usual. Dad and I settled at a wrought iron table under a red umbrella, the fabric faded from years in the sun. He squinted into the light and waved off my offer to switch spots.

"I like the sun," he said with a small shrug, unfolding his napkin onto his lap like it was a formal dinner. "Feels good on my joints."

"Well, you're not that old," I said with a smile, trying to lighten the air that still felt too heavy from earlier. My cheeks had finally cooled, but my stomach was tight with nerves.

A waitress came over and took our order—chicken salad sandwich for me, turkey club for him, two iced teas. We handed over the menus, and I glanced across the table as he leaned back with a little sigh, stretching his legs like a man twice his age.

We were quiet for a minute, both watching a couple two tables over arguing in hushed tones. I felt like I should say something, but the words got tangled up behind my teeth. So I went for the obvious.

"I'm glad you came today," I said, though I wasn't sure I meant it. "Felt like old times for a second."

He smiled faintly, but it didn't reach his eyes. "Yeah. We used to do this more often, huh?"

"Back when you were at Next Gen all the time. You barely had time for coffee, let alone lunch."

"I miss it sometimes," he said, drumming his fingers on the edge of the table. "Then I remember the stress and the twenty-four-hour workdays, and I come to my senses."

I laughed, but there was something distant in his tone. Like he was holding something in. I reached for my tea, letting the straw click against the glass just to have something to do.

"You sure you're comfortable at my place?" I asked carefully, eyes on the condensation ring he'd left on the table. "I know it's not exactly a luxury suite, and the couch has that weird spring that jabs you—"

"You don't have to say it," he said, cutting me off gently. "I know you'd rather have your space back."

That made my stomach twist. "That's not what I meant."

"But it's what you feel." He gave a shrug that tried to look casual.

"It's okay, Amelia. I didn't plan to stay this long. I'm heading back tonight."

"What?" I sat up straighter, caught off guard. "No, Dad, you can't. The door's still—"

"I'll figure it out," he said quickly. "Get it replaced this weekend. Or board it up. I just ... I need to be in my own space again."

There was something brittle in the way he said it, like he was trying not to break open in front of me.

So I softened my voice, leaned forward a little. "Did the insurance company say when the contractors are coming out?"

He made a face like he'd bitten into something sour. "They're still arguing over the quote. Apparently, the first contractor inflated the labor costs, so now it's a whole back and forth. Nothing's scheduled yet."

I sat back frowning. "And the front door? What, are you just supposed to wait around indefinitely with a plywood slab and a broken lock?"

"I told you, I'll figure it out," he said again, but it sounded thinner this time.

"Okay. But even if you do figure that out—what about the alarm system? Shouldn't it have gone off during the break-in?"

He hesitated. Long enough that I noticed.

"It was off," he said finally, voice flat. "Has been."

"What do you mean it was off?"

"I didn't pay the bill," he muttered, not quite meeting my eyes. "Canceled the autopay a few months ago. Didn't have the money for it, and it seemed ... optional."

"Optional?" I blinked. "Dad, that's literally why it's there."

"I didn't think someone was going to actually break in, Amelia."

My throat tightened. He sounded defensive now, like a kid who knew he screwed up and was trying to justify it.

"But even if I had kept it on," he added quickly, as if reading my mind, "the electric's going to get shut off anyway. I got the final notice this morning. If I don't pay by Monday, I won't have lights. No power, no fridge, no heat. So the alarm wouldn't work regardless."

I stared at him. "Why didn't you tell me any of this?"

"Because it's not your responsibility." His jaw clenched, and he looked out toward the street. "You've got your own life. I didn't want to drag you into my mess."

"But you're already in my apartment," I said, not unkindly. "And now you want to go back to a house with no door, no electricity, and no security system?"

He didn't answer that.

He just picked up his tea, took a slow sip, and set it down again—hands steady, expression blank.

I leaned forward. "What about your profit share? You said when you officially retired, that was going to keep you afloat."

He paused—just long enough. "I spent it," he said finally. His tone was flat. "Took a gamble, literally. Casino. Thought I could stretch it into something more, but I didn't know when to quit."

I stared at him. "You what?"

He wouldn't meet my eyes. "I know. It was stupid. I thought maybe I'd hit big and not have to lean on anyone. I lost more than I could afford to." A lie. Or half of one, at best. Something about the way he said it—quick, rehearsed, vague. And he never talked about gambling before. Not even recreationally.

I sat back in my chair, trying to breathe through the slow flood of shock. "How much do you need?"

He let out a sigh and rubbed his jaw. "To catch up on utilities? About six hundred. But to get ahead again—to get the door fixed, and pay off what I've put on cards ... I don't know. Ten? Twelve?"

"Twelve thousand?" I choked on my sip of tea. A few heads at nearby tables turned.

"I've been working," he added quickly, like that would soften the number. "A few part-time gigs. Just enough to stay ahead of the worst of it. Deliveries. Some warehouse work overnight a few times a week."

My heart ached. "Why didn't you tell me? I could've helped sooner."

"Because I'm not your kid," he said, too sharply. "I don't need you putting food on my table. I just need a little help until things level out."

I stared at the tabletop. Twelve thousand dollars. I didn't have that kind of money sitting around. I definitely couldn't ask Xander for it. That wasn't the kind of favor you slipped in between pillow talk and quarterly projections.

"Okay," I said slowly. "Maybe it's time to think about selling the house." He stiffened. "I'm serious. You could sell it, get something smaller. Or—" I hesitated. "You could stay with me for a while. For real. Move in until you're back on your feet."

He looked at me like I'd just slapped him across the face. "What, so you can put food on my table?"

"No. So I know you're safe. So I don't come home one day and find out someone broke in again, or that you've been sitting in the dark for a week without telling me."

His eyes narrowed, voice rising. "Are you trying to put me in a home now?"

"What? No! That's not—Dad, that's not what I'm saying."

"Sure sounds like it," he snapped. "You want me under your roof so you can manage me like I'm some burden to organize."

I opened my mouth, then closed it. This wasn't about logic anymore. His pride was hurt. He was spiraling.

"You'd rather just rot in that house, sitting by candlelight with a baseball bat by the door?" I shot back, frustrated despite myself.

"I'd rather not feel like an old man with nothing to show for a lifetime of work!" he barked, pushing back his chair. It scraped loudly against the concrete patio. "I don't need you—or Xander—or anyone else telling me how to live."

"You brought Xander into this?" I asked, incredulous.

"He's your boss, isn't he? Or is that just part of it now?" he said, bitterly, and I flinched.

I stood slowly, palms flat against the table. "I'm going to help with the electric. Just—please don't go home until the door is fixed. That's all I'm asking."

He didn't respond. He just shook his head like he couldn't stand to hear another word from me, then turned and walked away—fast, too fast for someone who'd claimed his knees were giving him trouble last week.

I didn't follow. I sat back down, staring at the empty space across from me, heart hammering in my chest.

Something was wrong. He wasn't just broke—he was scared. Hiding something. The break-in didn't feel random anymore. And if he wouldn't tell me the truth, I was going to have to find it myself.

13

XANDER

A few days had passed since Laurence's surprise visit to my office. Amelia and I hadn't spoken about it, not so much as a passing thought. I had gotten so busy with the good problem of handling incoming inquiries for potential projects, I hadn't even called her to my office, and my body was feeling the strain of sexual tension.

From where I stood now, behind the tinted glass of my office window, I had a perfect view of the café across the street. My eyes had drifted there out of habit, and now they refused to move. Amelia was sitting at one of the umbrella-covered tables with Godwin, just two tables over from where she sat with her father a few days ago after that comical shock she had. I'd have liked to see how far she took her little striptease for me that day had we not been in her father's presence.

Today, however, the tension I felt wasn't eased by her smile or the way she seemed to glow in the sunlight. It only swelled as she laughed at Mr. Tharmor's jokes, touched his arm lightly, leaned in toward him to look at his phone screen. He ate up that attention like a man dying of thirst in a desert, while I watched on from several floors up with my hands fisted in my pants pockets.

I recognized his laugh before I even noticed her hand on his shoulder. Too familiar. Too comfortable. The way she leaned into him, the tilt of her head, that full-bodied laugh she gave him—it scraped something raw inside me.

She didn't laugh like that with me.

He said something and she touched his arm again, fingers curling briefly before pulling back. And it wasn't even the touch itself—it was how effortless it looked. So natural.

If she moved on, if she started dating someone like him, there wouldn't be room for our arrangement anymore. She'd have to commit to him, draw a line. End us.

And she looked like she could. From where I stood, the natural chemistry they had seemed so fluid that any moment she would lean into him and kiss him, give him that gaze-locked expression she held for me alone. Or had she? Had I been too blind to notice this intimacy she shared with him leading up to my request for a no-strings arrangement with her?

I turned away from the window with my peace rankled, sinking into the sofa across my office. My hands rose to scrub my face of stress, then slid upward to my forehead where my fingers tangled in my hair. I planted my elbows on my knees and let my eyes close to block out the image of her next to him, but my thoughts refused to obey me.

It wasn't just the way she looked at him—it was the way he looked at her. Like he understood her. Like he deserved to. That bothered me more than anything else. It felt unfair—how some people seemed to move through life forming bonds without trying, like emotional gravity just pulled people toward them. Meanwhile, I was stuck in this orbit I couldn't escape, watching from a distance. Too much history under my skin, too many walls built too high. I didn't even know what it felt like to laugh like that with someone.

Amelia had that. At least with Godwin, and it made me feel like an intruder in a life I only got to borrow in pieces.

Maybe I was stupid to think I could keep things casual with her. That we could have this thing and pretend it didn't mean more.

Because now that I'd had her—tasted the version of myself that existed when she was around—I couldn't look away. Couldn't not want it, even if I'd never say it out loud.

I leaned back on the couch, staring at the ceiling like it held some sort of answer. But all it did was press the silence deeper into my psyche and drive me insane. I hated this part—when I got too far inside my own head.

Something about watching Amelia so open with someone else scraped at an old wound. One I thought I'd buried deep enough to forget, but the scar of which was still permanently etched in my heart. But it came back, sharp and uninvited as the day I felt it the first time.

I was eight years old again. Standing at the front door in my pajamas, bare feet on cold tile, watching my mother zip up a suitcase with hands that didn't shake. I begged her not to go. I held her wrist. I remember that clearly—how small my hand looked against her skin. How tiny I felt knowing that no matter what I said I couldn't change her mind.

"Please," I'd said. "Please just stay. I'll be better. I swear."

She didn't cry. She didn't kneel down or soften. Her eyes were dry and hard when she slid her arm free from my grasp, not in an overly harsh way but not the kindness of a mother's touch either.

"It's time for you to be a man, Xander," she'd said. "You don't need me for that." Then she walked out. Just like that.

That was the day I learned what it meant to be a man: it meant being alone. It meant silence where comfort should be, pride where softness used to live. And I've carried that definition with me every goddamn day since.

Even now, with Amelia—especially with Amelia—I could feel it there between us like a wall I didn't know how to tear down. Wanting her didn't change the fact that I didn't know how to let her in. And God, I was furious about it.

Furious that everyone else seemed to know how to be close. How to be loved without it slipping through their fingers. Furious that after all these years, I was still that kid standing at the door—watching someone walk away.

My hands shook as I took out my phone. The surge of jealousy over her smiling laughter with Godwin Tharmor had me feeling impulsive, obsessive even. I sent her a message telling her I needed her as I rose off the couch and strutted to the window, already loosening my tie.

Xander 12:13 PM: *Come up*

Just two words. I didn't even add a period. Didn't need to. She'd know what it meant.

I stared out the window. My pulse was louder than it should've been. She was still at the café. Still laughing. But then she glanced down at her phone. I saw the shift, even from across the street—her smile faltering, hand retreating from where it rested on Godwin's arm. She stood abruptly, said something too quick to catch, then leaned in and hugged him. That made my jaw clench.

She didn't hug me like that.

Then Amelia turned and scurried across the sidewalk, weaving through traffic without waiting for the crosswalk light. She half jogged up the steps to our building, her hair catching in the breeze, her body tense with purpose.

Moments later, I heard the elevator ding and the soft click of her heels against the tile hallway. The door to my office opened without a knock. She stepped inside, cheeks pink, eyes searching mine.

"You texted," she said, breath slightly hitched.

And for a second, I forgot how to breathe.

I wanted her, and I had called for her attention, now here she was. She didn't hesitate to leave him sitting there alone, so that said something—but what? And when she reached behind herself and locked the door, I knew she understood why she'd been beckoned.

Except, it wasn't the sex that I needed right now. It was whatever she had been giving him—the closeness, the bond, the smiles. I wanted that. My heart craved that.

"Xander?" she asked, plucking one heel off then the other. "Are you okay?"

"Clothes off, now," I growled possessively, undoing my tie and tugging it off my neck.

She pursed her lips then dipped her head and began to strip. Slowly she undressed herself, beginning with the top, then the skirt, her silk stockings next followed by her panties, all of them discarded haphazardly on the floor. When she was naked, she stood there in front of me with her hands crossed over her chest, covering her breasts, as if she needed to hide her beauty from me.

I removed my shirt and pulled my dick out of my slacks, then gestured to the heavy oak desk behind me. "Bend over," I ordered.

Amelia's eyes widened, but she did as I said without question. She leaned over, revealing that luscious ass of hers—my favorite part of her body—and I couldn't help but spank it once, just because I could. A soft gasp escaped her plump lips and my cock throbbed in anticipation.

I wanted to own her in every way, especially in the ways I felt she had allowed someone else to own her. Specifically because she let him own her. And I hated him for it.

Amelia looked over her shoulder, using one hand to spread herself open and put her holes on display. It got a rise out of me, but not the right one for today. I stroked myself as I looked at her pouty lip, begging me to penetrate her, and my gut roiled. I wanted sex, but somehow this felt empty today. Hollow. Like we'd been missing something, and I had just figured out what it was.

"You know," I muttered as I walked closer, "this isn't what I want."

Amelia straightened, turning to face me. "You want me to suck you off?" Her hips perched on the edge of the desk where too many times I had taken her from behind, given her a few orgasms of her own, and sent her back to her desk. A few times she was on her knees for me without hesitation, admitting sex wasn't what she wanted. But based on the moisture between her thighs that I saw glistening against her core, today wasn't one of those days.

"No," I told her, grabbing her wrist. I tugged her from my desk, pulled her across the room, then spun her around and pressed her back against the windowpane, thankful the mirrored glass allowed me to indulge in another fantasy I had. "This."

My mouth covered hers in a steamy kiss as I gripped her hips and leaned in. My dick throbbed against her thigh, and she wrapped her fingers around it, stroking softly as I kissed her.

I reached between her legs, sliding a single digit inside her tight warmth and felt how wet she was for me. I knew what she was thinking—that this had turned her on too.

"Better?" she purred against my lips, her eyes fluttering closed.

I pulled back, my dick still hard and throbbing in her palm. "Not quite," I growled, unsure why I was acting this way. It felt like I had to prove to her that I was better than him, that she was somehow mine, even though I couldn't admit that was what I wanted. "Say the sluttiest thing you can think of." Amelia's eyes widened and her cheeks flushed pink, but dammit if it didn't make me harder.

I thrust my fingers into her core, through her thick moisture, and rubbed the heel of my palm against her clit. She whimpered and arched into it while clawing at my shoulders. Her hand continued to stroke my cock, but awkwardly now as she got more worked up.

"I ... Christ, Xander, I'm not like that. I don't know what you want me to say." She whimpered when I drove my fingers deeper into her, leaned forward and bit my shoulder.

"Tell me you're a slut and my cock is the only one that does it for you," I demanded, still unsure where this sudden change in my demeanor was coming from. Amelia hesitated, her eyes locked with mine, her pupils dilating as she bit down on her lower lip.

"I'm a ... slut ... and ... I can't." Her whimpers were music to my ears. I loved hearing her say those words. The dirtier she was with me, the more I loved it. The more it boosted that part of my ego that needed to be stroked to get me off. She was enraptured by my actions too, unable to stroke me anymore, but her hand lingered on my dick anyway.

"Say it now, Ms. Johnson." My eyes flashed with lust as she whined.

"Your cock is ... the only one that ..." she panted. As she did, her body began to pulse, and an orgasm ripped through her. Her core tightened around my fingers, teeth sinking into my skin again, and I smirked as I watched how those words brought a flush to her cheeks and her climax in the same breath. Seeing the release had my cock dripping.

When her body began to calm, I pulled my hand free, bringing it to her lips. "Suck them clean, now," I ordered, stopping short of calling her a slut. It was the last thing I wanted to do, humiliate her or insult her. But my God was she incredibly hot when she was so nasty with me.

Amelia's jaw dropped, tongue lazily licking up the moisture off my digits. When she was finished, I brought my lips to hers and kissed her hard, tasting her juices on her tongue. I wanted to be inside her and feel her pulse around me, but I wanted to feel that closeness first, when she and I both let down our guards and we're fully raw, primal, the core of us exposed to the other.

"You want to be a whore for me?" I asked her, afraid of how naked I felt by saying the words.

"I want to be the only slut you bend over your desk …"

Her words triggered a cascade of something inside my chest. I spun her around, pressed her tits to the glass, grabbed a handful of her hair, and slid into her pussy from behind, thrusting so hard she whimpered. The way she fit me like a glove made every jealous, possessive cell in my body explode. I was drowning in her. I wanted to own every inch of her.

"Say it," I growled against her ear. "Say you're mine."

"Only yours," she breathed, fogging the glass. I gripped her hips hard, driving into her even harder, and she wriggled her hand between her legs to rub herself.

The idea of pinning her against the window and screwing her raw while the city below watched us only made my arousal suck me closer to the edge. Every one of her exhales fogged the window more, and I leaned into her ear and whispered, "Louder, Ms. Johnson. I don't think heard you all the way in New York ."

"I'm yours," Amelia moaned as her second orgasm broke, making her face rock against the glass. I couldn't hold back. My body was poised to flood her, so I let go with a grunt, my hand still wrapped around her torso.

Amelia's fingers pressed against the glass, her orgasm milking every last drop of my seed from my body as we both panted for air. The thought crossed my mind that I never wanted to let her go, and for the first time in my life, I felt like I needed someone. Like I wanted something more with them, something I'd never be able to admit to her because I had drawn a hard line in the sand already.

I pulled out, leaving her breathless against the glass, and turned away from her to hide whatever emotion was still on my face. The thought of her walking out of this office and returning to any sort of interaction with Godwin Tharmor terrified me, but it surfaced as anger.

"Whoa," she said, stumbling away from the window. She walked to my desk, took out some tissues, and wiped herself clean, then she picked up her clothing and began to dress as I put my dick away and zipped my pants.

She was so casual, so relaxed. Her hair was a bit mussed, cheeks still flushed from excitement, and when I found my shirt and slid it on, she turned to me with a furrowed brow.

"What's wrong? It wasn't good? Did I say the wrong thing?" Her desire to please me was more than I expected. This sort of thing usually didn't happen. We didn't lie around talking for a while after sex; that was something couples did, and we weren't a couple.

"It was fine," I grumbled, beginning to button my own shirt. "But I'd like a change to our agreement." I didn't have to see it to know my eyes had darkened. She dipped her head, appearing to draw back a little as she slid on her stockings and avoided eye contact.

"Alright?"

"If we're going to keep doing this, I don't want you having sex with anyone else." Her eyes popped up at my words, surprise written there for a second before it vanished. Her lip quivered like she wanted to say something, but I continued before she could. "For health reasons

—you get it. We commit to only having sex with each other, so we don't share bugs ..."

I knew controlling her actions would not control her heart, and if she wanted to fall in love—or stay in love—with someone else, I couldn't stop it. Something inside of me, however, felt the urge to protect my own heart, to limit her ability to hurt me.

"Yeah, that makes perfect sense ..." Amelia smiled softly and walked to where her shoes lay on the ground. I followed her, tucking my shirt in, and when she had one hand on the doorknob, the other brushing across her hair, I leaned in to kiss her.

Again, not something we ever did after sex. Normally she just waltzed out and that was that. My body felt like it was on autopilot, like I was mimicking what I'd seen her do with Tharmor, and I felt so out of place. I even wrapped my arm around her in an awkward hug, and she chuckled to diffuse the strange tension.

"I—"

Her phone buzzed, she pulled it out of her pocket. I looked down to see Tharmor's image on the screen as she swiped to look at his message and laughed. I stopped short of reading what he said, but anger surged through me as she snickered.

"I gotta run ..." Her eyes were full of mirth. Mine were certainly full of possessive, jealous anger. "I'll be by around two for our meeting."

Amelia snuck out and quietly shut the door, while I stomped to my desk and hit the cup that held my extra pens right off it. It slammed into the bookshelf behind my desk, and the pens went in every direction.

Why couldn't I be normal? Why did I have to be the broken one that couldn't connect with people? My mother had destroyed my heart, and all I wanted was to feel something other than cynical anger and fear.

I should just end the arrangement because I knew I would never be able to give her what she wanted, what she already had with Godwin. If she was with me, she would only feel neglected and alone, probably empty. And she deserved better than that.

I was incapable of loving her.
So why couldn't I let her go?

14

AMELIA

A few days had passed since Dad moved back into his house. He'd fixed the front door himself—not professionally, but well enough—and insisted I stop worrying. I'd covered his electric bill just enough to keep the lights on and the fridge running, but I couldn't afford the full amount to get his security system back online. He told me not to worry about it, said he didn't need it anyway. But I could tell he was lying. Something about the way he rushed through his sentences, the forced lightness in his voice—it didn't sit right.

So I showed up today with a dish of baked ziti and a gnawing sense of dread I couldn't shake. The smell of it in the car made my stomach turn, and by the time I pulled into his driveway, I was swallowing hard to keep the nausea down. I told myself I might be coming down with something, but the truth was, I'd been feeling off for days. Restless. Uneasy. Like something bad was coming, and I was the only one who didn't get the memo.

When he didn't answer the door—front or back—I started to feel the familiar pinch of anxiety settle in. I knocked again, harder this time, and waited. Nothing.

Letting myself in through the back door wasn't new. I'd been doing it since I was a teenager, and he never minded. The kitchen was exactly the way I expected it to be: clean enough to pass but not spotless. A coffee mug sat in the sink, yesterday's newspaper folded neatly on the table. The chair was pushed back like he'd just stood up and wandered off. But the house was quiet. Too quiet. And he wasn't answering his phone.

I tried calling again and listened as it rang twice before going to voicemail. I didn't leave a message.

Something felt off. It wasn't any one thing—it was everything. The too-tidy kitchen, the silence, the unanswered phone. My gut had been buzzing since I woke up, and now it was screaming.

I left the dish on the counter, wiped my palms on my jeans, and walked down the hallway. The framed photos hadn't changed. They still followed my life from kindergarten to graduation and beyond. They still made the house feel like it belonged to someone who had been proud once, before things got ... complicated.

Dad's office door was half closed, like it always was. He didn't keep it locked. Never had.

I pushed it open and flipped on the light.

The space was neat, unnaturally so. No clutter, no takeout bags, no piles of mail or sticky notes tacked up on the corkboard. His laptop sat closed but plugged in, perfectly centered on the desk. For a man who used to leave everything out where he could see it, the whole room felt like it had been scrubbed down for show.

I hesitated, standing behind the chair, then pulled it out and sat. My fingers hovered over the laptop for a second before I opened it. It blinked to life immediately.

It blinked to life immediately, but then the login screen appeared, and my stomach sank. The username was already filled in, but the password field waited, blinking expectantly, as if daring me to try. I sat there for a moment, thinking maybe it would come to me—something obvious, something personal. I typed in a few guesses: his birthday, my name, the name of our old dog from when I was a kid. Nothing worked. I tried the company name, a few variations of his favorite sports team, even the street we grew up on. Every attempt was met with a polite but firm error message.

After the sixth or seventh try, I leaned back and exhaled slowly through my nose, annoyed at myself for even thinking it would be that easy. I wasn't angry at him, exactly—not for protecting his privacy. He was allowed to do that. But it stung, in a quiet and specific way, to realize he'd drawn a line between what he was willing to share and what he wanted to keep hidden. Especially from me.

I pushed away from the desk slightly and glanced toward the drawers, reaching instinctively for the nearest handle. The first two slid open without resistance—one held a couple of pens, a pad of yellow sticky notes, and a half-used pack of batteries. The second had an envelope from the water company and a folded grocery list scribbled on the back of a paper napkin. I pulled on the bottom drawer and felt resistance right away. I tried again, a little harder, but it was locked.

My fingers tightened on the handle as I stared at it, frustration rising in my chest. I understood he had a right to keep things to himself. I wasn't trying to invade his life. But after everything that had happened—the fire, the break-in, the bruises, the sudden spiral into debt—it was getting harder and harder to believe this was just about privacy.

He hadn't been himself for weeks. Months, really. Always deflecting, always minimizing, never quite answering when I asked him what was going on. And now this—the password I couldn't guess, the locked drawer he never used to lock—it all felt like pieces of a puzzle I didn't have the image for yet.

I sat there in the quiet, looking around the room, trying to slow my thoughts. Nothing looked out of place. Nothing was technically wrong. But that was the problem. There was no explanation for the break-in. No arrest. No security footage. He had no real plan to catch up on his bills, and yet he wouldn't ask for help. He was keeping something from me.

I reached into my bag again, this time pulling out the small tin I kept tucked in the inner pocket. Inside were a few emergency bobby pins, and with a quiet sigh, I slipped two into my hand and crouched beside the drawer.

I'd picked locks before—just once or twice, mostly as a teenager when I was curious or bored. Dad never caught me, and I never admitted it. I felt guilty now, but the worry twisting in my stomach overrode my hesitation.

It took a little longer than I remembered, but finally, I heard the soft click. The drawer creaked open.

At the top was a bundle of photographs held together by a rubber band. I eased them out carefully, immediately recognizing my mother's face. There were pictures of her in the garden, laughing with a glass of iced tea, arms wrapped around me during some long-ago birthday. I hadn't seen these in years. The sight of her caught me off guard—something in my chest gave a sharp tug. She died when I was eighteen, but seeing her like this, full of color and movement even in still images, made the grief feel startlingly fresh.

I almost closed the drawer and left it at that. But a yellow notepad caught my eye, tucked beneath the photos. I pulled it free and began flipping through. It wasn't a journal or casual notes. It was a ledger—lines of numbers, dates, and what looked like repayment amounts. Near the middle of the pad, a number had been underlined twice—$574,000.

My mouth went dry.

If I was reading this right, my father owed someone a very large amount of money.

As I flipped another page in the notepad, a business card slipped out and landed face down on the floor. I picked it up, expecting something familiar—a bank logo, a company I'd recognize—but it wasn't. The card was unbranded, plain, with a name I didn't know, a phone number, and an email address. On the back, in small, tight handwriting, someone had scrawled a single line: *Monthly, or we escalate.*

Before I could even begin to make sense of it, I heard the back door open. The clatter of keys hit the counter, followed by the unmistakable sound of a bottle being pulled from the cabinet. The creak of a cupboard door, a glass being set down—my heart jumped into my throat. He was home.

In a rush, I shoved the notepad back into the drawer, trying to make it look untouched, and pushed it closed. I didn't bother trying to relock it. I slipped the business card into my coat pocket just as his footsteps thudded heavily down the hallway.

He appeared in the doorway, glass in one hand, half-empty bottle in the other. His face was red, his expression unsteady, and his eyes didn't look quite focused. The smell of whiskey hit me before he even spoke.

"What are you doing in here?" he asked, voice thick, words slightly slurred.

I stood up from the chair slowly. "I came by because I was worried. You weren't answering your phone."

He looked past me, toward the desk. "You went through my desk?"

I hesitated too long, and his jaw tightened. He took a drink before slamming the glass down on the edge of the desk, liquid sloshing over the rim.

"You think you get to come in here and dig through my life like it's yours to fix?" His voice rose, shaking with anger.

"You're in over half a million dollars of debt," I said, the words escaping before I could think better of it. "I saw the ledger."

For a moment, he didn't move. His expression flickered between rage and something else—fear, maybe, or shame—but it hardened just as quickly. "It's none of your damn business."

I took a step toward him. "You're my dad. Of course it's my business."

He pointed toward the hallway with the bottle. "Get out. You don't belong in here. You don't know what you're doing."

"I'm trying to help," I said, voice trembling now.

"Well, I don't want your help. Just go home. I've handled worse than this without anyone holding my hand."

I didn't look back. I walked to the car with my vision blurred, my chest tight, the weight of everything pressing in from all sides. Once inside, I sat for a moment, staring out at nothing, the silence around me louder than anything he'd said. I had come to check on him, to feed him, to make sure he was okay—but all I'd done was open something I wasn't prepared for. And now I couldn't unsee it.

I started the engine and pulled away from the curb, not knowing where I was going, only that I couldn't stay. I felt hollow, shaken, like a thread had snapped inside me. I had never seen him like that. I had never felt so far away from him. I drove without direction, hoping the motion would steady me, but the farther I went, the more lost I felt.

15

XANDER

The call rang through to voicemail at least four times, and I had all but given up trying to reach Mr. John Smith—the man I'd met for dinner that turned out to be a very awkward glass of wine shared over a tense table. After several days of client calls and meetings where I'd been shot down every time, I was following up on a few prospective clients I hadn't gotten confirmation out of yet.

The phone lay on my desk facing up, screen alight with Mr. Smith's number scrolling across it as it rang through. I wasn't holding my breath. I knew when he gave me his name, it was most likely an alias, and I didn't expect much from it. And after the strange way I saw him sneaking a look at my phone over the table, I didn't know if we would even make a good fit. What I did know was that direct sales through our website for our project management software were our golden ticket item right now, and the days of handling clients' individual builds seemed to be fading. I hated it.

"Hello?" I heard, but it wasn't the voice of a man. From the sounds of it, it was an older woman.

"Hello, yes, my name is Xander Blackwell, calling from Next Gen Solutions. I'm calling to speak with Mr. John Smith. Is he available?" I paused long enough to click the phone over to normal mode and picked it up. When I pressed it to my ear she was already speaking.

"... Mr. Blackwell, but I'm not sure I know a John Smith. My name is Harriett Gershom. I live here alone." The shake in her voice betrayed her age, probably some eighty-something widow whose husband had passed on years ago, and now she lived alone hoping her kids would come to visit.

"My apologies, Ms. Gershom, I was given this number by mistake." My tone remained pleasant, but my inner calm was rankled. I scowled at nothing in particular and let my shoulders drop.

I'd had four rejections already this morning, and though I somewhat expected this, it felt like another blow to the gut.

John Smith had been a long shot anyway. The last follow-up call I had was to Gerard Millet, who may or may not have signed with one of my competitors by now. He was leaning that way anyway, and I didn't have any wiggle room in the budget to undercut any of them. Laurence kept our profits tight in order to pay our team what they deserved. It was more than enough cushion for me, considering I had a cushy salary, but at times like this it punched me in the gut.

"I'm so sorry, Mr. Blackwell. I do hope you find the person you're looking for." Harriett sounded like a sweet old lady, but she wasn't the sort to be in the market for a website or app build.

"Good day, Ms. Gershom," I told her before hanging up.

This crappy situation had started to wear me down mentally, on top of several other large stressors I'd been carrying around. Dad insisted I meet his latest fling, and dinner hadn't gone well with them. Turned out Candy was years younger than I even thought and probably believed Dad was oozing money based on his designer suits and flashy car with driver. A gold digger if I ever met one, but try to tell my father that.

Still, I wasn't a quitter. And I wasn't going to let these rejections get me down. Worst-case scenario, I would have to go to Laurence and have him coach me on how he roped clients in hordes. If that didn't work, the entire focus of our business would have to change, which wasn't something I looked forward to telling our team.

With renewed determination, I dialed Gerard Millet's number and held the phone to my ear. The last time we talked, he had mentioned ProForge or Tacticon and their lower prices. I prayed at the time that Next Gen's quality would shine over both of my lesser-known competitors, but Gerard hadn't confirmed with me.

The phone rang through to his secretary, whose chipper voice annoyed me. "Millet and Sons, how may I direct your call?"

"Yes, Gerard please. Tell him Xander Blackwell is calling from Next Gen." I sat straighter, leaned over my desk rubbing my forehead with my thumb and forefinger. Gerard took his good time getting to me, and when he answered he sounded rushed.

"Yes, Blackwell, how's it going?" There were voices in the background, this call taken on the fly. He wasn't expecting me, clearly.

"Mr. Millet, I'm doing fine. How are you today?" The tension in my body wouldn't let me relax. I was starting to get a complex, feeling like a total failure at this job with as many contracts as I had lost in the past nine months.

"I'm doing alright, Xander. What can I do for you?" He was playing coy, nonchalant like he didn't know what I wanted, when he knew darn well I needed him to commit to me.

"I'm calling to follow up with you after our meeting a few weeks ago. Did you decide on a final design for the app build?" I knew one of the tricks was to direct them toward a decision about the project, not to ask them directly if they were choosing to go with my company. It didn't work though. He sighed hard, and I felt like I was the one annoying him now.

"Listen, Xander, I tried. I have the board breathing down my neck and investors chirping about every red cent. ProForge offered us almost a 40 percent discount over what you were able to give. I had to go with them. You understand, it's just business."

"Just business," I repeated, careful not to take a tone with him. "I do hope your build goes well and that your app is successful. If you need a good UX team to demo their work, I'm your man." My heart sank like the Titanic.

"Sure thing. Thanks for understanding." He hung up before I did.

I sat back in my seat and let the phone drop to my lap. Another call, another deathblow to my confidence. What was I doing wrong to let so many clients slip through my fingers? Laurence had no problems getting people to pay a bit more money for the professionalism and higher quality service we provided.

I was too on edge, too frustrated to sit here and think about work stuff anymore. If Amelia hadn't already gone home for the day, I'd have had her bent over my desk with her butt in the air, but she mentioned taking her dad some dinner, and I didn't want to intrude on a father-daughter moment. I knew how he'd been struggling, how concerned she'd been. I didn't, however, want to sit here a second longer and stew over things. It would only make me more tense and my need for release grow.

I grabbed my wallet and house key, put on my suit jacket, stuffed my things in my pocket, and then started toward the elevators. I made a habit every day of passing by offices with doors open and shutting them. I heard once that it lessened the risk of fire spreading through a building quickly, and ever since then, it had been my normal thing.

When I saw Godwin's office door cracked, I scowled at it and walked over there, reaching for the handle. Everything about the man irritated me and reminded me of how cozy he and Amelia got while working, like a bug crawled under my skin and into my ear whispering invasive thoughts meant to anger me. The intrusive thoughts didn't help my focus at work or the way I felt about myself after my long day. And when I peeked through the door to make sure his lights were off, I saw a screensaver playing through a photo collage.

Most of the pictures that flashed on the screen were images of him and people I assumed were friends or relatives, but when one came on the screen of him and Amelia I froze. I shouldn't have been there staring at his computer screen, shouldn't have cared that he had a picture of her. They were friends, anyone could see it. But I couldn't unsee it.

The image of her leaning in, smiling at him, pressing her hand on his arm over lunch was seared into my conscience. And the way I took her against that window, as if announcing to the whole world that she was mine had been my retaliation. Except, no one saw it. No one could. And I couldn't stake a claim and tell the world anyway. What we had was no strings attached; our original agreement made sure of that.

Now grumbling, I slammed his door, pushed the button for the elevator a little too hard, and rode down to the parking garage below the building. I never thought I had an anger problem in my life, but the more frustrated I got with the work situation, the more I realized how capable I was of wanting to hurt people or scream like a lunatic. It wasn't healthy at all, though it had only gotten this bad when I started sleeping with Amelia. Never pegged myself for the jealous type either, but here I was.

The parking garage was quiet, not very many cars left. I passed by a few sedans on my way toward where David parked normally. He had his hat down over his eyes, likely dozing lightly while he waited. But something else caught my eye across the garage.

Amelia's car sat there, not running, lights off. She told me she was going to have dinner with her father, so I didn't understand why her car was still here. I stopped for a second, wondering if I should be nosy and snoop around or just go home and blow it off. A million things could've happened. She could've gotten a flat tire, a dead battery. Laurence could've picked her up or maybe she got a ride home with—Godwin.

The thought made a new surge of anger flood me, propelling me —against my better judgment—toward the car. Every step that took me closer made my blood boil hotter. I fully expected to see her car empty, and a million accusations flew through my mind. I specifically asked her not to sleep with other men if we were going to keep doing this and while her car being here might've meant she got a ride home, it didn't immediately mean she was disregarding my request. But tell that to my irrational thoughts and the defense mechanism I'd had since Mom walked out on Dad.

The way I stomped up to the car, I was shocked Amelia didn't throw her door open and run away. I probably looked like a rabid dog about to attack. But when I strolled up and saw her head down, realized she hadn't seen me approaching, and that she was, in fact, in the car, something inside me softened instantly. She was crying, hands cupping her face.

Any thought of anger vanished as I tapped on the glass. My insides felt like lead, my heart a stone. I was a fool for letting my insecurities run away with my thoughts, but if Godwin Tharmor was the reason she was crying, I was going to have a word with him. A very loud word.

Instead of rolling down her window, Amelia opened the door. She sat there swiping at her eyes, forcing a smile to her face as she turned and set her feet on the ground. Her heels were off, stockinged feet seeming smaller than I remembered. Her entire frame seemed smaller now, like she was shrinking in on herself.

"Hey," she chirped in a less-than-happy tone.

"Amelia, are you okay?"

"Oh, I'm fine." She waved her hand in a dismissive gesture, but more tears sprang to her eyes. I wanted with everything in me to pull her into my arms. I knew it was what Laurence would do, but Amelia and I didn't have that sort of relationship really. I wanted to, but we didn't.

"You're not fine. You're crying. What's wrong?" I wished I had a handkerchief to give her. My father would've had one. Any grown man worth his weight in marbles would've had some way of helping her. But I stood there with clenched fists and a scowl I was unable to shake.

Her shoulders drooped and her head dropped. "I had an argument ... I'm fine. Really."

She said she was fine, but her body language screamed that she wasn't. Nothing about this seemed fine—not her tears, not her posture, not my inability to even function. This was why I was incapable of having a real relationship. When things like this happened, I stood staring, gawking the way my father did at me when I was a child and I skinned my knee.

The only thing I knew to do was the thing that I knew helped me.

When she was stressed out, she sent me a text—albeit fewer times than I had texted her for a hookup, but she had. However, it felt cold, callous even, to offer her a quickie for stress relief in the face of so much deep emotion.

Amelia wiped tears off her face again and looked up at me. "I uh ..."

"Came here to M-4-S?" I said carefully, unsure if that was what she wanted. She had been somewhere and argued, or maybe she argued here. Either way she was missing dinner with her father, and I hoped Godwin Tharmor was to blame for her mood.

She licked her lips and sighed, then looked thoughtfully up at me. "Yeah, I think so. I think that will help."

"My place?" I said, feeling a surge of hope shift my entire mood.

"Should I follow?" she asked.

"Ride with me ..." I waited, holding out my hand to her. She turned and grabbed her shoes and purse, then locked her car and took my hand. Now we were getting somewhere. And I was going to get her to tell me exactly what Tharmor had done to hurt her, and then I was going to make sure he never did that again.

16

AMELIA

Xander walked me from his car to his front door where he unlocked and guided me inside. It wasn't the first time I found myself in this situation, but the last time had ended so awkwardly I wasn't sure what to expect this time, especially considering he drove me here. I couldn't just get up and leave this time.

"Want a drink?" he asked as he shut the door behind us. I set my purse on the table in his entryway, turning to face him.

"Can we just ..." I reached for him, pulling him by the tie closer to me. His tie was loose, hair disheveled like he'd run his hand through it one too many times. If I didn't know better, I'd have said he was on the verge of texting me for this booty call anyway.

Xander's hands rose and rested on my shoulders, massaging away the ache. After seeing Dad in such rough shape, it made me appreciate this situation with Xander that much more. Maybe he just wanted something off-the-books, so to speak, but sexual tension added to my overall stress level. Getting relief from that made dopamine replace the negative feelings with happy feelings, at least for a little while.

"You want to talk about it?" he asked softly as he rubbed my shoulders. I wasn't sure what to say because it wasn't like we had that sort of relationship. When he tried to hug me goodbye that day in his office, we almost bumped heads. It wasn't that I didn't want it. God, I wanted it so desperately, but he was the one who laid down the rules, and I didn't want to step on his toes, tell him I was falling for him, and ruin the whole thing.

"It was Dad," I breathed sadly, splaying my palms on his chest. "He just refuses to let me take care of him. We argued and he was really angry."

A flash of anger in his eyes resolved to disappointment and then worry in such a fleeting moment, I almost didn't believe I'd seen it. It felt like he hoped I was arguing with someone else, or maybe he was feeling frustrated that I even felt like talking. I was here for a quickie, not for an emotional venting session.

"But we don't have to talk about it."

Xander's hands slid down my arms to my hands. He cradled them in his grasp and licked his lips, backing away a few inches. "Amelia, we don't have to do this. I can see you're not into it."

"Are you kidding?" I asked, forcing a chuckle. No, I wasn't into this. I didn't want bend-me-over-the-desk sort of hot, nasty sex we did in his office. I wanted hold-me-in-your-arms sort of making love where two souls intertwined their hearts until they became one. I couldn't tell him though. "What problem can't be solved by three good orgasms?" I grabbed his tie again and pulled him down until his lips met mine. He seemed stiff at first, hands lingering on my hands, until I pulled one away and rubbed the outside of his slacks. He was semihard and swelling, and the action seemed to snap him out of his funk.

"I mean it, Amelia. If you're not into this, I don't want to pressure you."

"Take me now before I change my mind, sir." I wagged my eyebrows, backing toward his bedroom, but he changed course, gripping my hips, turning me toward the kitchen.

I stumbled backward into a bar stool, and he leaned me against it, kissing me hard, taking my breath away. His hands were already at work stripping my clothing off, leaving it piled on the floor. I reciprocated the favor, fumbling with the buttons on his shirt, eager to feel his bare skin against mine. The intensity of his kisses and the urgency with which he undressed me made my core ache.

His mouth traveled down my neck, leaving a trail of heated kisses as he knelt in front of me. He hooked his fingers into my panties and pulled them down, tossing them onto the countertop, exposing me. His hands gripped my thighs as he brought me closer to him, his eyes locking onto mine.

"I've been dying to taste you again," he growled before he dipped his face between my thighs. "Tell me you're a bad girl, Amelia. Tell me how bad you are."

Xander's words vibrated my core as he abused my clit mercilessly with his tongue, flicking it back and forth. I arched my back, moaning his name as he lapped up every drop of my arousal, hands gripping the bar stool for support. My thighs squeezed his head; I uttered guttural groans when his tongue rubbed just inside my entrance, and something rose up in me that made me feel so nasty, so bad.

"I'm a little whore for you, Xander. I love it when you eat my pussy so good." I bucked against him, grinding my hips against his face. He growled and sucked harder as he teased my holes with his fingers. "God, my pussy wants you so bad."

He looked up at me with that intense gaze of his, exposing just how much he desired me as well. "I've been fantasizing about you in this position since our last little ... encounter," he said, his voice gruff with need.

"Oh God Xander, you're driving me insane," I panted, running my fingers through his hair.

"Mmm, look at how wet you are for me, Amelia." He continued teasing my clit with his tongue and fingers before sliding them inside me. I moaned—a primal sound that I didn't know I was capable of making. His fingers found a sweet spot, and I felt an orgasm tightening my coil.

"Yes, right there. Don't stop. Don't ever stop."

He groaned and the vibrations of his voice against my center sent me over the edge, coming apart on his face. I grabbed his hair as my body started shuddering, but Xander held me up, slowing his movements so my orgasm would last longer, and the aftershocks rippled through my body. I jolted and shook, my belly cramping, my toes curling, and when my body calmed, I was breathless.

He stood, his pants already undone and his erection jutting out. I expected him to bend me over the counter or table, but he scooped me up and pulled me against his chest. His strong arms carried me across the room, down the hall to his bedroom where he flipped me over and pinned me face down on the bed.

"Tell me the kinkiest thing you've ever done …" The rasp of his voice made goose bumps rise on my arms. I felt his hand on one shoulder, elbow on the other weighing me down, and I felt his hand stroking his dick. It was hot, though a little intimidating.

"I … uh …"

"Come on, Amelia. You've done bad things. Tell me the naughtiest one." He nipped my ear, pelvis now grinding on my backside as he spread my cheeks and slid his dock up and down my crack.

"Well, I fucked my boss against the window of his office." My mind raced, my body aching to have him inside me, and I had no clue what he wanted.

"Sounds like you're a bad girl … Maybe you need to be punished," he said, dipping his head into my soggy entrance. He thrust a little, slicking himself, but I knew what he wanted. "Maybe this needs to be punished," he growled, pressing his dick against my tight entrance. It'd been a very long time since I did anal, but the minute he touched me I wanted it.

"Maybe it does," I mewled, arching my hips upward into him.

He took it as permission, slicking his cock in my juices a few more times before lining up to the tight ring of muscles. When Xander started to thrust in, I clawed at the comforter, whimpering as he stretched me.

"Oh God, Xander!" I gasped as he went deeper. He hit something inside me that set off every nerve ending in my body. My pussy clenched around nothing, craving to be filled.

"So ... tight ..." he groaned, thrusting in and out of me, pulling almost all the way out before slamming home again.

"Yes! Don't stop!" I begged, unable to control the moans and whimpers that escaped my lips as he thrust so hard my entire body shook. There was nothing but him and this moment. When I felt him speed up, I forced my hand under my body, rubbed my clit with my fingertips.

"You like it when the boss punishes you, don't you?" he growled.

"Yes, sir, please punish me," I moaned, things I never thought I'd utter. It was hotter than anything I'd ever fantasized about. When he spanked my ass, lightly at first, and then harder when he picked up the pace, I whimpered in ecstasy. "Oh, God yes! Make me come!"

He roughly grabbed my hips and thrust into me so hard my body felt crushed, face pushing into the pillows. The plushness of the material muffled most of the moans that escaped my lips as my orgasm ripped through me, tightening around his own pleasure-seeking cock.

"That's it ... Be my little cum slut. Scream my name." His orders were impossible to follow. I could barely breathe, let alone speak, but just saying the words seemed to do it for him.

Xander thrust a few more times until I felt his cock pulsing. I couldn't feel his release—too absorbed in the waves of pleasure flooding me—but his body twitched, arm moved from my shoulders, and then he rolled to the bed next to me.

His chest heaved for a few minutes, body still taut, and I rolled to my side to face him. Both of us lay there catching our breaths, my body still pulsing with sensations. I closed my eyes and thought about why I drove to the office instead of home after that argument, about why my body just knew instinctively that being near Xander was the thing that would help me. Not the sex, just his presence. But I hadn't had the courage to walk inside.

"I thought about calling you anyway ..." he confessed, staring at the ceiling. One arm balanced over his forehead, the other lay draped over his belly. I propped myself up on an elbow and smiled the first genuine smile I'd had on my face since Dad went off on me.

"You did?"

"Yeah," he groaned. "I'm just really frustrated at work right now. Nailing down clients isn't my forte ..." He looked thoughtful for a second and then said, "And there's someone on staff that annoys the hell out of me. I can't fire them for being a total douche, but sometimes I wish I could."

I chuckled at his comment because there were a few people we worked with that made me feel like that too. I also chuckled because he grinned every time I did, and when he looked me in the eye and I saw the sparkle of emotion there, I felt like we were bonding finally.

"Yeah, I know a few people like that. You just want to throat punch them every time they open their mouths or something." My hand flattened on the mattress, inching closer. I wanted to hold his hand, but he'd have to make the first move. This was his arrangement. Though, if it had been mine, I'd have taken the no-falling-in-love clause off the table.

"More like helping their head meet the concrete," he said, and a deep belly laugh rolled up and out of him.

"I'm sure it's just a phase. Things are going well though." If work was where we had to start to come to a more personal ground, then I wanted to line up to the starting blocks because I was ready to race forward while he inched ahead.

"Things feel like they're falling apart, and maybe I'm just too worried about it, but sometimes I get the feeling I've made a mistake." Xander sat up and I followed him, scooting closer. The conversation seemed to take a more serious turn, like he was ready to bare his soul, but the moment I touched his arm he bristled.

"You haven't made a mistake," I told him, hoping to comfort whatever angst he was feeling.

Instead, he stood and grunted, "Bathroom." Then he left me sitting there wondering if I said something wrong. He vanished out the bedroom door instead of into the adjoining bathroom. I tiptoed to the door and peeked down the hall, watching as he walked into the bathroom off the kitchen.

I had said something wrong. But what? Or was it that I touched him? But we just had sex. How could me touching him upset him like that?

When I saw him coming back, I rushed back to the bed, perched on the corner of it. Xander strolled in wearing his boxer shorts, carrying my clothing. He set it on the bed next to me and walked to his dresser and pulled a drawer open.

"I shouldn't have been joking about personnel like that. I'm sorry. Won't happen again." He spoke with his back turned, tugging a pair of sweatpants out of his drawer.

"Xander, it's okay. Really. I can keep it confid—"

"My driver will take you wherever you want to go, home or maybe your dad's house. Just let him know where." I wanted to protest, to tell him it was okay to be vulnerable with me, but he didn't seem open to hearing what I had to say.

I felt a little better than I had when he knocked on my car window, but that mood was slowly spiraling downward again. I stood, started dressing slowly, and Xander went on.

"Remember our agreement—no one finds out, and no other sexual partners." He left out the part about no falling in love, but with the way he was acting right now my heart was picking up that red flag. He didn't need to announce it.

"Yeah, okay," I said, tugging my pants on.

"And thank you for coming." He strutted over to me, grabbed both of my biceps, and pressed a hard, chaste kiss to my forehead—the kind my father would. It was less awkward than that sideways hug he tried on me before, but it spoke something I didn't think he meant. Or maybe he did, and my stupid heart was too naive to believe it.

I stood there with my shirt in hand, watching him walk out of his bedroom. It was a big place, but not so large I couldn't chase him down, shake some sense into him.

For a moment, I let myself think he was going to be vulnerable with me, open up, maybe bond. And his actions snapped me back to reality really quickly. I was here to be his sex pet and get my needs met, nothing more. My heart screamed for more. My mind screamed louder—*No strings attached, dummy.*

I was doing this to myself and I had to stop. I thought being close to him would be amazing, even if I couldn't have him. But the closer I got to him on my end, the farther away he felt. How much closer could I get before he vanished and my heart was shattered?

I didn't think I could handle that at all.

17

XANDER

As soon as Amelia walked out the door, I could feel the anger rising in me. I shouldn't have let myself get so worked up. I shouldn't have felt so possessive when I thought it was Godwin, especially when it turned out to be nothing. But the thought of another guy having her—just the idea that he might be around her in that way—it set me off. I knew I was better than that. I told myself I was. But the truth was, I felt this gnawing in the pit of my stomach, something darker and uglier than I liked to admit.

The way she talked about her dad, how he kept making poor choices, how she had to be the one to step in—it hit home. She was talking about him needing someone to look out for him. I didn't just hear that. I felt it.

My dad had been making bad choices for years, especially with women. I couldn't tell you how many times I had to pick up the pieces after one of his relationships fell apart. He'd always tell me it was his fault, that he let things get too complicated, but I could see what went wrong every time. He trusted true love, and it failed him time and again.

Watching someone you care about make bad choices, not being able to stop it, felt like a kick in the gut. I'd seen it in her eyes when she talked about her father. And I felt it in my chest too. There was a spark there. A connection that I couldn't ignore, no matter how hard I tried.

But I messed it up. I should've been there for her. I should've told her I understood, that I was here for her, that she didn't have to carry that load alone. Instead, I pushed her away. I let my own confusion get in the way of something real, probably because I knew in my heart, I'd only screw it up later anyway.

Amelia had needed someone, and I'd been too proud, too wrapped up in my own guilt to step up when it mattered. All I could think about was how much I wanted it to be Godwin that she was upset with—so much so that I joked about him, and she joked with me. And when she touched me, I snapped. I felt like a fool.

I was a fool.

Strolling into the kitchen, I picked up my phone from the counter and unlocked it. My fingers hovered over the screen for a moment, then I typed out the message.

Xander 7:18 PM: *Thanks for coming by. Hope you're starting to feel better. If you need anything, don't hesitate to reach out. Take care.*

I stared at the message for a second before hitting send. Setting the phone back down, I poured myself a drink, the whiskey dark and smooth as it filled the glass. I leaned back against the counter, feeling the tension in my shoulders start to ease.

The sex with Amelia was easy, uncomplicated, just the way I liked it. No strings, no expectations—just two people satisfying their needs. But every time I walked away, there was a lingering thought. I wasn't sure if it was regret or something else. I'd convinced myself that this was all I wanted, but the truth was, I didn't know if I could walk away from her without feeling the weight of what I'd passed up.

It wasn't just the sex—it was the way she made me feel, the spark that flickered every time we were together. I told myself it was just physical, but deep down, I knew it was more. I wanted to be the kind of guy who could open up, offer more than just fleeting moments. But I wasn't built for that. So I kept pushing it down, kept telling myself it was fine, but something inside me kept hoping for more. A stubborn hope that didn't want to die no matter how many times I tried to crush it.

So I dipped into my bag of tricks, calling my father to help squash the little ember that refused to die. I grabbed my phone and dialed my dad's number, tapping my fingers against the table while I waited for him to pick up. The sound of the line connecting felt almost too loud in the quiet kitchen.

"Hey, Dad," I said once he answered, leaning back in my chair. "How's everything?"

"Same old, Xander. How about you? You holding up alright?" Dad sounded chipper like always, and like always it made me feel tense. How could he be so happy when life kept kicking him when he was down?

"Yeah, just …" I sighed, trying to find the right way to put it. "Work's been a mess. I've been striking out with new clients, and I'm feeling like nothing's working lately."

"Ah, you're too hard on yourself. You always are. Look, when are you going to stop letting work situations get to you so much? You've been all over the place lately."

I rubbed my jaw, staring out the window. The light was fading outside, the day winding down. "Maybe, but it's getting frustrating. I feel like I'm failing, and it's not sitting right with me." I knew it wouldn't sit right with Laurence either, and while I had nothing to prove to him—he didn't own the company anymore—his opinion did matter.

There was a beat of silence on the other end before Dad spoke again in a lighter tone. "You need to take a step back, son. Relax a little. When are you going to settle down, huh?"

I could feel my jaw tighten at the mention of that. "Settle down? Like you? You've been chasing whatever woman comes your way for years. That's the solution? Just keep doing the same thing?" This was the very reason I had called. I knew the topic would come up and my heart would get the beating it needed.

His voice went defensive, but not in a way that surprised me. "You're not getting it. You need someone who can help you, Xander. Someone like Candy. She's different. You should think about it."

I stared at the floor, biting back my words. "Candy? How many times have you said that about the women before her?" The dozens of women ... I shook my head and massaged one temple.

"Well, this time is different," he insisted, his tone soft but firm. He always insisted, always tried to say this one was *the one* and convince me love was real and within my reach.

I let out a sharp breath, leaning forward on the table. "Yeah, right. You keep saying that, but you've never held onto any of them. You've jumped from one to the next, and now you want me to follow the same playbook?"

"Stop twisting it, Xander. It's not like that." Now he was angry. I hadn't meant to anger him; I just wanted the swift kick in the pants that would keep me from doing something stupid with Amelia.

"No? Then why'd Mom leave, Dad? If women are supposed to be this amazing solution, why did she walk out on us?" Things went quiet. I had pushed the wrong button and I knew it.

I could feel him pull back on the other end, the silence thick before he finally spoke again, his voice low and tight. "Don't bring your mother into this."

"I'm just saying, Dad," I pressed, "if women were the answer, you wouldn't be in this cycle."

"Enough, Xander. You don't know anything." I heard his breath quicken. "I don't have to explain myself to you."

"You don't want to hear the truth," I said quietly, the words sharp despite myself.

"Goodbye, Xander," he snapped, cutting the call without another word.

I stared at the phone in my hand, the sudden quiet in the kitchen feeling too loud now.

I stared at my phone, waiting for Amelia's response, but it never came. My thumb hovered over the screen, but I couldn't bring myself to press send again. I felt the frustration building in my chest. My dad's words echoed in my mind about how amazing it could be, how I should settle down. But what was the point? Everyone always left. They always would. Even Amelia. I couldn't shake the feeling that I was just waiting for the inevitable.

18

AMELIA

I rushed into the company bathroom, barely making it to the toilet before I bent over and puked everything I ate at breakfast. The greasy sausage roll I had from the fast food place this morning had been a terrible decision, and now my body was making sure I regretted it. I spent the next few minutes leaning over the toilet, my stomach heaving even when there was nothing left to come up. I could feel the cold sweat on my forehead as I sat back, waiting for the dizziness to subside.

After a while, the nausea started to fade, and I wiped my mouth, trying to breathe evenly. The bathroom was empty except for me, which was probably for the best. I couldn't deal with anyone seeing me like this. I leaned back against the wall, taking a deep breath before I flushed the toilet.

I stared at myself in the mirror, trying to pull myself together. My face was pale, and my hair had fallen out of place from all the retching. I looked like I hadn't slept in days, which wasn't the case. I was exhausted all the time. And the bargain breakfast? I'd never make that mistake again.

Just as I grabbed a paper towel to clean myself up, a coworker walked in and gave me a concerned look. I'd seen her around accounting, but I didn't know her personally.

"Hey, you okay?" she asked in a gentle tone. Her bag, slung over her shoulder, brushed over the counter as she turned to set it down.

"Yeah, I'm fine," I said, forcing a smile, though I wasn't fooling either of us. She could clearly tell something was wrong.

"You don't look fine," she said, pulling out a mint from her bag and offering it to me. "Here, this should help."

I hesitated but took the mint, grateful for the small gesture. It wasn't going to fix the way I felt, but it helped mask the lingering taste in my mouth. I nodded at her, forcing another smile.

"Thanks," I said, popping the mint into my mouth. I stepped away from the sink, still feeling a bit shaky, but managing to keep it together. I had to get back to Godwin who was waiting at my desk. I'd rushed off before we even got started going over the numbers.

I walked back to my desk, still feeling weak, but I couldn't waste any more time. The office hummed with the usual noise—people typing away, phones ringing, the steady buzz of busy coworkers. Godwin was sitting down as I approached, looking up when he saw me.

"You look like death," he said, his voice a mix of concern and amusement. "Did you drink too much last night?"

I shook my head, sitting down at my desk, trying not to slouch. "No. Just ate something bad for breakfast."

Godwin raised an eyebrow, not convinced. "Are you sure? Because you don't look like you're doing too hot."

"I'm fine," I said quickly, not wanting to linger on the topic. I had spent enough time agonizing over the nausea I was feeling. I wanted to blame the sausage, but I knew there was a possibility it was more than just a bad breakfast. Still, I tried to focus on what I was really stressed about. My dad.

I grabbed the card with Victor Hayes's name on it from my desk drawer where I stashed it this morning and handed it to Godwin. "I need you to look at something. Do you know this guy?" After coming down from my anxiety-induced panic after Dad bit my head off, I decided I had to look into this guy.

He took the card, his eyes scanning it before looking back at me. His expression changed from casual to serious. "Yeah, I know him. Victor Hayes. He's a loan shark out of Vegas."

My stomach flipped again, this time for a different reason. "A loan shark?" The words felt like tiny hammers drilling the truth into my brain very painfully. Dad hadn't mentioned needing a loan for anything. And why not borrow from Xander? Why a loan shark?

"Yeah," Godwin said, nodding slowly. "He's known for being really harsh with people who owe him money. He doesn't mess around. People get in deep with him, and things … don't always end well."

My pulse quickened as I absorbed his words. I hadn't expected this. "What do you mean, 'don't end well'?" Dad was in real trouble here. That ledger with the business card was serious business. More than half a million dollars of serious.

Godwin leaned in, lowering his voice. "There are rumors that people have disappeared, gotten in over their heads, things like that. He's connected, and he's not someone you want on your bad side."

I felt cold, and it wasn't just from the nausea that still lingered in my stomach. If Hayes was really that dangerous, why the heck was I digging into him? What had I gotten myself into? And what had Dad gotten himself into?

"Great," I muttered, feeling the weight of the situation settling on me. "Just what I needed."

Godwin leaned forward farther like he didn't want anyone to hear him. "Amelia, I'm telling you, Hayes doesn't mess around. I've heard stories—people who've had their hands cut off, families attacked. He's ruthless, and if your dad's in the middle of that, it's bad news."

I felt my stomach turn again, but not from the food. When I finally spoke, my voice was heavy. "I went through my dad's desk. There was a card with Hayes's name on it. And the numbers—those dates, the amounts—it's all there. My dad's been borrowing money from him. I'm sure of it."

Godwin's eyes narrowed. "So your dad's mixed up with him?"

"I think so," I said quietly. "The ledger I found—it's a record of debt. It's not just some coincidence. My dad owes him money."

Godwin let out a low whistle, leaning back in his chair. "That's serious, Amelia. Hayes doesn't let people walk away from that kind of debt."

I swallowed hard, trying to keep my voice steady. "I don't know what to do. I just know he's in trouble."

Godwin nodded, his expression grim. "We need to figure this out. Fast. Before things get worse."

Godwin was about to say something else when the door swung open with a thud. I looked up in surprise as Xander walked in; his expression was tight, almost unreadable. The way he moved had an edge to it, like something was off. He didn't even acknowledge me at first, his eyes going straight to Godwin.

"Could we have the office," he said with a calm voice but with a certain finality that made it impossible to ignore.

I froze. My heart skipped a beat. There was a sharpness in his tone I wasn't used to, a kind of command that made me feel instantly on edge.

Godwin didn't argue, but I could tell he wasn't thrilled about leaving. He glanced at me briefly, his eyes flicking between me and Xander, but without saying a word, he stood up and grabbed his things. "I'll be outside," he muttered before walking out, leaving the door open just a crack.

Xander walked over to my desk with precise movements. He dropped a stack of files onto the corner of my desk with a little more force than necessary, and the sound of the papers hitting the wood made me jump. The air in the room seemed to tighten, and I suddenly felt too aware of my own breathing.

"I was going to talk to you about these," Xander said, his voice clipped, almost cold. He paused, looking at me with a frown that made my chest tighten. "But maybe you'd rather discuss them with Godwin instead?"

I blinked, confused. I could feel my face heat up, but I wasn't sure if it was from embarrassment or defensiveness. My mind raced, trying to process his words, trying to figure out what was happening. His sharp tone was unsettling. I'd never seen him like this before. We had no strings, no expectations between us, but now it felt like there were invisible ones I didn't understand.

I didn't know how to respond, so I just said the first thing that came to my mind. "I ... I'm sorry if I did something wrong." My voice was small and uncertain. "I didn't mean to cross any lines."

Xander's eyes narrowed, and he shook his head slowly. His lips twisted into something that could've been a smirk, but it didn't reach his eyes. "I don't like what's happening between you and Godwin during company time," he said, his voice lower now, like he was trying to make a point.

My stomach dropped. I didn't know why, but the way he said it felt off. His words were a mix of frustration and something else I couldn't quite place. Jealousy? Maybe. But he'd made it clear that what we had was casual—no strings, no expectations.

I glanced down at the files in front of me, feeling exposed, like I was suddenly under a microscope. "I wasn't doing anything—"

"I don't care what you were doing," Xander snapped, cutting me off. "I just don't like the way things are going. If you want to have personal conversations with him, fine. But not here. Not on company time."

I felt the sting of his words, but it wasn't just that. It was the way he was acting—irritated, maybe even angry. Was this jealousy? Why did he care if I was talking to Godwin? He'd said it didn't matter, hadn't he?

I felt rattled, upset, but I tried to keep my voice steady. "I'm sorry," I repeated, my tone quieter this time. "I didn't realize it was a problem. I won't talk to him again during work hours."

Xander didn't respond right away. He just stood there, staring at me, his jaw clenched like he was fighting to keep his emotions in check. I had no idea what was going through his head, but I couldn't shake the feeling that something had shifted between us.

"You don't get it," Xander said, his voice tight, but there was something else there too—something softer, maybe even unsure. "It's not about what you're doing. It's about respect. You're here to work, Amelia, not—" He paused, exhaling through his nose. "Not to get wrapped up in whatever this is. You need to focus."

"Focus?" I repeated, suddenly feeling defensive. "I'm focused. I've been focusing on my work. It's just that ... I needed to talk about my dad." My voice wavered, and I cursed myself for letting it crack.

Xander's face softened for a brief second, but it was gone just as quickly. He shook his head again, more to himself than to me. "Whatever. Just keep it professional, Amelia. I don't want to see this mess again."

With that, he turned on his heel and walked out, leaving the door open behind him. The silence in his wake felt thick, suffocating. I stared at the files on my desk, feeling completely off balance. His words kept echoing in my head: focus, respect, keep it professional.

I wasn't sure what had just happened, but I couldn't shake the feeling that things were about to get a lot more complicated between us.

I had been completely wrong about him letting his guard down and opening up to me before. And I was glad he hadn't heard the context of that conversation. Dad would hate me forever if Xander knew he was in debt to this Victor Hayes. Now my heart was broken, because I couldn't seem to make Xander happy, and I was losing my dad slowly.

Nothing felt right. The whole world felt like it was spinning out of control.

19

XANDER

I stormed out of the office with my mind clouded by anger, the kind that always made my chest feel tight and my fists clench. It had been building all day, but from the moment I saw Godwin talking to Amelia, it was uncontrollable. The way they were huddled together, whispering, exchanging looks—I wasn't blind. It was more than just business. I had let it slide once, but now? Now, it felt like a line had been crossed.

My thoughts were a mess as I marched straight for Godwin's office. The tension in my neck and shoulders was unbearable. As I reached his door, I didn't even bother to knock. I threw it open and walked in, my gaze locking onto him immediately. He was seated at his desk, looking up at me like he was surprised to see me. He shouldn't have been.

"Godwin," I said, my voice low, sharp. "We need to talk."

He didn't flinch, but I could see his eyes narrow slightly. He knew exactly why I was here. "What's going on, Mr. Blackwell?" he asked, his tone a little too casual for my liking. He had that look, the one where he thought he could talk his way out of anything. I wasn't in the mood for it.

"Cut the crap," I said, my teeth gritting. "I saw you with Amelia.

Don't act like it was nothing. I'm not an idiot." As I was speaking, I realized how irrational this was—I didn't take time to go through HR, didn't pause to admit my emotions could've made me see things that weren't there. I just saw through blind rage and jealousy.

Godwin leaned back in his chair with a relaxed face. "What are you talking about? We were just having a conversation. She needed help with something."

"Help?" I spat, my anger flaring. "You're fraternizing with her on company time, and you think I'm buying that? You're not fooling me. I know exactly what's going on."

He leaned forward, meeting my gaze with an expression of confusion that annoyed me. "Mr. Blackwell, calm down. You've got it all wrong. There's nothing happening between me and Amelia. It's just work. She was asking about some stuff, and I was helping her out."

"Don't lie to me, Godwin," I growled. My voice had dropped into that dangerous tone I used when I was angry. "I've seen this kind of behavior before. It's not just work. And I'm done pretending I don't know what's going on. You've been using company time for your personal interests. Don't think for a second I won't deal with this."

He stood up then, and the tension between us thickened. "You're overreacting, Mr. Blackwell. It was just a conversation." I could tell he was hiding something from me—something I felt the right to know about.

"I never said you weren't being helpful," I shot back, stepping closer. "But I know when someone's being shady. And I don't need people around me who can't be honest. So, here's the deal: you're going to be transferred to a different department. You've proven you can't keep it professional."

Godwin's face hardened, but he didn't argue. I could tell the idea of a transfer hit him where it hurt. I wasn't interested in playing games with him. The moment he'd crossed that line, he'd sealed his fate.

"I'm done with this conversation," I said, spinning on my heel and walking out the door before he could say another word. My blood was still boiling, my anger like a fire I couldn't put out.

I didn't want to deal with Godwin anymore. I needed to cool off, clear my head. I didn't know what had gotten into me, but I was furious. I wanted to believe them both, that it was just business, but everything about it screamed *red flag*. Amelia's presence in the office was messing with my mind, and I wasn't sure how much longer I could keep pushing it down.

As I stormed down the hall, I made my way to my office. I needed space, time to think. I had no idea how to deal with what was going on inside me, but I couldn't let anyone see how much it was affecting me.

I was just about to open the door to my office when I saw Amelia standing there, waiting, looking up at me with those eyes that seemed to see straight through me. It threw me, caught me off guard. I wasn't ready for this. I hadn't had a second to think since I saw her talking to Godwin. My thoughts were still tangled in knots, frustration still coursing through me.

I opened the door and followed her into the office, closing the door behind us. My eyes automatically went to her, though I didn't know what I was expecting. I had no clue why she had come to see me, but I didn't trust myself to speak right away. The image of her with Godwin lingered in my mind, nagging at me.

What was it about him that made her feel comfortable? Why did they get along so well? The thought grated on me. I hated the idea that she had a connection with someone else—anyone who wasn't me. It didn't matter that it wasn't expressly sexual in nature. There was something about the way they talked, the way she smiled, that made it feel personal. That made it feel like I was being rejected.

I knew I shouldn't feel jealous. We had an arrangement. Nothing more. Still, it stung, and I didn't know how to shake it. I couldn't let her see that, though. I was supposed to be the one who had control.

Amelia crossed her arms, her expression hardening as she took a step toward me. "What was that all about, Xander?" she asked, her voice sharp. "You walk in my office, eyes full of fire, acting like I'm the one who did something wrong. What's going on with you?"

I felt a sudden rush of irritation. Of course, she was going to call me out. She had every right to. I wasn't proud of how I had handled it, but I didn't know how else to express what I was feeling. And the more I tried to control it, the more it slipped out.

"Nothing's going on, Amelia," I said, my words careful. I didn't want to snap at her, but the frustration was still bubbling under the surface. "You're free to do whatever you want. I don't own you, but I won't share you either."

Her eyebrows shot up. "Share me? What does that mean?"

I ran a hand through my hair, trying to keep my cool. "You were talking to Godwin—on company time no less. That's not how this works." I winced at my own attitude toward her, then backtracked. "You can do whatever you want with whoever you want, just not while we're working. We have boundaries."

She blinked, clearly taken aback by my words. "Wait a second," she said, shaking her head. "You're mad about that? Godwin and I are just friends. Nothing's going on between us. It's not like that, Xander." She took a deep breath, exhaling slowly. Her eyes darkened, and I'd have sworn I saw pain in her expression. "Besides, this is NSA, right? No strings attached. You made that clear."

I felt a tight knot form in my stomach. She was right of course. We had an agreement. No strings. But her words stung more than I wanted to admit. "I'm not saying you're obligated to me," I told her, trying to control my voice, but my fight or flight response was going wild. "You can do whatever you want. I have no feelings for you at all." Just saying those words hurt me. "But don't throw yourself at men on company time. Keep it professional."

Her eyes narrowed with offense, the hurt in them so sharp it almost cut me. "Are you serious right now?" she demanded, stepping back. "I'm not some object you can control. I wasn't throwing myself at anyone. Godwin and I were talking about work. You really think I'm capable of doing that ... ?"

I saw her chest rise and fall, her breathing quickening with anger, and I knew I had overstepped. It didn't matter that we had an arrangement—what I said was out of line. It wasn't my place to tell her what to do, and the fact that I had made her feel that way made my insides feel like I'd been bludgeoned.

She took another step back, her eyes narrowing with indignation. "You know what? Forget this," she spat bitterly. "I'm not going to stand here and be judged for something that's none of your business."

Before I could respond, she reeled around and stormed out of the room. The click of her footsteps echoed down the hallway, fading as she got farther away. I stood there, frozen for a moment, my heart sinking in my chest.

It felt like a punch to the gut. I had pushed her away—pushed her to a point where she couldn't even stand to be in the same room with me. My fingers gripping the edge of the desk, I sank into my chair as I exhaled heavily.

What had I done? I'd let my jealousy cloud everything and twist it into something ugly. And now I felt like a complete fool.

I leaned back in my chair, staring at the ceiling, trying to get my thoughts straight. She was right to be offended. I didn't even know why I was so upset. What had I expected? That she'd just drop everything for me because I couldn't keep my cool?

I didn't know what I was doing anymore. I had no business being jealous. None at all. Yet, there I was—acting like a possessive idiot.

I rubbed my hands over my face, feeling the pressure of everything settling on me. If I didn't figure this out, I was going to screw up something good. Something I wanted. I was out of my mind with anger. Every muscle in my body felt tight, like a snake ready to strike. I couldn't control her. And she wouldn't let herself be controlled. Not by me, not by anyone. So why had I allowed myself to believe that NSA sex would work for us? That I could handle it? I hadn't even come close to handling it, and she appeared fine with the situation—unaffected by how I felt, unmoved in her own emotions toward me. It was just sex to her.

The whole situation, this whole arrangement, felt like a joke now. I was, tangled in something that was far more complicated than I ever imagined. And the worst part? I was the jealous one, not her. I didn't want to be, but I was. She was free to do whatever she wanted, and that was the problem. I wanted her to be free, but I couldn't tell her. I couldn't keep her from talking to Godwin or anyone else. And that realization gnawed at me, like a poison eating away at my soul.

I had let myself believe I could do this—keep things light, detached. But the truth hit me hard: this was too much to handle, too intense to keep pretending I could control it.

20

AMELIA

The kitchen felt quieter than usual as I worked to set the table. Dad stood by the counter, pulling out half-empty bottles of liquor, trying to look like he was contributing to the Easter brunch preparations. It wasn't much. He couldn't help with much these days.

"I'll pay you back for all this," Dad mumbled again, breaking the silence as he wiped a glass clean. I didn't look at him when I responded, focusing on arranging the plates and silverware. The soft clink of the dishes seemed louder than it should have been.

"It's fine, Dad," I said, trying to keep my tone even. I had paid his light bill last week, bought all the food for today. I wasn't expecting anything in return. But it was hard not to feel bitter. He said he'd pay me back every time, and every time, he didn't. It wasn't just about the money—it was about him not being the man I used to know. The man who'd take care of things.

"You don't have to do all this, you know," Dad added, his voice lower this time. He set the glass down and rubbed his face. "I'll get back on my feet soon. I'll figure it out."

I stayed silent, not trusting myself to say anything. I wanted to tell him that I didn't believe him, that I knew how much trouble he was in. But I didn't. It wouldn't help. It would just make him retreat further into himself.

I set the napkins down carefully, trying to keep my movements steady. "Dad," I said, voice quieter, "Are you sure you're okay? After what happened with the car ... with those men watching you?"

He stiffened but quickly masked it with a casual shrug. "I'm fine, Amelia. Nothing to worry about."

I didn't believe him, but I couldn't force him to admit the truth. He was trying to protect me, I knew that much. But it wasn't working. I couldn't just pretend everything was fine. Not after what Godwin had said about Victor Hayes.

The doorbell rang, cutting through the tension. I looked at him, but he had already gone to answer it. I heard Aunt Julia's voice as she greeted Dad, then Aunt Claire's softer one following. The usual chatter began to fill the house lightening the mood, and I hoped it would shift the way I felt about the entire situation.

My aunts swooped in like they always did—coats barely off, voices already high and warm, arms flung around me before I could dodge them. Lipstick kisses on my cheek, powdered cheeks against mine.

"Look at this table," Aunt Julia breathed, touching a napkin fold like it was a piece of art. "Amelia, you outdo yourself every year."

Aunt Claire stepped in behind Julia, her arms full of a covered dish and that worn canvas tote she brought to every family gathering. She smiled at me like I was still ten years old and winning spelling bees. "Oh, sweetheart, this is just lovely," she said, setting the dish down. "You have such a gift—really. Your mother would've been so proud." They shed coats and settled in, voices overlapping as chairs scraped and plates clinked.

Dad lingered near the counter, fingers tapping against the side of his glass. He watched us for a moment, then cleared his throat and crossed the room. He pulled out a chair slowly, like he was unsure if he was allowed to sit, and eased into it with a tight smile, eyes down.

My aunts filled their plates like they hadn't eaten in days. Aunt Julia hummed as she scooped up eggs and sweet potatoes, the way she always did when food met her approval. "This ham," she said, fanning herself dramatically, "Amelia, it's divine. You really do too much."

My aunt Claire gave my hand a quick squeeze before reaching for the rolls. "Your mother would be proud," she said softly, not looking at me when she said it, which somehow made it worse.

They passed dishes back and forth, praising the balance of seasoning, the way the carrots still had bite, how the green beans "weren't mushy like some people make them." My hands stayed busy —straightening a fork, refilling water, pretending I wasn't unraveling inch by inch.

Dad sat hunched at the far end of the table, nodding along, swirling what was left of his drink. He hadn't touched his plate. His smile flickered on and off, like he was trying it out and still hadn't decided if it fit.

My aunt Claire passed Dad the breadbasket and asked in a soft tone, "You holding up alright these days?"

Dad nodded, slow. "Yeah. One day at a time."

Julia reached for her glass. "It's still so strange without her, Laurence. Easter was always her favorite, wasn't it?"

Dad smiled, faint and far away. "She'd be chasing everyone out of the kitchen by now." I winced at the mention of my mother. They didn't have to say her name and it still hurt.

They laughed briefly. I kept my eyes on my plate. The steam rising from the ham made my stomach turn. I shifted in my chair, trying to breathe steady. When Dad said, "She'd be proud of you," I nearly gagged.

My mom would be appalled by my father's behavior lately, and the idea that he wanted to speak for her frustrated me. I gripped the edges of the wooden chair I sat in and scowled at my plate as nausea made my stomach roll. It'd been this way for days, and I'd been blaming it on that breakfast sausage last week, then my nerves, then the disagreement I'd had with Xander.

"What's wrong, dear?" Aunt Julia asked as she slathered butter on her breakfast roll. "You look green."

I forced a tight smile and reached for my water. The glass felt too cold in my hand, slick with condensation.

She pointed at the sausages piled on the platter in front of her. "I used to love these," she said, laughing softly. "When I was pregnant with Max, I couldn't even look at one without gagging. Morning sickness hit so hard, I had to open all the windows just to make it through breakfast."

The room felt smaller suddenly. My stomach flipped, then tightened like it was holding something in.

She went on, still amused. "And that was it. Never again. Haven't had one since."

I stared down at my plate, watching the edge of my egg yolk slide toward my toast. My chest felt hot. My breath caught halfway in.

Claire added without missing a beat, "Jenna's going through the same thing. Barely eight weeks and sick as a dog. Poor girl can't even keep crackers down."

The sound of my pulse rose in my ears.

I hadn't had a fever, but I hadn't been sleeping well. That was normal for someone who was so stressed about things. With everything happening with Dad, I couldn't rest if I tried.

Still, Xander and I never used protection, but I was on the pill, so it didn't feel like a risk. I hadn't had a period in months though, which was expected, and the idea of being pregnant didn't make sense to me. It didn't line up. But as they kept talking about morning sickness, the thought started to settle in my mind. I tried to push it away. I kept telling myself there was no reason to worry, but the more I tried, the harder it was to believe.

"Sometimes you don't even feel sick until week eight," Claire said, and my mind started tallying the weeks now. It was the second week of April; Xander and I had sex on New Year's Eve. Again, two weeks later when I was just getting over bronchitis, and then a week later we started our arrangement. That was almost ten weeks ago now. My God ...

The roll on my plate looked pale and dense and wrong. My fingers curled under the edge of the chair, gripping hard. I couldn't tell if it was the smell of the sausage or the weight of their voices, but I knew I needed to leave the room.

I pushed back my chair, careful not to knock anything over. "Excuse me," I said, barely hearing my own voice. No one looked up right away. They were still laughing about something Claire had said, still passing dishes like nothing had shifted. No one stopped me.

The hallway felt longer than usual, the light dimmer. I kept my steps quiet, steady, even as the pressure in my stomach built with every breath. The bathroom door stuck in the frame, and I had to shove it open with more force than I meant to.

I dropped to my knees and leaned over the toilet just as the nausea tipped past its breaking point. The retching was sharp and sudden, leaving my eyes stinging and my throat raw. I stayed there with my palms pressed against the cold tile, waiting to see if more would come up, but it didn't. I wiped my mouth with a tissue and unsteady hands, then sat back against the wall. I tried to slow my breathing, but the thought had already taken hold.

This wasn't just stress or bad food. I couldn't explain it away as easily as I had the last few days. I didn't want to believe it could be possible, but now I couldn't think about anything else. I wrapped my arms around my stomach, not sure if I was trying to hold something in or keep something out. Fear threatened to keep me planted on the bathroom floor, but the last thing I wanted was for them to come looking and find me a nervous wreck, so I pushed myself up and returned to the dining room.

I fought through the rest of brunch with a smile that didn't fit. The food on my plate stayed mostly untouched, but I moved it around to make it look like I was eating. My aunts didn't notice. They were too busy talking about Claire's oldest grandchild and the price of honey hams. Dad barely looked at me. He kept fiddling with his silverware, stacking and unstacking the knife and fork between sips of whatever he'd poured himself.

When the last plate was cleared and the laughter started to quiet, I stood and grabbed my coat. I told Dad I wasn't feeling great and needed to get home. He offered me a distracted nod and told me to drive safe.

I didn't go home, not right away. I drove straight to the pharmacy, hands gripping the wheel so tightly my knuckles hurt. I parked and sat there for a few minutes before I could force myself inside. The test was on the second shelf, next to the allergy meds. I didn't read the box, didn't compare brands. I just grabbed it and paid.

The apartment felt too empty when I stepped through the front door. It felt wrong to do this alone when most happy couples were together and celebratory during something like this. I hated that feeling. I didn't even take off my shoes; I went straight to the bathroom, ripped open the box with trembling fingers, and followed the directions without letting myself think.

I didn't pace while I waited. I sat on the edge of the tub and stared at the floor, at the grout between the tiles. I could hear the blood rushing in my ears. I set a timer on my phone and when it went off, I reached for the test with a hand I barely recognized as mine.

Two lines.

I blinked, hoping I had read it wrong. I read it again. And again.

I pressed my hand to my mouth and started shaking. I didn't mean to cry at first, but the sound came out anyway. Then everything spilled over. I sank to the floor and curled in on myself, sobbing until I couldn't breathe.

This couldn't be happening. I had done everything right. Or enough of the right things. I told myself it wasn't possible. I had believed it. And now everything felt out of control.

Xander had made it clear from the beginning. No strings. No plans. No future. I hadn't expected anything from him, but I never imagined this. I thought at some point I'd fall in love, and he'd figure it out and end things, and I'd be heartbroken, quit my job, and be out of work and desperate. Not this. Not a baby.

My phone lit up, buzzing softly on the counter and I almost ignored it. However, I saw Godwin's caller ID and knew he would help me. I didn't want to pick up and expose my shame, but my hand moved before I could stop it. My heart knew what I needed.

"Hey, happy Easter," he said. "Just checking in—"

"I'm pregnant." The words came out strangled. "I'm pregnant, and I don't know what to do."

There was a pause on the other end, just long enough to make me think I shouldn't have said anything. The way I word vomited on him probably shocked him.

Then his voice came back with a firm tone and the strength I needed in that moment. "Hold on. I'm coming. We'll figure it out. I've got you."

The line went dead. I clutched the phone to my chest and curled back into the corner, tears running hot down my cheeks.

I didn't know how this could get worse.

21

XANDER

Amelia hadn't been in since last week. At first, I thought maybe she was taking time off. It was a long weekend, after all, and she had earned the break more than most. Tuesday came and went. Nothing from her. No message. No ping on Slack. Just silence. By Wednesday, the silence had started to feel deliberate.

Now it was Thursday morning, and her office was still empty. Not just empty, but untouched. The blinds were half open like they always were. The chair tucked in. Notebooks stacked neatly. It looked less like someone on leave and more like someone who had vanished in the middle of a workday.

I stood outside her office door for a few seconds, letting the hallway traffic move past me. Phones were ringing somewhere down the corridor. A printer clicked and whirred. I could hear someone down in Records laughing too loudly about something that probably wasn't that funny.

I stepped inside and tapped the trackpad of her computer. Still locked. No one had logged in. I checked her calendar again, though I already knew there wouldn't be anything there. No personal day request. No doctor's appointment. No out-of-office message.

Amelia wasn't the kind of person who just didn't show up.

I left her office and walked the long stretch toward the south end of the building, toward the corner offices. I didn't walk quickly, but my steps felt heavier than usual against the polished floor.

I didn't knock when I got to Godwin's door. He looked up from his monitor, his mouth already tightening. The desk in front of him was clean except for a mug and a stack of papers with tidy notes scribbled down the margin. He'd been doing that more lately—keeping things organized, keeping things quiet. Like if he moved slowly enough, he might avoid attention. After my verbal beating last week, I didn't blame him.

"Amelia hasn't been in all week," I said, not bothering to sit. "Do you know where she is?"

Godwin kept his face even. "Maybe you should ask her that yourself."

"I've tried," I said. "She hasn't answered. Not one message. Not even a read receipt."

He didn't say anything, just kept his eyes on mine like he was waiting for something.

"She's part of this team. Disappearing without notice isn't normal for her," I said. "Are you covering for her?" I felt the words stick in my throat.

He leaned back in his chair. "I'm not covering for anyone. I'm respecting someone's privacy."

"You've already had a warning about this," I said. "You want another write-up?"

There was a long pause. He didn't move. He didn't fidget. Just sat there like a stone.

"If you're hiding something that affects this office, you'll be fired." I heard the edge in my voice and couldn't quite soften it. "I'm not playing games here." It was an empty threat, but he didn't know that. I was the boss; he just took orders.

Godwin gave me a look I couldn't quite read. Then he leaned forward, resting his arms on the desk like he was settling in. "I've already told you," he said quietly, "I'm respecting her privacy."

I stepped forward. "If she's sick, or something's happened, and you're sitting on it like it's not your problem ..."

"I don't know what you think I know," he said, not looking at me now, eyes drifting toward the corner of his desk. "I'm not dating her or sleeping with her." His words slapped with accusation. Had she told him about us when she promised to keep our arrangement confidential?

"You've already had a warning," I snapped. "This is exactly the kind of thing that put you on thin ice in the first place—crossing lines you weren't invited to cross."

Godwin's fingers tightened slightly around the edge of his mug. He still didn't meet my eyes.

"I'm not crossing any line," he said. "I'm staying out of it."

"Which is funny, because you're not out of it," I said. "You know something. You've been talking to her."

"I didn't say that."

"You didn't have to."

He finally looked up. "You want to help her? Then stop trying to do it through me. You're not going to get what you're after here."

I took a breath and exhaled through my nose. "If she's not back in by Monday, I'll escalate it. I don't care who likes it or who doesn't. This stops being a personal matter if it starts affecting her performance—or yours."

He nodded once, slow and silent, like he'd expected that. I stared at him another beat, waiting for anything—regret, worry, even fear—but he gave me nothing. I knew if I stayed there talking to him, I'd tear into him again and make myself look even more foolish, so I walked away scratching my head, worrying that what I'd said the last time I saw her really had hurt her that badly.

I'd sent a half a dozen messages to her already asking her to reach out, but she'd said nothing. Any other time, she'd have been in my office with her panties down waiting, and thinking that only made me feel like the sleazeball I was. Who in his right mind would ask a woman to have sex with him whenever he wanted and think emotions wouldn't get mixed up in it?

I went back to my office, closed the door a little harder than I meant to, and dropped into the chair behind my desk.

The screen was still up from earlier—some report I'd been picking at all morning—but the numbers didn't mean anything now. I scrolled through two paragraphs of data before realizing I hadn't read a single line. My mind kept drifting, circling the same thing over and over. Where the hell was she?

I minimized the window and grabbed my phone from the corner of the desk. There were three unread emails, one flagged report, and a calendar invite I didn't remember accepting. I ignored all of it. I opened my messages and scrolled until her name appeared. There were already four unanswered texts from earlier in the week. A simple **Hey, you good?** on Tuesday. Another one on Wednesday—**Need to talk. Call when you can.** Nothing back.

I stared at the blinking cursor for too long before I allowed myself to send yet another message.

Xander: 8:23 AM: *Where are you? What's going on? Are you coming back to work?*

I hit send and watched the message go through.

Then I started another one. Deleted it. Typed it again.

Xander: 8:27 AM: *I need you.*

It didn't sound like me, not even in my head. It sounded like something I wouldn't say unless I was drunk or dying. But I stared at it, thumb hovering over the screen, and I knew if I didn't send it now, I never would. I sent it.

It sat there on the screen, blue bubble, no reply. I waited. I kept waiting, telling myself she was just busy, or maybe asleep, or out. But she always had her phone on her. Always.

I tossed the phone face down on the desk and leaned back in my chair, rubbing my hands over my face. My palms were cold.

I didn't know what I wanted her to say. I just wanted to know she was there. I'd told myself, from the beginning, that this wasn't anything serious. That it didn't have to be complicated. But it was. It had been for a while. She didn't feel like something casual anymore. She hadn't for a long time, and I'd been lying to myself about how often I looked for her in the office, or how much I liked hearing her laugh when she forgot to be careful around me. That message wasn't just me checking in. It was me giving something away. And she wasn't responding.

I picked up the phone and checked it again, throwing out another fast message.

Xander: 8:39 AM: *Please just let me know you're okay.*

No dots. No read receipt. Just silence.

Eventually, I set it beside the keyboard and turned back to the screen, trying to shake it off. There was work to do. Reports piling up. People waiting on decisions. I opened the file I'd meant to finish earlier, the same one I'd been pretending to care about for the past hour. The numbers looked the same. The language was just as dry. I scrolled halfway through it, not taking in a word, then clicked out of it again.

An alert popped up in the corner of the screen—a new email. My eyes flicked to it automatically.

The subject line was simple—ordinary.

From: Amelia Johnson

Sent: 8:41 AM

Subject: Resignation

At first, it didn't register. The personal address threw me—one I hadn't seen since the early months, back when we were still keeping things casual, when she sent over project notes late at night and always followed up with a sarcastic emoji. I stared at the screen, my hand frozen on the mouse.

I clicked.

Dear Mr. Blackwell,

I am writing to formally tender my resignation from my position, effective immediately. I have ensured that all of my current assignments are either completed or appropriately delegated, and I have collected all of my personal belongings. There is no need for further contact regarding my departure.

I would like to take this opportunity to express my appreciation for the time I spent with the organization. The experience has been valuable in expanding my skills, and I am grateful for the trust and responsibility I was given during my tenure. I will carry the lessons learned here into my future endeavors.

Please consider this letter my final communication regarding my role. I wish you and the team continued success.

Sincerely,

Amelia Johnson

I read it once, then again, slower. My stomach dropped halfway through the second reading and didn't stop. There was no explanation. No softness. Nothing to suggest she'd even hesitated. She was gone. Just like that.

I leaned back in my chair, staring at the screen like maybe it would change if I waited long enough. But the words stayed exactly the same. Clinical. Final.

She hadn't told me. Not when I asked where she was. Not when I said I needed her. I thought that message meant something, that maybe it would shift something in her, open a door that had been stuck halfway shut. But she hadn't even read it. She'd already decided.

I sat there, barely breathing. There was no anger in me, not yet. Just a slow, growing weight in my chest, like something was being lowered into it, one brick at a time. I thought I had more time. I thought this wasn't over. She didn't feel like something temporary anymore, not in the way she used to. I didn't even notice when that changed, not really, but it had. And I had no idea what to do with the way it hurt to realize I might never see her again.

I hadn't said how I felt. I hadn't figured out how to say it. I wasn't even sure I fully understood it until now.

But she was already gone. And I was in love.

22

AMELIA

I showed up at Dad's house because I wasn't going to keep tiptoeing around this anymore. No more guessing, no more waiting for him to bring it up on his own—he wouldn't. I needed to hear the truth about Victor Hayes straight from him, and I wasn't leaving until I got it. Every part of me knew something was wrong, and after seeing the ledger and the business card, it wasn't just *bad choices* or some passing debt. This was serious. Dangerous. And he might not understand how much it could drag him—and us—under.

The lights were off like the house was empty, which I half expected. Lately, he'd been bouncing between a couple part-time jobs, nothing steady. Delivering things, some light warehouse work when he could get it. Basically, whatever would take him without background checks or long-term contracts. He'd probably say he was just *keeping busy* if I asked.

I let myself in with my key; the house was quiet. Not suspiciously quiet, just … normal. "Dad?" I called out as I shut the door behind me.

No answer. Just the muffled hum of the fridge and the soft tick of the kitchen clock. I didn't hear the TV, which was rare. Usually, it was playing old westerns or the same news loop over and over, even when he was gone. Today—nothing.

I wandered farther in, glancing down the hallway toward the back bedrooms. Still nothing. His bed was made, mostly. A couple of empty glasses on the nightstand. No sign of where he'd gone or when he might be back.

Maybe I should've waited. Called first. But no—he'd had plenty of time to come clean on his own. Instead, I got bits and pieces, vague assurances, brushed-off questions, and that tight smile he wore when he didn't want me to dig deeper. It wasn't working for me. He was in deep and hiding it from me. And now, with nothing to lose, I had to know.

I moved toward his office. The door was slightly open, same as last time. It always looked the same—bookshelves crammed with papers, folders he probably hadn't looked at in years, a few framed photos pushed to the side like an afterthought. I stepped in and immediately noticed something different.

His computer was on. Not just glowing in sleep mode—actually on. Desktop lit up, mouse blinking softly like someone had just stepped away. No password screen, which wasn't like last time. I'd been shocked when I found it locked, which made this all the more suspicious. Where had he gone in a hurry?

I sat in his chair without thinking twice. If I was going to get answers, this was where they were hiding.

I clicked open the email tab first. It loaded automatically, already open to a message thread. Subject line: *Balance Due*. The sender's email was vague, but I suspected it was Hayes. Didn't come with a letterhead or signature—the way a man like Hayes would work if he were doing illegal things. Probably untraceable too.

I started reading. At first, it was standard collections speak. Numbers, late notices, interest piling up. But it shifted fast. The emails turned aggressive, layered with threats. Stuff like *You don't want this to get physical,* and *People get hurt when they think I'm playing games.* Another one just said *Clock's ticking, Laurence. You've run out of time*. I felt my stomach lurch but forced myself to keep scrolling through the nausea. I had to know what was going on.

There were dates and figures listed. Dad owed more than I realized—way more. The loan was tied to the startup money for Next Gen, which he'd already sold. But he hadn't cleared the debt, just passed the problem along like he was hoping no one would notice. And now someone had noticed—someone who wanted their money back with interest.

I leaned back, trying to make sense of how this all happened. He'd told me the sale went fine. Said he broke even. That was a lie. Or maybe not a total lie—he probably covered the business expenses, sure—but the loans? They were personal. Hayes wasn't after the company. He was after Dad.

I glanced around the room again. The framed photo of Mom was dusty in the corner. I didn't think he looked at it anymore.

"You could've just told me," I muttered. "I would've helped."

I didn't know how to help though. This wasn't the kind of mess you helped with by loaning someone a few hundred bucks or bringing them dinner. This was serious—illegal—and getting worse by the second.

I closed the email tab carefully, like maybe that would undo it somehow. My hands were colder than they should've been. I stared at the desktop background for a while—some stock photo of a mountain lake that didn't even look like anything he'd pick. Maybe it came with the computer.

I stood slowly, running my palm down the front of my shirt. My fingers itched to call someone—to do something—but I didn't know what the right thing was yet. What I did know was that when I left that room, I wouldn't be coming back just to check in. The next time I saw Dad, we were having this conversation for real. Whether he wanted to or not.

I left Dad's office quietly and pulled the door shut, still unsure what I was going to do. My heart was pounding, but not in that adrenaline way you get when you're excited or even angry. This was something else. My fingers wouldn't stop twitching. I kept brushing my palms on my jeans like that would ground me, but all it did was remind me that I was still standing here with no plan.

I walked down the hall slowly, one step at a time, thinking maybe I'd sit at the kitchen table and just ... think. Not that I expected an answer to fall out of the ceiling, but I needed a second. Just one second to breathe, to stop my mind from jumping between worst-case scenarios and whatever came after them. I wasn't going to cry. Not yet.

I turned the corner into the living room just as the back door opened.

It didn't creak. It didn't rattle. It opened like it belonged to them.

At first, I thought it might be Dad. My brain reached for that explanation because it was the only one that made sense. But when I turned, it wasn't Dad at all.

Three men stepped in like they'd done it before. No hesitation. No fumbling. The first one was older, maybe late forties, with short, graying hair and a clean-cut look that didn't match the moment. His coat was too nice for someone just dropping by. He looked straight at me and smiled in a way that didn't touch his eyes.

"Hello, Amelia," he said, as if I'd invited them in.

I froze halfway into the room, the kitchen light still casting a line across the floor behind me.

"Who are you?" I asked, though I already knew. I felt it in my throat, in the knot forming at the base of my spine.

"Is your father home?" he asked casually, looking past me like I wasn't even there.

"No," I said, voice thin. I didn't recognize it.

"Pity."

The two men behind him were taller, broader, dressed in muted, shapeless clothes. One wore gloves. The other had a thick scar under his chin that caught the light. They didn't look at me directly. They didn't need to. Their presence was enough.

"You need to leave," I said, but it came out shaky. "You can't be here."

The man in front took one step in, then another, his shoes soft on the floor.

"We wouldn't be here if he hadn't made it necessary," he said simply.

I backed up two steps, my foot catching the edge of the rug. "I said get out."

He didn't even blink. He nodded slightly toward the others. "Hold her."

One of them moved too fast. His hand grabbed my wrist hard and pulled. I screamed and yanked away, stumbling into the side of the couch, but the second one was already there. He caught my shoulders and shoved me down onto the cushions before I could brace myself. My elbow hit the armrest too hard. Pain flared up my arm.

"Get off me!" I shouted, kicking, twisting, trying to push them away. "Let go—let go of me!"

The man in the blazer crouched to eye level in front of me, his voice calm like we were discussing the weather. "We just need a little message from you," he said. "Something your father can watch when he gets home."

"No!" I was crying now, sobbing so hard my shoulders shook. One second I was yelling, the next my face was soaked, my chest heaving like I'd run a marathon in the middle of a blizzard. "Please, don't do this—please. He doesn't have anything. I saw the emails. I know. I know how bad it is, but this isn't the way—"

He didn't react. He just lifted his phone and tapped the screen. "Camera's on," he said. "Let's make it count."

One of the men tightened his grip on my arm while the other leaned in closer. My whole body was shaking. My mouth opened, but nothing came out at first except a strangled breath.

"You can't do this," I gasped. "You don't have to do this."

"You want to stay calm," the man holding me said quietly. "You really do."

"I—I can't—" My throat closed. I could barely see through the tears. Everything was blurred—his face, the light, even the phone. It didn't matter. I knew what I was supposed to say.

I looked at the camera, trying not to sob, trying to keep my voice from breaking completely. "Tell Daddy Dearest who has you, sweetheart." His voice was angry and menacing, not at all matching his words. "Tell him what we'll do if he doesn't pay what he owes me." My blood ran cold, goose bumps rising on my arms. This was Victor Hayes?

"Dad," I stuttered, the word barely audible. "They're h-here ... They've t-taken me."

I sucked in a breath that felt more like sludge than air. My hands were trembling so badly it felt like my whole body was about to come apart. "Please, Daddy," I continued, every word harder than the last, "they'll hurt me. Please—just ... please fix this."

He turned his phone away, stopped the recording. I dropped my head forward and cried into my hands, too weak to move, too sick to think. Then the vomit came, bursting up through my mouth onto his shoes and Dad's carpet. I couldn't stop it, no matter how much I wanted to. My body lurched and shook, and when it was over, I coughed, choked, and spat the nasty taste out of my mouth.

They didn't say anything after that. The two men yanked me up again, one gripping my arm, the other walking behind me. I stumbled trying to keep up with their pace, my feet barely catching the floor. The hallway blurred past me, the kitchen light flickering slightly as we passed.

I saw my reflection in the microwave door as we passed it. My cheeks were red, streaked with tears, hair clinging to my face. I didn't recognize myself.

I didn't fight them as they opened the back door again. I couldn't. My legs barely worked.

But somewhere, underneath the fear and the shaking and the mess I'd become in the last five minutes, I was thinking. I was watching. I was memorizing the way the car looked at the end of the driveway. The license plate. The patch on the taller guy's jacket. The sound of the engine when the door opened.

The car door slammed shut behind me, and before I could even shift my weight, one of them tied my wrists tighter and pulled a gag across my mouth. The seat was cold and stiff under me. My body twisted on instinct, trying to get away, but there was nowhere to go. I couldn't breathe right. I could barely think.

The man in the front passenger seat tapped something on his phone. The driver stared straight ahead. Neither of them looked back at me. It was like I wasn't even a person, just cargo.

I pressed my forehead to the back of the seat, shaking, wishing I had never opened Dad's office door. I should've walked away. Pretended I didn't see the emails. If I had just left it alone, maybe this wouldn't be happening.

Or I could have asked Xander. He wouldn't have liked it, but he would've done it. He had the money, the influence. He could've ended this with one phone call. It wouldn't have meant anything to him. Just a favor, a transaction. We didn't have a relationship. Not a real one. I told myself that over and over, but it didn't stop me from picturing his face. I wanted to believe he'd care. That if he knew, he'd come for me.

But he didn't know. No one did.

I thought of Dad. What he'd do when he saw the video. Would he panic? Would he finally tell someone the truth?

And then the worst thought landed in the center of my chest.

What if I never saw either of them again?

My hand curled against my stomach. I was going to die. Alone, in the back of a stranger's car. And my baby would never take a first breath.

23

XANDER

Monday came and went like a haze. The office was quiet in the way that made people more tense, not less. Amelia's absence was starting to stretch into something that couldn't be ignored anymore. Her desk hadn't been touched. Her inbox had gone cold. She didn't respond to the resignation acknowledgment I sent last week, and I hadn't heard a word from her since.

It didn't feel right.

I sat at my desk with a half-written report open on one monitor and her old Slack thread open on the other. Still no green dot next to her name. Still no reply to the last message I'd sent asking her to just let me know if she was okay.

I stared at the screen a few more seconds, then grabbed my phone and scrolled until I found Laurence's contact. I didn't want to make the call—I wasn't even sure what I was hoping to get out of it—but if anyone would know where she'd gone, it was her father.

The line rang twice before he picked up. His voice sounded thinner than usual. "Xander. Yeah. Hey." There was some kind of background noise—like he was outside or pacing near traffic. His words came fast, uneven. I wasn't sure if he was distracted or just not completely sober.

"Hey, Laurence. I'm calling about Amelia," I said. "She hasn't shown up. She quit suddenly last week. No word since. Have you heard from her?"

There was a pause, then a sharp exhale. "She quit?" He sounded hollow, like he wasn't all there, but his voice ticked up a notch at the mention of Amelia's name.

"You didn't know?"

"No. I haven't talked to her. I figured she was just busy or something." His voice pitched higher again, unconvincing. Then suddenly, it was filled with fear and a tremor of panic. "Xander, listen—I need a favor. I need a loan. It's urgent. Can you get me half a million? Just temporary. Please. I swear I'll pay you back. I wouldn't ask if it wasn't an emergency and—"

I blinked. "Laurence, I—what?"

"I wouldn't ask if it wasn't serious," he said quickly. "It's a mess, but I've got someone breathing down my neck. It's not personal—it's business."

"That's not something I can just move around," I said slowly. "We don't have cash like that just sitting around. Even if I could get access, the business needs it. We're barely covering our pipeline projects as it is." My mind was reeling. Larry was in trouble with someone; I could hear it in his voice, and Amelia had been acting strange for a while, telling me she was scared for him, worried about him. My throat constricted as I wondered if she'd gotten involved, if that was why she suddenly vanished.

"I'll pay it back," he said. "You know I'm good for it."

I hesitated. "What happened to your December profit share? You got a lot of money, enough to last the full year. I signed the check myself."

There was silence on the line for a moment. Then I heard a small rustle, maybe wind, or fabric. "That's not enough," he said, and then—without warning—he hung up.

I sat there, staring at the phone. The call had lasted less than three minutes, but it left my thoughts scrambled. He sounded nothing like himself. And whatever trouble he was in, it was big enough to make him ask for money that he had to know I couldn't just produce.

Something was off. Way off. And now I had two people missing pieces of themselves—one who had vanished entirely, and another who didn't seem far behind.

I stared at my phone long after the call ended, still holding it in my hand like maybe something would light up or vibrate. Nothing did. Just a blank screen and the quiet hum of the office around me.

That conversation with Laurence left a strange echo in my head. His voice hadn't sounded right. Distracted, agitated—maybe worse than that. And the request for a half million dollars? That wasn't just out of character. It was desperate. If he had no idea where Amelia was either, and something had him so flustered he hung up without even a goodbye, then whatever this was, it went deeper than I thought.

I sat with that discomfort for another minute before standing up and heading down the hall.

I wasn't marching. I wasn't angry. I just needed clarity.

Godwin's door was open this time, but he was focused on his screen, typing with that sort of careful speed that meant he was solving something. He glanced up as I stepped in and then sat back in his chair, like he already knew why I was there.

"Hey," I said, keeping my voice even. "Got a minute?"

He nodded once, eyes narrowing slightly with caution. "Sure."

I stepped inside and closed the door behind me. Not for secrecy, just for the quiet.

"I'm not here to lecture," I said, lifting my hands a little. "I'm not coming down on you. I just ... need to ask something, as a friend. Or at least someone who's just trying to understand what's going on."

Godwin tilted his head, curious but not defensive. "Alright."

"I called Laurence," I said. "To see if he'd heard from Amelia. He hadn't. He sounded ... off. Like he was stressed, maybe drunk. He asked me for half a million dollars. Then hung up."

Godwin's expression didn't shift, but I could see something flicker in his eyes.

"I'm worried about her," I said. "Actually worried. And I know I don't deserve the benefit of the doubt with you, but I swear I'm not asking to control anything. I'm not looking for leverage. I just want to know she's okay."

Godwin folded his hands and looked down for a second before responding. "She hasn't told me anything lately. I don't know where she went."

I nodded, but didn't move.

"She's not in danger," he added, a little too quickly. "She needed time. That's all."

"Why does everyone keep saying that?" I asked, too sharp, then softened. "Sorry. I just ... what does 'time' even mean when someone ghosts their whole life?"

He took a breath. "Look, I don't know everything, and I wouldn't tell you if I did. But I can say this—when you came down on her in the office, when you accused her of things that weren't happening, it shook her more than you probably realized."

I let that sink in.

"You humiliated her," he said, not cruel, just honest. "Not publicly, but still. That day ... you were jealous. Possessive. And it made her question everything about the situation you two were in. She didn't say it exactly, but she didn't feel safe, emotionally."

I nodded slowly. I'd known that. Even when I was storming out of her office, I knew.

"We crossed lines," I admitted. "She and I. I never planned to. But I did. And I know I made it worse. But Godwin, if something happens to her, and I didn't act because I was worried about protocol—"

"She just needs space," he repeated, firmer this time. "Whatever she's dealing with, she's not asking to be found right now."

"I can't take that as an answer anymore," I said.

Godwin didn't argue. He just looked tired. Maybe he understood. Maybe he didn't.

I left his office without another word, grabbed my keys, and walked out into the late afternoon haze without checking my email or telling anyone where I was going. If Amelia wasn't going to come to me, I would go to her. I refused to be one of those people who let life walk right past and didn't say anything. It felt like something was wrong, that she might be in trouble, and what sort of man was I if I ignored that gnawing gut feeling?

The drive over to her apartment felt longer than I remembered. I knew the route by heart, but every red light stretched out like it was trying to test my nerves. My hands tightened on the steering wheel. I wasn't racing. I wasn't weaving between cars. I just ... needed to get there. I needed to see her place, to feel like I was doing something besides pacing around my own mind.

"You're being dramatic," I muttered under my breath, not even convinced. "She probably just turned off her phone. People do that."

But Amelia didn't. Not like this. She wasn't the type to disappear without so much as a goodbye. Even when she was upset, she didn't vanish. The resignation letter had been the only real sign she'd given me—and it had read more like a formality than a choice. Too clean. Too final. It hadn't sounded like her at all.

I turned down her street and caught myself scanning the sidewalks as if she might suddenly appear, walking her trash to the curb or checking her mailbox like nothing had happened.

"She needed space," I repeated Godwin's words, but they sat wrong with me. Space didn't look like this. It didn't sound like Laurence asking for half a million dollars and hanging up the phone like the house was on fire. And if she really was fine, if she really just needed a break, why did I feel like someone had yanked a wire loose inside my chest?

I pulled into the lot and rolled slowly to a stop. Her parking spot was empty. Not surprising, but not helpful either. I got out and walked into the building and up to her door—knocked and waited. I knocked again—nothing.

So, I sat on the floor outside her apartment door, right on that little welcome mat with the faded floral border. The hallway smelled like someone down the hall had just reheated leftover pasta, and I could hear a TV echoing through thin walls. Every now and then, a door creaked open somewhere on the floor, or footsteps passed behind me with slow suspicion. I kept my head down and my hands laced loosely between my knees.

Let them stare. I wasn't moving.

If Amelia was here, she wasn't answering. If she wasn't here, I'd see her when she came back. I didn't have a good reason to sit here like this. I just couldn't leave. It wasn't about control. And it wasn't pride. It was this gnawing sense that if I walked away now, I'd never see her again.

She had walked out of my life with no real explanation. Just that carefully worded resignation email that read like it had been copied from a template online. She never even acknowledged the messages I sent. She didn't fight. She didn't explain. She didn't even give me the chance to apologize.

And here I was. Sitting outside her door like someone waiting for an answer that might never come. I should have kept my distance. We were supposed to be temporary, clean, unattached. But somewhere between the office and the nights in my house and the way she'd slowly taken up space in my life, I started letting her in. I let my guard down, and now I felt stupid for it.

No, not stupid.

Abandoned.

It felt too familiar—that silence, the disappearing act. That final door shutting that you don't even realize is the last one. Like when Mom walked out of the house for the last time, and I never saw her again.

Amelia shut me out the same way my mother shut my father out. Quietly. Without discussion. Just gone. And maybe that's the part that hit hardest. The idea that I didn't matter enough to be told why.

A door opened down the hall, and an older woman with a laundry basket walked out. She stared openly, like she was memorizing my face in case she needed to describe me to a police sketch artist later.

I gave her a nod. She didn't return it.

I turned my attention back to Amelia's door, resting my arms on my knees, and let the hallway fall quiet again.

Maybe I was an idiot for caring this much.

Maybe I should just quit while I still had some dignity, go home, and admit I'd lost this one.

But I stayed. Because something inside me couldn't leave.

24

AMELIA

The room they put me in was nicer than most hotel suites I'd stayed in. That was the strangest part. Nothing about it felt like a prison, except for the locked door.

From where I sat—on a cream-colored bench at the foot of the bed—I could see nearly every polished surface in the room reflecting light like it had been cleaned twice this morning. The windows weren't barred. They looked out over a neat backyard with desert landscaping, all tan stone and low shrubs that looked expensive to maintain. Beyond the fence was another house, and another after that, all stacked up like dollhouses in a quiet cul-de-sac.

We were in Vegas. I never saw a sign or a street name, but I recognized the mountains and desert when we stepped out of the helicopter. Warm, dry, and heavy with dust. They hadn't blindfolded me or tied me down, though they did keep the restraints on my hands. Thankfully, they took the gag out of my mouth when I started dry heaving again.

One of them—always in a navy polo and slacks—came in earlier to drop off a tray with food. Bottled water, a sandwich, a few grapes. Like this was some strange spa retreat instead of a hostage situation. I stayed on the far side of the room when he entered and almost cried.

"As long as your father pays up, you'll be out of here in no time," he said, as if that was supposed to help.

I didn't respond. I just sat there with my hands folded in my lap, nodding like I agreed. He closed the door behind himself gently. It clicked when it locked, even though it didn't need to.

I hadn't touched the food.

They told me not to worry. That I'd be home soon. But they didn't know my father. Not the version I'd seen lately—the one barely keeping the lights on, pretending the walls weren't closing in. He had no money to pay up, and though I assumed he'd go straight to Xander, I knew that was a long shot too. Xander didn't care about me. He'd said as much the last time we spoke.

I looked out the window again. There were kids riding scooters a couple of houses down. A man hosing off his driveway. The world looked completely normal from here.

I stayed by the window most of the day, leaning my elbow on the sill, watching the ordinary lives unfolding just outside this strange bubble I had landed in. Somewhere beyond those tan walls and trimmed hedges, people were going to work, picking up groceries, making dinner plans. I was here. Waiting.

They weren't rough with me. No one raised their voice. No one made threats. They offered food, clean sheets, privacy. But it wasn't kindness. It was calculation. Like they wanted me calm so I wouldn't make their job harder. They never called me by name. Just "her" or "the girl." And the only thing they repeated was that it would all be over as soon as my dad "handled things."

I hadn't asked what that meant, not directly. I already knew. That number—the six figures I saw in his ledger—it wasn't going to vanish.

The door opened again midafternoon, but this time, it wasn't the man in the navy polo. It was Victor Hayes. He wore a tailored suit. Crisp white shirt, pale gray jacket, silver cuff links. Not flashy, just confident. His salt-and-pepper hair was neatly cut, and he didn't carry a phone or a file. Just walked in with both hands in his pockets and stopped a few feet from the center of the room.

"Miss Johnson," he said. "I hope you've been treated respectfully."

I stood up without meaning to. "You must be Hayes."

He smiled faintly. "You're sharper than your father." I didn't answer. He nodded toward the chair by the desk. "Would you mind sitting? I'd like to explain a few things."

I didn't want to, but I also didn't want to be standing in the middle of the room while this man towered over me. I sat carefully, crossing my arms over my stomach out of habit more than anything else.

"I imagine this situation has been ... unsettling," Hayes said, pacing a little but never turning his back to me. "I don't make a habit of involving family in business matters, but your father has left me with very few options."

"You're threatening his daughter," I said. "That feels personal."

He nodded as if I'd only just caught up. "It is now."

There was nothing hostile in his voice. No raised tone, no hard edge. It was a plain statement, spoken with the same rhythm someone might use when confirming the day of the week. That only made it harder to grasp. I wondered if he had children of his own, if they were in this house somewhere.

"You're here because I gave your father every chance to make this right," he continued, walking with slow, deliberate steps. "And he didn't. He took money—large amounts—on the promise of future earnings. Those earnings never came."

"He sold the company," I said. "Didn't that cover any of it?"

Hayes gave a dry laugh under his breath. "Your father was smart enough to structure the sale so it paid him upfront. What he failed to do was prioritize what he owed. That money was spent before the ink dried. Half a million dollars is not the sort of debt a person just walks away from."

"He doesn't have it," I said, holding his gaze.

"That's not my concern," he replied, calm as ever. He paused, turning his cold stare on me. To him this was just business, even dragging me into this.

"He can't give you what he doesn't have," I added, unsure why I was still trying to explain something that had probably been said a hundred times already.

His eyes narrowed further, making me swallow hard against a lump in my throat. "If I go easy on him, the next person I lend to will expect the same. And the next one after that. Generosity becomes softness in this business, and softness becomes failure. That's not how I operate."

It was hard to argue with the logic. His tone was too steady, his message too clean. I didn't like it, but I understood it. The man was protecting his reputation, not venting anger. This wasn't about rage. It was about rules. Anyone else would file a lawsuit, but in the end they would lose. The debtor would file bankruptcy.

Hayes tilted his head slightly. "You're not dumb. I'm sure you're sitting there wondering if there's another way out of this. Some other solution you just haven't considered yet."

"There isn't," I said, though it came out quieter than I intended.

He raised one eyebrow, like he didn't believe me. "There's always a way when someone's desperate enough. People mortgage their homes, call in favors, make promises they never imagined making. Resources come out of nowhere when enough pressure is applied."

I said nothing, and neither did he for a moment. Then his gaze narrowed, not in anger, but in the way someone watches for a reaction they expect to find. "Your father's not the only one with ties. There's that CEO ... Blackwell. You think he might be inclined to help? Maybe cut a check for an old friend?"

I kept my expression still.

"Your father used to brag about that partnership. Said Blackwell had a gift for building things. That he owed everything to the opportunity that came from that first sale."

"Xander doesn't owe us anything," I said. "He already bought the company. He moved on."

Hayes nodded slowly, like that answer fit whatever theory he already had. "But you know him. That's not a question. What I'm asking is whether he'd come through."

I glanced toward the window, giving myself something else to focus on. My heart started pounding harder, palms growing sweaty. This couldn't be happening.

Hayes didn't push the point. "You don't think he'd help," he said. "Interesting."

I could feel the tension knotting at the base of my neck. I wanted to speak, to say something that would shut the whole thing down, but nothing came out. There was no safe version of that conversation. I didn't know what Xander would do. And even if I did, I wasn't about to hand him over to this.

Hayes studied me for a moment longer. Then he turned toward the dresser and picked up something small—a hairbrush. He turned it over once in his palm, then set it down again without comment.

"You live alone, right?" he asked in a voice so casual it chilled me. "Nice little apartment. Second floor. Good light. Organized."

A quiet rush of nausea settled in my stomach. I didn't move.

"We were careful," he added. "Didn't take anything. Just wanted to confirm a few things. Make sure there were no surprises."

His eyes met mine again and he calmly stared at me. "Your vitamins were still on the counter. You keep your mail in a little wire basket by the door. Appointment card was sitting on the table, tucked halfway under a candle."

I felt something slip in my chest. Not a panic, exactly. Just that awful drop when you realize you're too late.

He smiled, just slightly. "Congratulations, by the way."

I stood without thinking, heart hammering. "Stay away from me."

"No one's going to harm you," he said. "We're not interested in hurting people. We're interested in results. But I imagine your father might think differently once he understands what's really at stake."

I took a step back, closer to the wall. He didn't move, didn't reach for anything, didn't raise his voice. He didn't need to. Just him being here was terrifying.

"You're a bargaining chip, Miss Johnson," he continued, adjusting the sleeves of his jacket. "You are leverage." My throat was tight, and my limbs felt heavy, but I didn't let him see it.

Hayes gave one final glance around the room before walking to the door. "We'll give him a little more time," he said. "But not much."

He stepped through the doorway and pulled the door closed behind him. I heard the lock engage with that same clean, mechanical click I had started to hate.

I sat down slowly on the edge of the bed, placing both hands on my stomach. The fabric of my shirt bunched under my palms. I pressed lightly, trying to steady my breath.

They had been in my home. In my space. They knew everything now, and I couldn't take any of it back. They knew about the baby. They sorted through my trash ...

And whatever came next, I had no idea how to stop it.

I leaned forward, resting my elbows on my thighs and folding my hands tightly together. My fingers wouldn't stop moving, tracing invisible lines across my palms like I could smooth this feeling away.

The fear wasn't loud anymore. It had settled somewhere deeper, coiled and quiet inside my chest. But it hadn't gone. They knew. They had been in my apartment. They had touched my things, seen my appointment card, understood what even I had barely accepted. And now they could use it—use me—in whatever way made the numbers work.

I could handle being here. I could stomach the threats, the silence, the uncertainty. But the thought that they might reach for Xander next, that they'd hold the pregnancy over him the same way they were holding it over me—it made my chest lock up.

He didn't know. He wasn't supposed to. And if they told him—if they turned this into some twisted form of pressure—I didn't know what he'd do. I didn't know what that would make me in his eyes.

This wasn't supposed to touch him. I kept him out of it for a reason.

I stood again, restless, pacing from the window to the bed and back. My reflection caught faintly in the glass, and for a second, I didn't recognize myself. I looked tired. Smaller somehow.

If they told Xander, it wouldn't just ruin whatever thread of peace I had left. It would pull him into this storm I never should've been in to begin with. And I didn't know if he'd walk away from it, or walk toward it, or if that decision would break both of us in ways we couldn't fix.

I pressed my fingers to the windowpane and closed my eyes.

I had no way of knowing what they'd do next, but I knew now I was afraid of more than just them. I was afraid of what this would do to Xander too.

25

XANDER

I woke up with a crick in my neck and the smell of someone's microwave dinner lingering in the air. The hallway light above me buzzed faintly, flickering every few seconds. My legs were stiff from being folded under me, and my back ached from slumping sideways against Amelia's door. For a second, I couldn't remember where I was.

Then I saw the worn floral mat under me, the mail slot, the closed door I'd been staring at for hours. I sat up slowly and rubbed the side of my face. My drool had left a faint mark on the denim of my jeans and dried to my jaw. My phone was dead in my pocket. I must've fallen asleep sometime after midnight, maybe later. No messages. No footsteps on the other side of the door. No signs of life at all. Just silence.

A shuffle of movement pulled my attention down the hall. A woman carrying a folded newspaper and a chipped ceramic mug passed by. She was older, mid-sixties maybe, in a faded house robe and slippers with a sag to them. She slowed when she saw me, her brow knitting in quiet concern.

"You waiting on someone?" she asked.

I stood, brushing off the back of my pants. "Amelia Johnson. This is her place. Have you seen her?"

She shifted the mug to her other hand and squinted. It was an expression that revealed disdain, as if the folks who lived in this apartment building bound together and hated outsiders just for existing. "Not for a few days, no."

"Are you sure?"

"Pretty sure. I live two doors down. Usually when she's going out of town, she lets someone know. Leaves a note, asks for the mail to be brought in." She nodded toward a small stack of envelopes tucked under her arm. "She didn't this time. I figured maybe it was a quick trip, but it's been … four days now … I think?"

I stared at the mail. Utility bills, a magazine, something official-looking from a doctor's office. There were more letters, but the return senders' addresses were hidden. Still, nothing anyone would leave behind on purpose.

"Has anyone else been here? Someone picking her up, stopping by, anything like that?"

She tilted her head, thinking. "Well, there's that friend of hers, the one with the glasses. Comes by sometimes, nice enough. Little over friendly." She leaned in and spoke out the side of her mouth for a second as she narrowed her eyes in judgment. "Might be a poofter."

"Godwin?" I shook my head wondering what the heck that was supposed to mean, but I figured she knew and the expression on her face being one of criticism, I figured it wasn't good. People were so judgmental these days.

"That's the one. He's been around lately. Last week I saw him here twice in the same day." She frowned. "This just doesn't feel like her."

No. It didn't feel like her at all.

I nodded, thanked her, and watched her disappear around the corner. The door closed softly behind her, and I was alone again—privacy to obsess and stew in my own concern.

Godwin had said she needed time, said she wasn't in danger. I believed him when he said it. Or I wanted to believe it. But Amelia didn't just vanish like this. She didn't go radio silent, didn't quit a job she'd worked her fingers to the bone to earn, didn't let someone else collect her mail without saying a word.

And now I was standing here like some half-drunk idiot who'd passed out on a hallway floor instead of doing something useful. Instead of paying attention sooner.

I turned back to her door and knocked again, even though I knew it was pointless. My voice came quieter than I expected.

"Amelia."

No answer.

The silence didn't feel neutral anymore. It felt wrong.

I stepped back and stared at the lock, running over every conversation we'd had in the last few weeks. Every word I missed. Every shift in tone I should've questioned. Every moment she looked like she wanted to say something and didn't.

Space was one thing.

This was something else.

And if I was right—if she was in trouble—then I might already be too late.

I took the stairs down instead of the elevator, not sure why. Maybe I needed the movement, something to distract me from the quiet scratching under my ribs that said something was off. The building felt hollow. The hallway was still, and the city outside felt colder than when I'd arrived. I walked without rushing, hands in my pockets, the kind of tired that sinks into your shoulders and makes everything a little slower.

Outside, the street was still. My car was parked under the same dim streetlamp I'd left it under hours ago. I slid behind the wheel, turned the engine over, and sat there for a moment with my hands still on the ignition.

I pulled out my phone and plugged it in, then called Laurence. It rang once, then went to voicemail. I didn't bother with a message. He wouldn't hear it tonight anyway. I wasn't sure what I would've said if he had picked up. That I'd been camped out on Amelia's hallway floor like some idiot with no sense of boundaries? That her neighbor said she hadn't been home in days, and it didn't line up with anything I'd been told?

I dropped the phone onto the passenger seat, shifted into gear, and started driving. The streets were empty, traffic lights blinking yellow as I passed through intersections without stopping. I kept one hand on the wheel and the other curled tight around nothing, trying to ignore the way everything suddenly felt thinner—less stable, like whatever I'd told myself before had stopped being enough.

By the time I got home, the sun was beginning to edge up behind the hills, casting a dull silver light across the skyline. I didn't bother changing clothes. I dropped my keys on the counter, turned on a lamp in the living room, and sat down on the edge of the couch without bothering to lean back. I stared at the darkened windows across the room, waiting for some sort of clarity that never came.

The house felt colder than usual, or maybe it was my anxious tension, but I was shivering. I turned my phone over in my hand again and again, checking the lock screen every few minutes as if something might appear. There were no new messages or missed calls. I kept thinking maybe I had overlooked something—a sign, a detail, anything that might explain where she had gone.

But there was nothing.

I moved to the kitchen, poured a glass of water I didn't drink, and stood there with my hand braced against the counter for several minutes before I finally gave in and took my phone out again. I searched for the non-emergency police line, punched in the number, and waited through the usual list of options before someone picked up.

When the call finally picked up, the woman on the other end had a calm, almost mechanical tone—courteous but detached, like she'd been on this shift too long to bother with warmth. "Metro Police, Missing Persons Division. How can I help you?"

"I need to check if someone's been reported missing," I said. "Her name is Amelia Johnson."

There was a pause as she brought up a database. I could hear her typing, short bursts broken by the occasional click. "Can you spell the last name?"

"J-O-H-N-S-O-N. First name Amelia. A-M-E-L-I-A."

"Date of birth?"

"August 22, 1999."

"Alright," she said. "Give me a moment to check."

I leaned my elbow on the counter and rubbed the bridge of my nose, closing my eyes while I listened to the silence on the line. In the other room, the refrigerator kicked on, and a car passed outside with its headlights illuminating the street. It was almost five in the morning, and the city hadn't quite decided to wake up yet.

"Nothing's been filed under that name," she said finally. "There's no open case for Amelia Johnson at this time."

I swallowed a lump in my throat. "So no one's reported her. Not even her father." My stomach clenched as anxiety struck. Maybe Larry didn't know she was missing either.

"Not yet. Would you like to initiate a report?"

The question sat there between us. I glanced down at the counter, then at the small stack of unopened mail beside the toaster, like the answer might be buried somewhere between bills and coupons. If I said yes, the wheels would start turning. They'd ask more questions, open an investigation, start contacting people.

Laurence would be the first call. Then maybe Godwin. And if Amelia had just decided to disappear for a few days—if she was exactly where I suspected she might be—then I'd have dragged her whole life into something official, and she'd never forgive me for it.

"I don't think I'm ready to do that yet," I said, my voice lower now. "She's been gone a few days, but I'm not sure what's going on."

"Are you concerned for her safety?" the woman asked, her tone softening slightly now, like she knew I wasn't calling because I had nothing better to do. I heard her fingers still clicking on the keyboard, but I hesitated.

I didn't answer right away. I looked at the tile floor, then at the faint reflection of myself in the microwave door. "I don't know," I said.

"She's been ... not herself. But maybe she's just with her dad. I don't want to jump the gun."

"Understood," she said. "If anything changes, call us back."

I ended the call and set the phone down face-first on the counter, then stood there with my arms crossed over my chest. I didn't sit—didn't move. I just stood there, breathing slow and even, trying to convince myself that this wasn't turning into something else. If she was with her dad, then at least she wasn't alone. That was the only thing I had to hold onto, and I was holding it tightly.

I plugged my phone in as soon as I walked into the bedroom. The battery icon blinked red, clinging to 1 percent. I set it on the nightstand, screen down, and pulled the blankets back without bothering to undress. The room was dim, the curtains still open just enough to catch the first hints of daylight, but I didn't get up to close them. Lying still felt like the only thing I could manage.

Sleep didn't come. I wasn't even close. I kept replaying the same useless thoughts, waiting for something to shift. The ceiling fan ticked softly every time the blades swung past the same spot. I stared at that point like the noise might line up with something, but it didn't.

The phone vibrated once, then lit up. I turned toward it with my heart lurching in my chest, and for a second I didn't move. The message came from a restricted number—no name, no contact, just text across the lock screen.

Restricted: 5:04 AM: *The police can't help you. If you want to see Amelia alive again, talk to Laurence.*

I sat up slowly and picked it up, reading it again just to be sure I hadn't imagined it. There was nothing else—no demand or instructions. Just a line that landed exactly where it was meant to.

The message was real, and whoever sent it knew exactly what they were doing.

I swung my legs over the edge of the bed and grabbed my keys from the dresser. There was no chance of sleep now. Not after a message like that and no way of knowing who sent it. I checked my phone again—still nothing. I tried Laurence one more time. It rang until it didn't, then went to voicemail just like before. I ended the call without leaving a word.

Whoever sent that message wanted me unsettled. It worked. There was no reason to wait around for another cryptic threat to show up. If Laurence knew something—and I was starting to believe he did—then I was done guessing.

I slipped my shoes back on by the door and grabbed my jacket from the hook. The house was still dark as I locked up behind me, but the air outside felt different now.

I was going to his house.

26

AMELIA

I didn't realize we were headed toward the Strip until I saw the skyline shift. The familiar glow of the big-name hotels started bleeding through the tinted windows, distant at first, then close enough to pick out the casino names. We passed a few without slowing—bright, polished places that looked clean enough on the outside to pretend nothing dark ever happened inside. Then the car turned off the main road and took a narrow side entrance tucked between two loading docks.

The lights were dimmer here, service access hidden from the front-facing glamour. It smelled faintly like motor oil and too many cigarette breaks. The man in the passenger seat didn't speak. The driver didn't either.

They parked in a concrete bay behind an unmarked service door, and without a word, one of them got out and opened the door on my side. I didn't move at first, but he didn't touch me—just waited, like the silence was enough to push me forward. I stepped out slowly, the soles of my shoes making soft contact with the damp pavement. I wasn't gagged or handcuffed anymore, but the freedom was fake. I knew that.

The man with the scar on his chin led the way. We entered

through a door held open by another guy I didn't recognize. There were no signs, no names. Just a long hallway lined with aging wallpaper and worn carpet that looked like it hadn't been vacuumed in weeks. I kept walking and didn't ask questions. They hadn't answered the last ten I'd tried, and I doubted this would be different.

After several turns and a short ride in a freight elevator, we passed through a back room that opened into a private lounge just off the casino floor. I caught a glimpse of the flashing lights through tinted glass, just long enough to see a group of men gathered around a craps table. They were loud, laughing too hard, their movements loose and wild like they didn't know the rest of the world existed. If I screamed, they wouldn't hear me.

We moved quickly. One of the men placed a hand on my back—not rough, just firm enough to keep me moving. I kept waiting for someone to say something, but no one did. The hallway narrowed, then ended in a dark wooden door that looked too solid for this place. It opened before we reached it.

The room beyond was small, windowless, and cold. It felt like the kind of space that absorbed every bad thing that ever happened inside and kept it all a dark secret. A metal chair sat in the center of the room—nothing else—and they gestured for me to go in. I did, and the door shut behind me. The sound of the lock clicking into place caused goose bumps on my arms.

I stood for a while before sitting. My knees felt too loose, like I wasn't entirely in my body. The air smelled like dust and something metallic. My fingers curled around the edge of the seat. I didn't cry or scream. I just waited, even though I didn't know what I was waiting for.

Dad looked more tired than I remembered. His hair had been cut since the last time we spoke, and the circles under his eyes had sunken into the bone. His clothes were unsoiled but rumpled, like he hadn't slept or changed in a day or two. When his eyes landed on me, something cracked behind them. He stepped into the room, and the door shut again.

"Amelia." His voice broke on the second syllable, but he didn't reach for me right away, like he wasn't sure he was allowed.

I stepped into his arms and wrapped mine around his middle. He held me tighter than I expected—shaky, desperate, like maybe he'd already prepared for the worst and this moment wasn't real.

"I'm sorry," he whispered. "I'm so damn sorry."

I pulled back enough to look at him. "What is this? Why are we here? What's happening?"

His mouth opened, but nothing came out. He reached into his jacket and pulled out a thick envelope, folding it in his hands like he didn't know what else to do with it. I recognized the posture. It was the same one he'd used when he sulked into the dining room at Easter brunch and sat down with guilt all over his face.

Before he could speak, the door opened again. This time, Victor Hayes walked in. He didn't bring anyone with him, which surprised me. I expected the cavalry to file in with their weapons blazing. He wore the same suit as before—pressed, quiet, expensive. His hands were in his pockets, and when he looked between us, there was no curiosity or anger, just the sense we were being evaluated.

"Well," he said, with a small nod. "Isn't this touching."

Dad turned toward him, stepping slightly in front of me, one hand still holding the envelope like it was going to change something.

"I have twenty thousand," he said quickly. "It's everything I could pull together. Insurance paid out on the car; I liquidated my accounts, sold what I could. I even—" He stopped short, voice faltering. "It's what I have right now."

Hayes didn't respond. He stepped farther into the room and let the silence do the work. My father's hand tightened around the envelope. His breathing was louder now, labored. I stepped forward.

"Please," I said. "He's trying. Just let us go. I'll get the rest. I can find a way—if you give me time."

Hayes finally looked at me. "It's not about trying, Miss Johnson. It's about results. Twenty thousand doesn't undo half a million in debt, especially when the clock ran out months ago."

"You said this was about leverage," I said. "You have it. You've proven you can get to him and that this is very serious. What more do you need?"

He studied me, like I was part of a negotiation instead of a person. "We need guarantees. You leaving would be a variable we can't afford."

I stepped closer to my father, whose shoulders had started to cave inward. I could see it now—the full collapse of whatever pride he had left. He'd walked into this room knowing he had nothing to offer, but he came anyway.

"You said I wouldn't be hurt," I said quietly. "You said that wasn't your business."

"And it isn't," Hayes replied. "Which is why you're still standing here. But let's not confuse patience with forgiveness. You're here because your father has failed to meet his end of a contract. That has consequences."

Dad took a half step forward, his eyes glassy now. "I'll get the rest. I swear to God. I have a contact. He's good for it. He just doesn't know yet."

Hayes arched an eyebrow but said nothing. He didn't need to ask who. We all knew. My heart sank just thinking of it. It made the mild nausea I'd been feeling all day ramp up. I thought I might vomit on Hayes's shoes again.

"I'll talk to him," my father added. "He'll listen."

"No, he won't," I said before I could stop myself. "Not if you come at him like this. Not if you drag me into it again."

Dad looked at me, broken in ways I didn't know how to describe. "I didn't know they'd take you. I didn't know it would go this far."

"But it did," I said, and my voice didn't shake. "And now we're here, and twenty thousand isn't going to solve anything."

Hayes stepped back toward the door but paused before opening it. "You have forty-eight hours," he said. "After that, the terms change." When I thought he would walk out, he stepped into the hallway, hand on the knob, and said, "Better run to Mr. Blackwell ... let him know his unborn child needs his help."

I blanched, guilt swelling up to choke me, and watched the door shut. The lock slid into place behind him a second later. The silence that followed was too heavy to name.

I sat down on the edge of the metal chair and pressed both palms against my thighs, trying to ground myself in something, anything. My father didn't speak for a long time. When he did, it was barely above a whisper.

"I'm going to fix this."

I looked up at him, at the man who used to keep change in his coat pocket for vending machines after school, who once drove halfway across town to find me the exact notebook I wanted. I believed he meant it. But meaning something didn't promise it would happen. Half a million dollars was more than he'd ever seen in his lifetime outside of bank numbers. To come up with that much cash in forty-eight hours was an unreasonable expectation on Hayes's part.

"How?" I asked.

"I told you," he said. "I have a contact."

"You mean Xander," I answered, my voice flat. "You dragged him into this."

He didn't deny it. He didn't have to.

His jaw tightened, and then he looked straight at me, eyes bloodshot and raw. "You're pregnant, and you didn't tell me?"

The words hit hard, louder than they needed to be. I stayed in the chair, frozen for a second before I could speak. "That's not the point."

"It is to me," he said, stepping closer, voice hoarse. "They told me. Hayes told me. Said they saw the doctor's card, your vitamins. Do you know what it felt like hearing it from him?"

My chest tightened as I sat up straighter. "I was going to tell you when it mattered. When things were calm. You don't get to be mad about timing now."

"Timing?" he said, laughing once in a bitter sound. "You think that's what this is about? I failed you. I know that. But you're my daughter. And now Hayes knows you're carrying Xander's kid. You think I'm not going to lose my mind over that?"

My stomach turned. I hadn't wanted it said out loud, hadn't wanted that particular truth in this room, with these walls and this threat around us. "You were never supposed to involve him," I said. "You don't get to wave my relationship around like it's a bargaining chip."

"I'm not using it," he snapped. "I'm trying to protect it. Him. You."

"You offered them twenty thousand dollars, Dad. That's not protection. That's proof we have nothing left to give."

His shoulders sagged, like he'd spent the last of whatever strength he had getting that envelope into his hands. "It's all I have. It's everything. I got the car insurance money, cashed what was left of my savings, took money from a warehouse job I'll probably get arrested over."

I didn't say anything. I couldn't. The weight of what he'd done, and that it still wasn't enough to fix it, sat like stone in the room.

The door opened behind him, and a guard stepped in without ceremony. "Time's up."

Dad glanced back, then turned to me one last time. "I'll figure it out. I'll get what he wants. Just hold on."

He left before I could respond, and the door closed again, sealing me back into a room that felt like a prison.

27

XANDER

I hadn't meant to fall asleep. The car was like a furnace by the time I came to—stifling hot, my shirt clinging to my back, the leather seat radiating warmth through my jeans. I pushed the door open partway and leaned against it, blinking against the sunlight that had shifted to a hazy late-afternoon angle. The windows were already down, but it hadn't helped. The air inside was stale and dense, the kind of heat that clings to your skin even after you step out of it.

I sat up straighter and squinted down the street as a car turned the corner and headed toward the driveway. My pulse jumped before my brain caught up. It was Amelia's car. My hand went to the door handle, breath already caught halfway in my chest. She'd finally come home. I didn't care what she had to say—I just needed to see her step out of that car and know she was okay.

But it wasn't her.

The driver's side opened too hard, and Laurence stumbled out. He looked wrecked. He barely got the door closed before pacing in a frantic, disjointed loop near the curb. I was already out of the car and walking toward him when he saw me.

"Xander—God, okay. Okay. You're here. That's good." His voice was too loud, too fast. "I've been driving since this morning. I just got back. They let me see her. I saw Amelia."

I stopped short. "What do you mean you saw her?"

"She's alive, but she's not free. They've got her. Hayes has her. I went to Vegas. They brought me into this room—I don't even know where—and I tried to offer them everything I had. Twenty thousand in cash. That's all I could get. I got the car insurance money. Took from the warehouse job. Emptied the last of my savings."

He kept pacing. He wasn't making sense.

"They laughed at me," he said. "Said it was a down payment on a funeral. I told them I'd get more, I told them I had someone—"

"What are you talking about?" I snapped. "Where is she?"

"They're holding her. And they know. They know, Xander. Hayes told me himself. They were in her apartment. They went through her things. He said ... he said congratulations."

I stared at him, not following.

He froze. "She's pregnant. With your baby."

I stepped forward. "What?"

"She's pregnant," he repeated, eyes wide. "And Hayes knows. He saw the appointment card. Her vitamins. Her mail. He said it like it was a game."

"You're not making any sense," I said. "Why would she be with Hayes? Why are you the one coming out of her car?"

"She came to my house," he said. "Found my emails. Started asking questions. And when I didn't come home, they got to her first. She's being used, Xander. As leverage. Because of me. Because I owe Hayes a hell of a lot more than twenty thousand dollars."

"You're rambling."

"I know," he said, voice cracking. "But she's in danger. Real danger. And it's not just her anymore."

My fists clenched before I even realized they had. I stepped into his path and grabbed him by the shoulders. "You're telling me you left town with her car, left her unprotected, and now you're standing here rambling about cash and Vegas and leverage like I'm supposed to know what any of this means?"

"I didn't mean for it to happen like this," he said. "I didn't think Hayes would go this far. I didn't even know about the baby until—"

I didn't think. I just reacted.

The slap landed hard across his face, my hand stinging from the contact. He staggered a half step back, blinking at me, stunned.

"Get it together," I said. "Right now."

He brought a hand to his cheek but didn't swing back. "I deserved that," he muttered. "I do. But we don't have time. They gave me forty-eight hours. Less now."

"To do what?"

"Come up with half a million dollars," he said. "Or she disappears."

My mouth went dry. I couldn't feel the heat anymore. Couldn't hear anything outside the sound of my own breath and the blood pulsing behind my eyes.

"You're telling me Hayes is holding Amelia hostage. And now you're dragging me into this because you've run out of options." Laurence didn't argue. He just stood there, breath uneven, hands half raised like he didn't know what to do with them.

The name sat heavy in my head—Hayes. I'd heard it before, a few times. Quiet, offhand references in conversations that dropped off when someone walked into the room. A name people didn't want to say too loud. I'd never met him, but I knew he had money. I knew he wasn't the kind of man who forgave mistakes. But I had no idea Laurence had borrowed from him—no idea Amelia had been caught in the crossfire, and no idea I was next.

I opened my mouth, then closed it. I turned away from Laurence and stared down the street, trying to focus, to push my brain into lining up all the pieces. But it was all still noise. Heat, sweat, panic—none of it let me think clearly.

Then one word cut through everything else—pregnant.

I turned back to him. "What do you mean she's pregnant?"

He blinked at me slowly, dumbfounded. "You didn't know?" he asked, staring at me like I was a fool. And I was a fool—a complete total idiot.

My chest tightened. Something lodged behind my ribs like a stone. I took a step back and dropped my hands to my sides.

"No," I said slowly. "She didn't tell me. When did you find out?"

"Vegas. Hayes told me. He said they found her appointment card, the prenatal vitamins, some other things in her apartment. He said it casually, like it was just another pressure point."

The edges of my vision felt too sharp, like everything had suddenly gone high definition without warning. The baby—a baby—wasn't just some threat to throw around. It was real. She'd kept it from me. I didn't even know what I felt first: anger, confusion, fear, or something worse that didn't have a name yet.

Laurence watched me like he expected me to blow. Maybe I did too. But nothing happened. I just stood there, cold in the middle of all that heat, trying to remember how to breathe.

"She didn't tell me," I said again, mostly to myself.

"She didn't?" His blank expression enraged me. "Maybe she was scared …"

I almost said I would've helped her, but the words stuck. Because help wasn't what this was anymore. We were way past that.

Laurence shifted, his voice quieter now. "They won't let her go without the money. Half a million, or she disappears. That's what they told me."

I looked at him, really looked at him, and for once there wasn't anything else left to say. I nodded once. "Get in the car."

He hesitated. "What?"

"Get in the damn car, Larry. We're going to the bank."

"You have that kind of money?" He scurried, two-stepping as fast as he could around the front of my car.

"I don't know yet," I snapped, "but we'll figure it out on the way."

He didn't argue again. He followed me without another word, and we both climbed in. The moment the doors shut, the cabin felt too small. My hands were slick on the steering wheel. I turned the key, and the engine caught, the air conditioner kicking on with a slow wheeze that barely cut the heat.

I didn't wait for traffic. I pulled away from the curb too fast, tires skipping slightly on the hot pavement. The street blurred past as we drove, but I barely saw it. All I could hear was Laurence's voice on a loop, repeating things I hadn't wanted to hear. Amelia's name. A baby. Hayes. Half a million dollars or she's gone.

Gone.

I pressed harder on the gas.

Laurence stayed silent beside me. He looked hollowed out, like the panic had worn down everything else. But mine was just catching up. It was spreading fast, rising in my throat, settling behind my eyes, locking up every thought that wasn't *get to her.*

She was pregnant.

She hadn't told me. I didn't even know how far along she was. I didn't know if she was scared, if she was okay, if they were treating her like someone carrying a child or just another pawn in their game. That thought hit harder than anything else.

My child was out there—at risk. Held by people who didn't care whether they were threatening a woman or a life she hadn't even had the chance to protect yet.

I gripped the wheel tighter, knuckles white. We were going to fix it. I didn't know how. But I wasn't going to sit back and wait for another message to show up, or for some clock to run out.

I didn't care what it cost. I would burn every cent I had. I would clear out accounts, sell off assets, mortgage everything if I had to. I was going to be a father. And the person who should've been able to tell me that was locked in a room with strangers who knew it before I did.

That was going to change.

We didn't speak for the rest of the drive. I didn't need him to say anything else. We were already too far in. And this time, I wasn't handing it off to anyone else to clean up.

We were going to the bank.

And I was going to bring her home.

28

AMELIA

I was back in the same room, and everything about it felt worse this time. The walls looked cleaner, the sheets were fresh, and someone had laid out a folded towel on the bench like I was staying at some mid-tier resort—but none of that changed the fact that I couldn't leave. The windows were still locked. The lock still clicked every time someone left, and now I was too sick to pretend I had control over any of it.

I'd thrown up twice already. First in the bathroom, then in the corner wastebasket when I couldn't get there in time. The food on the tray sat untouched, same as yesterday. Just the smell of it made my stomach curl up. I knew they noticed. I didn't care.

The maid came in again just after noon. Older woman, mid-fifties maybe, with calm eyes and soft hands. She didn't speak much, not unless I asked something directly. Today, she carried a tray with a bowl of broth, two slices of bread, and a sealed bottle of water. She set it down on the small table like it was routine and glanced at the untouched plate from the day before.

"You need to eat something," she said gently.

"I don't want it." My voice came out rough, dry at the edges.

"Broth is light," she added. "Won't upset your stomach."

"I already threw up twice. I'm not risking a third."

She didn't argue, just picked up the old tray and carried it to the corner. I watched her the way I'd been watching everything lately—careful, waiting for some sign of help that hadn't come.

"Why are you here?" I asked suddenly. "Why do you stay?"

She hesitated, then straightened the towel on the bench like it mattered. "I clean. I cook. I don't ask questions."

"But you know what he's doing." I wasn't shouting, but my voice tightened in my throat. "You see people like me—locked in here, crying, scared out of their minds—and you just walk out like it's a job."

She didn't meet my eyes. She touched the edge of the tray and adjusted the spoon. "Mr. Hayes pays me well. I mind my business. That's how people stay safe around here."

I sat up straighter, nausea still turning in my gut. "Is that what this is to you? A paycheck?"

Her gaze flicked to mine for just a second. There was something there—regret, maybe. Or pity. "If your father does what he's supposed to, you'll be fine."

"And if he doesn't?"

She didn't answer. Just turned toward the door and opened it without rushing. "Drink the water," she said, and then she left.

The lock slid into place again, sharp and final. I sat still for a long time after she was gone, breathing slowly, trying not to let the fear crawl too far up my spine. I didn't know how many more days I could survive like this, but I knew one thing for sure, if no one came, I wasn't getting out.

The third time I threw up, it left my throat raw and my skin clammy. I leaned over the wastebasket, gripping the edge like it could steady me. Nothing came after the first heave, but my body kept trying anyway. I stayed on my knees for a while before I forced myself up and rinsed my mouth out with water. The taste lingered.

The tray of food sat untouched on the table. I didn't look at it for long. Even the thought of broth or bread made my stomach churn.

The only thing I could get down was water, and even that only stayed down through sheer will.

My hands trembled as I sat on the edge of the bed. I had stopped crying hours ago, not because the panic had gone away, but because there were no tears left in my body, no moisture. I waited. I counted every second by the ticking of the clock across the room. At some point, I stopped believing someone would come for me.

Then the door opened.

Two of Hayes's men stood in the hallway. They didn't speak, but one of them motioned for me to follow. I stood slowly, taking a breath to keep myself from swaying.

They led me down a different hallway than before. The temperature was colder here, and the ceilings felt lower. Every surface was spotless. At the end of the corridor, they opened a door into a room that looked like it belonged in a magazine. Dark wood floors, leather seating, a table set in the center with a silver case on top.

My father was already there. He stood when he saw me, and I could tell he'd been crying. He crossed the room in three strides and pulled me into his arms. I didn't hesitate. I leaned into him, pressing my face into his jacket. He held me tighter than I expected.

"You're safe now," he said. "It's over."

I didn't know if I believed him, but I didn't let go.

Victor Hayes poured himself a drink behind the bar. He glanced at the suitcase but didn't touch it. One of his men stepped forward and flipped it open. Inside were clean stacks of cash. Each bundle was neatly wrapped in bank sleeves, indicating the value of each stack.

"This is the full amount?" Hayes asked without turning around. For a man so hell bent on getting what was owed him, he seemed uninterested in this part.

My father nodded. "Half a million, all in cash. Nonsequential, unmarked."

Hayes raised his glass but said nothing. One of the guards scanned the serial numbers. Another examined the bundles under a blacklight. I stayed beside my father. He hadn't let go of me, and I didn't want him to.

Hayes gave a slow nod, then tilted his head toward the case. "Count it."

One of his men stepped forward, pulling a small machine from a black duffel. He set it on the table next to the cash and plugged it into the outlet along the baseboard. The other man began removing the stacks one at a time, peeling away the bands and feeding the bills into the counter in batches. The machine whirred to life, steady and loud, ticking through the notes at a pace that almost drowned out the sound of my heartbeat.

A third man pulled out a digital tally sheet and began logging totals. Another walked in with a second machine, smaller and sleeker, and set it next to the first. They moved with practiced coordination, no wasted motion, no spoken instructions. This wasn't the first time they had processed a payoff.

I stayed rooted beside my father, one arm looped through his, the other pressed protectively against my stomach. He didn't speak. He just watched them work, jaw tight, shoulders stiff.

Hayes poured another drink and turned toward us. "You want one?" My father didn't answer. Hayes lifted the second glass anyway and extended it toward me. "You look like you could use something to settle your nerves."

I shook my head. "No."

He gave the slightest shrug and took a sip himself, then walked over to stand behind the men at the table. The machines clicked and spun, counting down to silence, one stack at a time. It took nearly ten minutes for them to finish. When the final total appeared on the display, the man with the tablet nodded once.

"Verified. Five hundred seventy thousand. Clean."

Hayes exhaled through his nose and set his glass down. "Good. That's what I like to hear."

I could feel my father's body relax half an inch, just enough to tell me he'd been holding his breath. I leaned against him a little more, trying to breathe normally. I didn't. My heart was racing, and my thoughts had started to tangle again.

I knew Xander had paid. This wasn't warehouse money or something my father scrounged from wrecking his car. This was Xander stepping in and handing over half a million dollars without blinking. He knew what was happening here, the shame of what my father had gotten himself into, and instead of calling the police, he decided I was worth something. I just didn't know why.

I didn't know what he was thinking now. I didn't know what this meant for us, or if he even wanted to see me again. But he had done this. He had saved me.

My father cleared his throat and looked Hayes squarely in the eye. "It's done. This is finished."

Hayes looked at him for a long time before answering. "You're lucky it is."

He stepped away from the table and walked toward us, hands in his pockets, expression flat.

"You took from me. Then you ran. You ignored my calls. That isn't just business, Laurence. That's betrayal."

My father's jaw tightened. "I paid."

"You paid late." Hayes's voice sharpened, but only slightly. "And if it weren't for that extra twenty, I wouldn't be so generous." My father opened his mouth, but Hayes cut him off with a gesture. "I don't want an apology. I want you to understand what this was. You borrowed, you defaulted, and someone else had to clean up after you. That doesn't make you a man, Laurence. That makes you a coward."

My father didn't argue. He just nodded with slow control.

Hayes turned his attention to me. "And you," he said, voice measured. "You're lucky he still matters to someone."

I didn't say a word. We were done with all of this. All I wanted was to get out of here.

Hayes motioned toward the door. "Take your daughter. Get out of my house."

No one moved to stop us. The men at the table returned the

counted stacks to the case. One closed the lid and locked it. Hayes didn't spare us another look.

My father guided me toward the exit. I held his arm tighter than before, keeping one hand against my stomach. I didn't speak until we were outside, and even then, I wasn't sure I could.

We stepped out into the fading light, the door clicking shut behind us. The temperature had dropped, but the air still felt dry against my skin. I stayed close to my father, one hand locked around his forearm, the other braced over my stomach like it could shield me from whatever came next.

We were halfway to the edge of the driveway when I saw him.

Xander stood beside a black SUV parked at an angle near the curb. His arms were crossed, and his weight rested back against the driver's side door. He didn't move when we appeared. He just stared.

I stopped walking. My father slowed beside me, then turned when he noticed. He followed my line of sight and muttered something under his breath, but I didn't catch it. My whole body had gone rigid.

Xander was in a dark button-down and black slacks. His sleeves were rolled up. His jaw was locked. He looked like a man trying very hard not to let something crack through the surface.

I didn't know what to say. I didn't know what he wanted from me, if he wanted anything at all. He had paid. He had stepped in when no one else could have, and I hadn't even been the one to ask.

His eyes met mine across the length of the driveway. They didn't soften.

I forced myself forward again, one foot at a time. My father gave a slight squeeze to my arm before letting go and walking to the door of the SUV. I expected Xander to linger, to say something to me. I secretly hoped he would, but he turned and climbed into the driver's side, and I was left to swallow the rising bile in my throat.

Nothing was ever going to be the same between us again.

29

XANDER

The helicopter lifted off with a slow, shaking rumble that settled into something steadier as we cleared the rooftops. I kept my eyes on the skyline for the first few minutes, pretending I needed the view, but I was watching them through their reflection in the window as the lights of the city passed beneath us.

Amelia was curled against her father's side. He held her close, one hand on her shoulder, the other bracing her thigh. She hadn't looked at me since we boarded. I wasn't sure she would.

No one said a word.

The cabin wasn't large. The soundproofing helped, but the engine was still loud enough to make conversation feel like a chore. Maybe that was for the best.

Laurence hadn't even looked in my direction since he helped her into the seat. His jaw was tight, his eyes fixed on some point outside the window. He was doing what I couldn't—keeping it together, acting like he had a right to hold her like that after what he'd put her through. And the worst part? He probably did.

I sat across from them, hands folded, staring at nothing.

I had her back. That was the only part of this I could hold onto. Everything else had gone sideways.

She'd said it would be simple. She told me she was on the pill. She told me it wasn't serious. No strings. No mess. I believed her. I let myself believe that I could have her without the fallout. And then I made the one mistake I swore I wouldn't make—I got attached.

Now she was here, sitting two feet away and holding someone else's arm like it was the only thing keeping her from falling apart. And I didn't know what I was supposed to feel. Relief? Anger? Grief?

I couldn't even look at her without wondering what else I didn't know.

She was pregnant. That part wasn't a question anymore. And I didn't have it in me to doubt that it was mine. But knowing it and being ready for it weren't the same thing. I kept thinking about everything Laurence had done to get them into this mess. Every decision he made, every shortcut that turned into a trap. And I asked myself if I would've done the same. If I already had.

Could I protect her? Could I protect a child? Could I keep myself from turning into the same kind of reckless idiot, pretending I had control when I didn't?

My hands wouldn't stay still. I folded and unfolded my fingers, shifting my grip until I had to look away from them entirely.

I didn't want to fail her. But I knew I would. I'd seen what it looked like to be left behind. My mother walked out like it was nothing. Quiet, calm, final. She didn't scream. She didn't fight. She just decided. One moment she was there, and the next she was gone.

What if Amelia left too?

What if I gave her everything, and she still walked away?

I stared at her reflection in the window, her face half lit by the cockpit lights. She was pale, worn thin by whatever had happened in that house. She didn't look like someone who'd meet me in my office and pour her heart into satisfying me. And she didn't look like a woman who wanted to run. But neither did my mother, right up until the moment she did.

The rot doesn't show at first. It starts slow.

And now I was sitting here, wondering if I'd already lost something before I ever got to keep it.

The helicopter touched down just after eleven. Amelia moved like her legs didn't want to hold her, leaning into her father as they stepped onto the landing pad. She didn't look at me, not once. Laurence kept one hand on her back like she might disappear if he let go.

I drove them to his place. No one said anything.

When we pulled up to the curb, Amelia reached for the handle, but I stopped her with a look. "Stay in the car," I said, and she listened.

Laurence got out and stood there, waiting like he expected something else. I stepped out after him and followed him halfway to the door before he turned.

He didn't apologize at first. He didn't explain, and I didn't expect him to. There was nothing left to say that wouldn't make things worse. He'd gambled with her safety, with her life, and she was the one who paid for it. I hadn't forgotten that. I wasn't sure I'd ever be able to.

Laurence shifted like he might say something. "I didn't want—"

"Don't," I snapped. "Don't pretend this wasn't your fault." He flinched, but I didn't stop. "You let them take her without a clue what would happen. And you didn't fix it. I did. Half a million. My money. My name. You stood there and let her suffer while I bled to clean it up." I could've punched him, but I restrained myself for Amelia's sake.

He opened his mouth again, but I took a step forward. "If you ever put her in danger again, you'll wish Hayes got to you first."

Then I turned, walked back to the car, climbed in, and slammed the door shut.

The drive to her place felt longer than it was. I kept both hands on the wheel, staring straight ahead, chewing on everything I didn't say to Laurence. I didn't look at her. I didn't ask how she was doing. I didn't ask if she wanted music or if the heat was too high. I didn't trust myself to open my mouth. If I said one thing, I'd say too much.

She stayed quiet beside me, folded in on herself. Her knees were drawn up slightly, her hands tangled in the hem of her sweater. Every so often she sniffed, soft and quick, like she was trying not to be heard.

The city blurred past. Lights turned gold against the windshield and flicked off the sides of parked cars. I hit every green light and still felt like we were crawling. When we finally pulled into her lot, I killed the engine and stepped out first, circling the car before she had time to unbuckle. She didn't argue when I offered my hand. She just took it.

We walked to her door in silence.

She fumbled with the keys, her hands shaking. When the lock clicked and the door swung open, she stepped inside first. I followed her in, and the second it closed behind us, she turned.

"I'm sorry," she said, and the words hit fast, like she'd been holding them back the entire drive. "I'm sorry about my dad, and for disappearing, and for quitting like that. I didn't know how to explain it. I didn't know how to face you, especially not after—"

She stopped and pressed her hand to her chest like she needed to hold herself together. Her eyes were red, lashes wet, but she wasn't trying to hide it anymore. The room around us was dim. A lamp glowed in the corner, silhouetting her body.

"I never meant for any of this to happen," she said. "I didn't even know I was—"

I stepped forward before she could choke on the words. "Is it true?" I asked. "What Hayes told your father. About the baby."

She bobbed her shoulder and then dropped her head. "It's true."

I stared at her, heart beating too fast again. "You didn't tell me."

"I didn't know at first. I thought I was just off because I was sick. I had bronchitis. The doctor put me on antibiotics, and I didn't think—I was on the pill. I swear I was. I never would've done that to you on purpose." Her voice broke. "I love you."

I froze.

I hadn't expected that at all. It landed harder than everything else I'd heard in the past few days.

I didn't say anything right away. She just stood there after it came out—*I love you*—like it was supposed to fix something. I moved past her, too restless to stay still, and rubbed my hand along the back of my neck.

"You should've told me the second you knew," I said.

She turned, still near the door. "I was going to."

"But you didn't." My voice was sharper than I meant it to be, but I didn't take it back.

She stepped toward me. "I didn't want to screw things up."

I gave a short laugh, no humor in it. "Too late for that."

Her jaw tightened. "I didn't choose this."

"No, but you handled it without me. And now I'm just supposed to catch up, like the last two weeks didn't happen?"

"I didn't know what to say. I was scared."

"Well, congratulations," I said. "Now we're both there."

She took another step, not backing down. "You think this was easy for me? I was locked in a house with strangers, thinking I might die, knowing you didn't even know I was gone. You think that's something I planned?"

I looked at her—really looked at her—and saw the weight of it all. The fear. The guilt. But I was still holding too much anger to drop it.

"Then why hide it?" I asked. "Why not give me a damn chance?"

Her voice dropped, not weaker, just tired. "Because you told me this wasn't serious. You said no strings. I thought if I told you, it'd be over."

I didn't have a response to that. I turned and sat on the edge of her coffee table, bracing my elbows on my knees, head down. My skin felt too tight, like I couldn't get enough air. I heard her shift her weight, then the soft scrape of a chair on the floor. When I looked up, she was sitting in front of me, close, watching my face.

"I didn't do this on purpose," she said. "I had bronchitis. The antibiotics must've—"

"Amelia." I cut her off, quiet but firm. "This isn't about blame."

"Then what is it?"

"It's the part where I'm supposed to be ready for something I don't even know how to be."

She searched my face, then reached for my hand. I let her take it.

"You think I know how to do this?" she said. "You think I'm not scared too?"

I didn't answer, but I didn't pull away.

She moved closer, close enough that I could feel the heat of her knees against mine. "I know what this looks like. I know it wasn't what you wanted. But I love you. And I'm not going to disappear."

I shook my head, not to argue but to clear the static. "You say that now."

"I mean it."

Her hand tightened around mine, her other palm sliding up to my jaw, grounding me. I didn't want to let any of it in. But I was already too far in.

"You think I'll walk away like your mom did," she said.

I swallowed hard. "She didn't just leave. She erased herself. One day she was there, and the next, nothing. No note. No goodbye. Just quiet. My dad—he didn't recover. He shut down. That's who raised me."

"I'm not her," she said.

"I know."

"I won't do that to you."

I didn't answer. I didn't need to. She leaned in and kissed me. It wasn't soft or hesitant—it was steady, sure. I grabbed her waist and pulled her to me without thinking, without planning, without trying to protect myself from it.

She tasted like mint and salt, familiar and something else entirely. Her body fit against mine like it was made for me. I couldn't make sense of anything as her teeth grazed over my lower lip, her hands pushing my shirt upward. I was too caught up in the feeling of her against me—the way her body fit to mine, like she'd always been there. I couldn't remember a time when she didn't feel this way.

I pulled her onto my lap, heard the coffee table creak, and let her straddle me. Amelia's fingers moved to the button of my pants, and I stopped her. "Wait."

Her eyes darkened with want, but she didn't move. She pulled her hands away, letting them rest on my thighs. "I can stop," she said, though it was clear she didn't want to.

I shook my head. "I don't want our first time to be like this."

Her brows drew together. "Our first?"

"Yeah," I said, meeting her eyes squarely. "Our first."

She stared at me, searching for something I couldn't name. I wasn't even sure if I knew what it was myself. Fear? Security? The knowledge that whatever happened next, we'd do it together? What I did know was that I wanted her more than I ever had. Wanted to press her against the wall and feel her and know that she was really here.

"I don't understand ..." she said, her eyes searching me.

"As a couple," I said softly, bringing her knuckles to my lips and kissing them.

Amelia smiled and curled her fingers around my hand, pulling me as we stood up. "Come on."

I let her pull me down the hall, too lost in the way her bottom swayed ahead of me to come up with any more objections. Everything inside me protested in fear, but the tiniest little voice in my heart urged me forward. I knew this was the right path. I just prayed it didn't hurt like hell later on.

30

AMELIA

In my bedroom I shut the door, turned to press my palms against Xander's chest. His heart was pounding, probably in shock or fear, or uncertainty about the vocalized change to our relationship. No more no-strings-attached sex, this had developed into something we both felt but I had never been brave enough to speak about.

"Kiss me," I whispered to him, and his hands, resting on my hips, gripped me firmly.

Xander's lips descended on mine, searching me with stubble and teeth scratching.

My lips parted under his desperate onslaught, teeth clashing lightly as Xander's tongue invaded my mouth, coaxing me further into the kiss. I could taste hunger in him, and something else, something raw and untamed that unleashed a primal response deep inside me. Moaning softly, I wrapped my arms around his neck and pulled him closer. He responded by sliding one hand up my shirt to fist in my braided hair, angling my head back. Using this newfound access, Xander devoured me, the other hand roaming down my spine to settle on my butt cheek, squeezing tightly.

I felt like melting into him, but there was too much adrenaline pumping through my veins—pure need and want took over my senses. Breaking the kiss, I bit his lower lip, lingered for a second, then mewled, "Come with me."

This time I didn't take his hand. I walked toward my bathroom, undressing as I walked, and started the shower. It'd been days since I felt clean, and the intimacy of being totally exposed with him, lights on, eyes open, was what I wanted.

He followed me. I felt his eyes pinned on me the entire way. By the time the steam was rolling through the bathroom, I was nude, and he was shucking his pants.

As Xander pulled off his socks, the outline of his erection straining against his boxers was readily visible. Eyes locked, I pulled him into the shower with me. The hot water pelted our skin, steam fogged the glass door. Xander cupped my face under the spray, running his thumb around my chin and down my jawline and kissed me softly. "I didn't know if I'd see you again," he confessed hoarsely.

His admission, coupled with his heated gaze, sent a wave of liquid heat between my legs. I leaned in closer until our foreheads touched and our breaths mingled together with the steamy air. His hands caressed my back; mine slid around his body and pulled him closer.

"I don't plan to leave ever again." The nightmare, as far as I knew, was over. Hayes was a thing of the past, and the threat he posed was over. The only mess left to sort out was being sorted out right now between us. "I meant when I said I love you, Xander."

His jaw clenched, and rather than saying anything, he kissed me hard, pinning me against the shower wall. My hand slid down to his dick, fingers curling around its girth. Xander growled out a low groan, his hand tangled in my damp hair as I slid his cock against my wet core.

Xander groaned, his grip on my hair tightening as I teased him mercilessly. I rubbed him against me faster and faster, his tip just inside my entrance.

"I missed this," I mewled out past the pleasure consuming us both.

"Jesus—Amelia," He groaned helplessly against my ear, his hand cupping my breast and pinching my nipple, heightening the sensation.

"I want you," I whispered, guiding him inside me with a shaky breath.

Xander obliged, burying himself, his hand shaking with restraint as he pressed against the shower wall to brace himself. "I need you," he growled as his hips rocked into mine in a primal rhythm as the water rained down on our intertwined bodies.

Eyes locked with mine, he bottomed out, only to pull back and drive in again, and again. Greedily, I took everything he had to give me—every thrust, every groan, swallowed every sweet word he whispered like it was my last meal. The intensity grew sharper as our breathing quickened with each thrust, hands clenched tighter, and kisses became more desperate. Soon enough we were both panting, kissing sloppily between moans and gasps. His hand tangled in my hair had me angled just so his thrusts hit that spot deep inside that sent sparks of pleasure radiating along my spine.

"God—Amelia," Xander gasped above me, his neck straining with exertion as he pistoned in and out of me, and the way his pelvic bone rubbed my clit, I was on the edge of coming undone.

With a soft keening sound I came apart, and stars exploded behind my eyelids. Xander's grip on my hair, the wet wall against my back, and then nothing but pure pleasure washed over me like a wave. The sensation of being so completely connected to someone after days of isolation had my vision doubling as I clung to him for dear life.

I twitched and jerked, clung to his shoulders trying not to draw blood. My pussy clenched around him, and he slowed to a glorious syrupy pace that had my insides melting, and his lips covered mine again. His stubble was rough on my skin, but the way I nipped at his lips repaid him for what little discomfort it was.

He let my legs find their composure before he pulled out and turned me around. With my chest pressing against the shower wall, he grabbed my hips and placed soft kisses on the back of my shoulder.

"Jesus," I panted loudly, "Xander that was—"

"Shh," he cut me off, kissing each vertebra all the way down my spine, keeping me on my tiptoes as his hand roamed between my thighs, seeking out my wet core.

"I'm not done with you yet."

Glancing over my shoulder, I saw him kneel. His teeth nipped the back of my thigh and he buried his face there, stubble scratching my most sensitive places.

"Xander," I gasped out barely coherently. He ignored me and kept teasing me with featherlight touches and slick kisses that had my toes curling and my hands fisting on the wall for support.

"Xander," I held my breath as he circled my entrance with the tip of his tongue, before lapping up my juices. "Oh God, that feels so—"

He continued to torment me relentlessly, increasing my pleasure. At one point I was sure I would pass out from the sensation of his warm tongue on my core. When his fingers slipped into me and teased that rough patch of skin, I felt a second orgasm crest.

I moaned, my back arching off the wall as he toyed with me. His talented tongue and fingers worked in combination until I was a quivering mess against him, caught up in the devilishly delicious sensations he evoked in me. I grunted hoarsely as I shattered around his fingers for the second time, the aftershocks making me twitch against him.

When my knees threatened to buckle, he held me up. My palms splayed on the shower wall, my hips bucking back into his face. The convulsions were stronger than the last time, and pleasure radiated into each of my limbs, down to my fingertips and toes.

As the orgasm passed, he licked me clean, then rose, keeping his hands on my hips, and guided himself back into me.

"Christ," I gasped.

"I know," he growled in my ear, and then the only sound was the water pelting our skin, and our harsh breathing.

Xander drove into me relentlessly, stretching me to the brink and beyond, and my inner muscles clenched around him, milking him greedily. I needed him inside me, needed this connection like I needed oxygen.

One hand left my hip, pressed on my lower back to bend me over, and he backed up as he pulled me toward him. The spray of water hit my hips as he began thrusting into me again.

His increased fervor had me biting down on my lip to stifle the moans, but he sucked the life out of me with each thrust, drawing moisture from my very pores. As if he sensed my surrender, his hands tightened along my hip bones and he thrust roughly into me, as I reached between my legs to rub myself.

"Amelia," he called out hoarsely above the drumming water.

I felt him pulse inside me and clenched around him tighter before pitching over that precipice for the third time in as many minutes into the abyss of sensation overload. He pumped into me as I came down from my high and when he pulled out and I straightened, he turned me in his arms. My head rested on his shoulder; he washed my back. Then we traded places in the water and he washed my hair.

After we dried off, he led me to bed where I curled up and he coiled around me like a serpent with its prey, not letting me go. His arms wrapped around me, his breath in the crook of my neck as I drifted off into deep thought.

His chest rose and fell against my back, like he was trying to breathe around something heavier than air. I didn't speak. I didn't move. I stayed tucked into his chest, waiting for whatever he needed to say. There was a pause before it came, the kind that meant it had been living inside him for a long time.

"I asked her to stay," he said. "I stood at the door, and I asked her not to go. I didn't cry. I didn't yell. I just asked. And she left anyway."

I shifted just enough to look at him. He wasn't looking at me. His eyes were on the ceiling, the lines in his forehead soft but drawn. He looked like someone remembering a scar.

"I didn't see her again," he said. "No phone calls. No letter. She didn't just leave the house. She erased herself. My dad never talked about it. I think he thought ignoring it would help, but it didn't."

I reached for his hand and found it resting near the hem of the blanket. When I laced my fingers through his, he held on like he needed to.

"I thought maybe I wasn't enough to stay for," he said. "That's the part I couldn't shake. I think I stopped letting people get close after that."

He said it simply—no drama, no attempt to draw sympathy—just the bare truth. I swallowed the knot forming at the back of my throat and leaned in a little closer.

"I'm not going to make promises I can't keep," I said. "But I'm not the kind of woman who gives up when things get hard."

He didn't answer. His thumb moved slowly against mine. "Then why'd you quit?" he asked. "No warning. No call. Just gone."

I expected the question. Still, it landed harder than I thought it would. I pushed myself up a little and turned toward him so I could see his face clearly.

"Because staying started to feel like lying to myself," I said. "I was pretending it didn't mean anything when it did. I was in love with you, and you made it clear from the beginning that it wasn't supposed to be more than sex. I didn't know how to keep showing up like it didn't hurt. And then the baby ..."

His brow furrowed, just slightly. He didn't speak, so I went on.

"I wanted you to be happy, even if it wasn't with me. I saw how it bothered you—when I was around Godwin, when we left meetings together. You didn't want anything more from it, but it still got under your skin. You said you had zero feelings for me."

He exhaled through his nose, the corner of his mouth twitching like he might argue but couldn't.

"And then I found out about the baby," I said. "That was the last thing you needed. If I'd told you, you would've stepped in. You would've felt obligated. And I didn't want that. Not from you. Not when I didn't understand what you felt at all."

He looked down at the space between us, then back at me. "What was going on with Godwin?"

I smiled for the first time since the conversation started. I had to fight back a chuckle, but the snicker still escaped, and the grin came despite my reluctance. "Godwin is so gay, Xander," I said, and a quiet laugh slipped out. "He came out to me over microwave popcorn in the break room a month after he started. He makes playlists for his boyfriend's cats. There was never a threat there."

Xander let out a quiet, embarrassed laugh. "I hate that that makes me feel better." I loved the way his smile reached his eyes.

I traced a small circle against his shoulder with the pad of my thumb. "You don't have to be jealous. It was always you. Even when I didn't want it to be. Before we even had this dumb agreement."

He looked at me again, his expression unreadable. "You love me?" he asked.

I nodded. "Yes."

"I don't know how to do this," he said. "I've been single for a long time. I don't know what it means to share space with someone—really share it."

"You don't have to figure it out all at once," I said. "We can take this one decision at a time."

"I've never had to think about anyone but myself."

"Well, that's definitely over," I said. "There's no version of this that's going to be NSA from here on out."

That pulled another real smile from him. He leaned back, eyes still on me, and for the first time since we crawled into this bed, he looked a little lighter.

"And you can be patient with me while I figure it out?" He searched me with his eyes and I nodded at him.

"Gotta practice having a mother's patience sometime …"

We didn't say anything else for a while. He pulled me close again, my cheek against his collarbone, his hand smoothing along my back like he was still making sure I was real. And I stayed there, wrapped in the quiet, wondering how something that had started as casual could have ever felt small.

Xander slept beside me, one arm resting across my ribs. I lay awake, watching the shadows shift across the ceiling. My body ached in the way that came after fear had drained out and left something hollow behind.

I kept thinking about my father.

He had tried to fix it. He'd walked into that house with a suitcase full of money and the look of a man who already knew it wasn't enough. I didn't know how he would repay Xander. I wasn't sure either of them had thought that far ahead.

It wasn't just the money. That part could be counted. What Xander gave me was harder to name. He'd come for me when I didn't ask him to. He had done it without conditions, without waiting to be needed. That wasn't something my father could ever return.

And now there was the baby. The silence between us when we parted earlier had said more than anything. I didn't know how Dad felt about it. I didn't know if he saw it as a burden or a second chance. I didn't ask. I wasn't ready to hear if he was afraid of what it meant for me, or worse, ashamed.

I couldn't forget that he was the reason I ended up in that room at all. Even though I'd forgiven him, I still didn't know how to carry it.

There was love between us. I believed that. But love didn't erase the things we had to face.

And there were still so many things left to face.

31

XANDER

It had been nearly a month since Hayes let her walk out of that house. A month since I stood in Laurence's driveway, furious and exhausted, wondering what the hell we were supposed to do next. Now it was the end of May, and he'd invited us over for dinner like we were just another family getting together for a quiet meal.

I said yes, partly because Amelia wanted to go, but also because I needed to see him in person. Amelia sat beside me in the car, watching the side mirror more than the road. She hadn't dressed up for the occasion. No makeup, just a soft cardigan over a cream blouse. She looked calm, but I could feel her tension from where I sat.

Laurence opened the door before we reached the top step. His face didn't give anything away—neither tense nor friendly. He stepped back without a word and let us inside.

"Dinner's just about done," he said, finally breaking the silence. "I made too much."

We followed him into the dining room. The table was already set. He'd laid out actual napkins. Not paper. Silverware lined up perfectly. The dishes were simple—roast chicken, seasoned vegetables, mashed potatoes in a serving bowl with a real spoon instead of something plastic. I didn't know if it was effort or guilt, but either way, he'd gone through the motions like it meant something.

We sat. Amelia to my right, Laurence across from me. The air between him and me was stiff, but it wasn't angry anymore. We had both lived through the kind of mistake that burned too much out of you to hold onto rage. What was left now was quieter. Complicated.

Amelia picked at her food, though I noticed she ate more than she had in days. She complimented the seasoning, and Laurence gave a soft thanks but didn't look up.

We were halfway through the meal when he set his fork down. The scrape of metal on ceramic pulled both our eyes to him.

"I know I said it already," he started, voice rough, "but I need to say it properly this time."

I didn't speak. Neither did Amelia.

"I should've told her everything," he said, looking at his daughter, not at me. "I should've asked for help before it got that far. I kept thinking I'd fix it on my own, and then I didn't, and it was too late. That's when I got stupid."

Amelia reached across the table and touched his hand. "I know, Dad. It's okay."

"It's not. You were the one who paid for it. And Xander—" He finally looked at me. "You cleaned it up. All of it. I put you in an impossible position and then handed you a bill for something you never owed. I'll never forget that."

I leaned back slightly, resting one arm against the edge of the chair. "No one was keeping score, Laurence. You would've done the same for her if you could've. I know that."

"I should've protected her," he said. "Instead, I let her walk into something I should've seen coming. And then I made her feel like it was her fault. That day she showed up at my house—when she found the emails—I was awful to her. I didn't know how scared I was until she was gone."

The room fell quiet again. Not empty—just full of everything none of us could fix.

"I don't expect you to forgive me," he said. "But I wanted to say it all the same."

Amelia gave his hand a squeeze. "I already did."

I didn't say anything right away. I looked at him and saw the same man I'd known for years, but smaller somehow. Not physically. Something inside him had worn down. Maybe it was shame. Maybe it was just age finally catching up to the way he lived. Either way, he meant it. That counted for something.

"I appreciate the words," I said. "But this doesn't get fixed with an apology. It gets fixed with what happens next."

Laurence nodded slowly, like he expected that to be the end of it. He shifted in his seat, reaching for his glass of water. His hand didn't quite shake, but there was something cautious in the way he moved. Then he cleared his throat.

"I meant what I said about paying it back," he told me. "Even if it takes the rest of my life. I'll figure it out."

I shook my head before he could get any further. "That's not what I want."

His brow tightened. "What do you mean?"

I looked at him, really looked, the way I used to in meetings when I needed to make sure someone understood the weight behind my words. "You can keep the money. What I want is your partnership. Back on paper. Back in the room."

He stared at me, confused.

"You were the magic man," I said. "You were the one who brought the clients in, made them feel like they belonged. I've got spreadsheets and a good pitch, but that's not what made us work. You did. And ever since you stepped away, we've been holding steady, not growing. I don't need my money back. I need my closer."

Laurence blinked like I'd slapped him. My mind went to the day he left, and how confident I'd felt. But after losing so many clients, I no longer felt that way.

"You'd give me a salary," he said. "After what I pulled?"

"I'd call it a job," I said. "Not a favor. But yeah."

He didn't speak. He just sat there with his mouth half open. I glanced over at Amelia. Her hand had come up to her mouth, and her eyes were glassy. I gave her a small smile.

"Don't cry yet," I told her.

She let out a quiet laugh that sounded like she was trying not to fall apart entirely.

I turned back to Laurence. "There's one condition."

He looked wary now. "What's that?"

I stood, reaching into my jacket pocket. My fingers closed around the box. It had been sitting there since last week, waiting for the right moment. I didn't know if this was it, but I wasn't waiting anymore.

"I want your blessing," I said. "Because I want to marry your daughter."

The silence hit harder than I expected. Amelia froze. Laurence blinked. I opened the box and set it on the table between them, the diamond catching the light in a way that felt almost too on the nose.

"I know it's fast," I said. "I know she's younger than me. But I also know what I want. And I'm too old to waste time not having it."

Laurence stared at the ring, then at me. His mouth opened, but it took a second for anything to come out.

"She's ..." He stopped, then started again. "You're serious?"

"As a heart attack," I said. "Half a million might as well count as a dowry, right?"

That broke the tension. Amelia made a noise that was half laugh, half sob. I grinned, and then she burst into laughter, and I joined her. Laurence looked between the two of us, then leaned back and rubbed a hand over his face. When he pulled it away, he was grinning too—like an idiot. The joke simmered all the negative vibes in the air and eased my anxiety.

"She's got a mind of her own," he said eventually. "Always has. And I won't pretend I'm not still trying to wrap my head around all of this. But if you're in this for real—if you're going to treat her like she matters every day, not just when it's easy—then you have my blessing."

Amelia let out a breath like she'd been holding it for hours. I walked over and took her hand. She stood slowly. When I got down on one knee, her lips parted like she couldn't believe I was doing this here, in her father's dining room, right after mashed potatoes and a confession.

"Amelia Johnson," I said, holding her hand in mine, "I want to spend the rest of my life with you. And this kid. And probably a few more, if we're not careful. Will you marry me?"

She nodded so fast it made me grin. "Yes. Of course yes."

I slid the ring onto her finger, stood up, and pulled her into me. Her arms wrapped around my neck, and when I looked over her shoulder, Laurence was smiling, his eyes damp.

She held my hand like it was the easiest thing in the world. Like I hadn't once made a habit out of keeping people at arm's length, or burned every bridge before someone else could. All my life, I told myself it was safer to want nothing than to risk losing something I couldn't get back.

That started the day my mother packed a bag and walked out. I'd asked her to stay. I meant it. I was twelve, barely old enough to understand what was happening, but I still knew what goodbye looked like. She didn't answer. Just walked out the front door and never looked back.

Since then, I'd made a career out of being untouchable. I built walls. I stayed in control. I kept things casual, kept people at a distance, and convinced myself it was enough. I told myself I liked it that way. I didn't owe anyone anything, and no one could disappoint me.

And then Amelia happened.

She walked into my office, confident and capable, and I didn't think twice. I thought I could keep her in that same safe category—attractive, competent, off-limits. But somehow she made me forget I had limits in the first place. She didn't ask for anything. She didn't press. She just stayed. Even when I gave her reasons not to. Even when I made it harder than it had to be. Even when I didn't deserve it.

Now she stood next to me in her father's kitchen, the ring on her finger catching the light above the sink. She hadn't stopped smiling since she said yes, but it wasn't a big, giddy kind of smile. It was quiet. Certain. Like she wasn't afraid anymore, and maybe she didn't think I would be either.

I looked down at our hands, still laced together. I could feel the weight of everything we'd been through sitting in the room with us—Hayes, the money, the months of miscommunication and almosts. All of it had led here.

And for the first time in my life, I wasn't trying to run from what I felt. I wasn't trying to contain it or bury it under something easier. I had someone. I had her. And I wasn't going to lose that.

Not to fear. Not to pride. Not to the past.

She turned slightly and looked up at me, eyes steady, waiting for whatever came next.

I didn't need to plan the words. They were already there.

"I love you," I said, and my voice didn't shake. "I mean it. I love you."

Her eyes went wide for a second. Then she smiled in that soft way she did when something truly mattered to her. She didn't rush to fill the silence. She didn't smother the moment. She just leaned in and rested her forehead against mine.

"I know," she said quietly. "And I love you, too."

We stood there for a while in that little kitchen, hands clasped, her father somewhere down the hall giving us space he didn't used to know how to give. The past wasn't erased. It was still there. But it wasn't running the show anymore.

This was real. It was ours. And for once, I wasn't bracing for the moment it would slip away.

I was holding on.

EPILOGUE: AMELIA

The wedding planner kept asking if I wanted more time, but I just smiled and told her I was ready. Truthfully, I had been ready since the day Xander told me he wasn't going to lose me. Everything after that had felt like waiting for this moment—one final, sunny afternoon surrounded by family, friends, and a dress that somehow still fit, even with the baby bump just starting to round out under the silk.

Aunt Julia adjusted the flower comb in my hair for the third time while humming something I didn't recognize. She had a mouthful of safety pins and absolutely no intention of letting anyone else near my veil. Claire stood behind her holding the backup bouquet, chatting with the makeup artist about how proud she was of me. Their energy made the bridal suite feel a little like a parade float in motion—chaotic, loud, and entirely full of love.

I glanced at the mirror and gave my reflection a nervous once-over. The dress wasn't traditional. It had a square neckline, simple sleeves, and no train. I didn't want anything that would make me trip. The bouquet sat waiting on the table, pale peach and ivory roses bound with silk. My stomach did a small flip—not nerves, just the baby reminding me I wasn't the only one excited to get down the aisle.

The door opened, and my dad peeked in, already dressed in his suit and looking stiff enough to pass for royalty. Julia stepped back with a satisfied sigh as Claire gave me a quick hug.

"You look like a dream," my dad said as he crossed the room. "Like your mom would've wanted to see."

I took his arm, feeling steadier with him next to me. "Let's get married then."

The walk down the aisle was shorter than it looked in rehearsal. My eyes went straight to Xander, who stood at the other end of the archway like he was carved from certainty. He wore a crisp black suit and had this soft, knowing look on his face that made my heart skip and settle all at once.

As Dad gave me away, he didn't try to say anything poetic. He just squeezed my fingers and whispered that he loved me, which was all I needed to hear.

The ceremony passed in a blur of vows, quiet laughter, and whispered promises I never wanted to forget. Xander's hands never shook. Mine only did a little, and only when I said his name.

When we kissed, the crowd clapped like we'd just won a gold medal. Claire shouted something about finally, and Julia wiped tears from under her glasses, waving off anyone who dared to comment.

The reception was held under a white tent strung with fairy lights and flowers that smelled faintly like citrus. Xander and I sat at a long table while guests filtered in and took their seats. The food was warm and hearty—roasted chicken with herb butter, garlic mashed potatoes, grilled vegetables, and soft rolls that Claire declared better than any bakery in town.

Every time I turned around, someone had left a new glass of sparkling cider at my elbow. The champagne flowed freely for everyone else, and I didn't mind one bit. I was already tipsy from joy and hormones.

Dad kept hovering by the dessert table, claiming he was making sure the cake didn't melt. Julia and Claire had planted themselves near the dance floor and were telling anyone who'd listen that I'd been the calmest bride in family history.

When it came time for the first dance, Xander reached for me without saying a word. The music was soft, a classic tune played by a live quartet. I rested one hand on his shoulder and the other over his heart, letting him guide us in a slow circle that made the room tilt gently around us.

"You okay?" he asked, voice low enough that no one else could hear.

"I'm better than okay."

"You sure? You haven't stopped smiling since you walked down the aisle."

"I'm just afraid if I stop, I'll cry."

"Then don't stop."

I didn't.

After the dance, we mingled with guests, posed for photos, and managed to sneak two bites of cake before Claire noticed and brought us each a full slice. Dad made a speech that was equal parts sentimental and sarcastic, ending with a toast to "the man who spent half a million to marry my daughter and didn't even blink."

Everyone laughed, and Xander didn't deny it.

Then, just when I thought the surprises were done, Xander's dad took the microphone and cleared his throat with dramatic flair.

"Since we're already celebrating love," he said, glancing toward his girlfriend, Candy, "I'd like to officially announce that we're engaged."

A round of applause rippled through the tent, followed by delighted chatter from the older guests. Candy beamed and waved her hand, showing off a diamond that sparkled even in the soft light.

Julia and Claire immediately descended on her with questions about venues and dresses, dragging her halfway to the floral arch before the man of the hour could even finish his glass of champagne.

Xander leaned close and whispered, "Guess we're not the only ones stealing the spotlight tonight."

"I'm just glad someone else will be planning the next party."

As the evening wore on, I wandered from table to table, hearing every version of congratulations a person could imagine. Guests gushed over the food, the dress, and the music. Some of my cousins had started a dance line near the bar, and Claire joined them without hesitation. Julia held court with a group of women near the punch bowl, hands flailing as she retold every detail of the ceremony.

I felt full in every way a person could be full.

Later, after the sun dipped behind the trees and the fairy lights were the only thing keeping the yard from going dark, Xander took my hand and guided me toward the edge of the garden.

We sat on a bench away from the crowd, watching the last of the guests filter out. My feet ached and my back was tired, but none of that mattered. The weight of his hand in mine was grounding, and the way he looked at me told me I wasn't the only one quietly amazed we'd made it here.

"You did it," I said. "You made it through a wedding without any corporate emergencies or fire drills."

"There's still time," he replied. "Let's not tempt fate."

I leaned my head against his shoulder and sighed. "I think this was the happiest day of my life."

"I think it's just the start."

For once, I didn't worry about what came next. Not the nursery or the baby clothes or the long nights ahead. I didn't worry about how we'd juggle work and parenthood or who would do the dishes or if we'd argue over things like curtains and bedtime schedules.

I just sat there, full of cake and love and the kind of quiet peace that doesn't demand anything more than this—him, me, and the life we'd chosen together.

Claire found us eventually, dragging Julia with her, both of them carrying Tupperware full of leftovers and already arguing about baby shower themes.

"Don't forget to hydrate!" Claire warned as she handed me a water bottle.

Julia pressed a kiss to my cheek and grinned. "You're glowing, Amelia."

I smiled at them both and tucked myself a little closer to Xander.

"I really am."

Three months later

The hospital room was quiet except for the slow, steady beep of the monitor beside the bed. Outside the window, early morning light poured over the skyline, soft and warm against the white blinds. I could hear the faint shuffle of nurses at the station down the hall and the occasional squeak of rubber soles as someone passed by the doorway.

My entire world had narrowed to the small bassinet a few feet from my bed—and the warm, steady presence of the man sitting beside me.

Xander had barely moved in the past hour. One hand rested on the edge of the bassinet while the other propped up his chin. His eyes were fixed on the tiny, sleeping bundle inside like he still didn't believe she was real. I couldn't blame him. I had been holding her all night and I still wasn't sure any of this had really happened.

Our daughter.

The words still felt new, like trying on a name I hadn't earned yet. Everything about her seemed impossible. The way her fingers curled into little fists, how her nose wrinkled when she yawned, the perfect swirl of dark hair on the top of her head. She was seven pounds, four ounces of absolute wonder. And I was already wrapped around her tiny, wrinkled finger.

Xander reached down and adjusted the edge of the pink blanket tucked around her. He didn't say anything. He hadn't said much since she was born, just short, quiet sentences when the nurses asked questions, or when the doctor gave updates. It wasn't like him to be this still. But watching him now, I understood. This wasn't stillness. It was awe. Maybe even disbelief. We had talked about this moment for months, but living it was something else entirely.

He finally looked up and met my eyes. There were dark circles under his, and his stubble had grown into something just past charming. His tie from yesterday hung loose around his neck. His jacket was nowhere to be seen.

"She's asleep again," he said, his voice low and tired.

"I think she likes the sound of your voice," I said, smiling softly.

He glanced back at the bassinet, and a small smile tugged at the corner of his mouth. "That makes one of us."

I shifted carefully against the pillows and reached for the water on my tray. The soreness from labor was still present, a dull ache that stretched across my lower back and hips, but it felt distant now. I was too full of adrenaline and emotion to let it distract me.

"I thought you'd fall apart," I said, sipping slowly. "You've handled this better than I have."

Xander raised an eyebrow. "You're the one who pushed a human out of your body, and you're saying I've got the harder job?"

"You looked more nervous than I felt."

"I was terrified," he admitted, sitting back in the chair. "Every time a monitor beeped, I thought something was wrong. And when she finally came out, I just stood there like an idiot, waiting for someone to tell me what to do."

"You cut the cord without flinching."

"I flinched on the inside."

I laughed softly and watched as he rubbed his eyes with the heel of his hand. For all his worry, he hadn't left my side. Not once. Not when labor started, not when the contractions hit their worst, and not when she finally arrived, red-faced and wailing, her little fists swinging in the air. He had stayed, eyes locked on me, jaw tight, one hand gripping mine like a lifeline. And when the doctor handed her to me, his face broke open in a way I had never seen before.

"You cried," I said.

"No, I didn't."

"You absolutely did."

"I had something in my eye."

"You had a full breakdown in your eye, then."

He leaned back in the chair and crossed his arms over his chest. "Don't tell your aunts. Julia will write a song about it."

I smiled, remembering the look on their faces when we called them with the news. Julia had immediately burst into tears and demanded photos. Claire had sworn she was driving up with lasagna whether we wanted it or not. Dad had arrived with balloons and flowers and a copy of *What to Expect in the First Year* like we hadn't already read everything we could find.

He had also cried, quietly and without fanfare, while holding her for the first time. He didn't say much, but I saw the way his fingers shook, the way he whispered her name like a prayer.

We hadn't settled on it until we saw her. We'd had a short list— three names we both liked—but nothing felt right until she opened her eyes and stared up at us like she was already sizing up the world.

Lena Grace Blackwell.

It suited her. Strong, soft, timeless.

Xander reached for the small card the nurse had left and flipped it over in his hands. Her name was printed in neat handwriting, along with her weight and the time of birth. He read it again and again like it would change if he stopped paying attention.

"She's going to grow up here," he said. "In this world. With us."

I reached out and took his hand again. "That's the plan."

"I want her to have everything we didn't."

"She will."

"I'm serious."

"So am I."

He looked at me again, and the emotion behind his eyes made my chest tighten. "I want her to know she's safe. That she's loved. That we're not going anywhere."

"She'll know," I said. "Because you'll show her. The same way you've shown me."

He leaned forward and pressed a kiss to my forehead, then rested his against mine. We sat like that, tangled up in the silence, listening to the steady breath of our newborn daughter. There were no big declarations, no grand promises. Just the quiet certainty that we were in this now—for real, for good.

A soft knock came at the door, and a nurse peeked in with a clipboard in hand.

"Ready for discharge in the morning?" she asked.

Xander nodded. "We're ready."

The nurse smiled and stepped back out. The door clicked shut, and I looked over at the duffel bag in the corner. It was already packed. Clothes for me, a tiny going-home outfit for Lena, a pink blanket with her name embroidered on the corner. It was all waiting.

We were going home.

Home to a life I hadn't imagined a year ago. Home with a husband who had once sworn off love, and a baby who made every sharp edge in both of us a little softer. I had no illusions about what the next few months would bring. Sleepless nights, messy mornings, uncertain steps—but also joy. Laughter. The kind of moments we'd never be able to plan for.

I had everything I needed.

A family.

A future.

Love that stayed.

Continue the steamy romance with the next book in the Billionaire Baby Daddies series: ***Daddy's Accidental Babies***

Want exclusive content and new release updates? **Join my newsletter here.**

ALSO BY SOFIA T SUMMERS

Billionaire Baby Daddies
Knocked Up by the Silver Fox | Silver Fox's Twin Babies | Daddy's Double Surprise | Daddy's Dirty Little Secret

Forbidden Fantasies
My Irish Billionaires | Toy for the Teachers | Three Grumpy Bosses | Feasting on Her Curves | 4 SEAL Daddies | Ice Cold Hearts | Nanny for the Bratva Daddies | The Professors' Plaything | Age Gap Academy | Snowbound with the Santas | The Naughty Elf | Pucked and Pregnant | Power Play with My Brother's Irish Friends | The SEALs' Single Mom Baby Surprise | Campus Daddies

Forbidden Doctors
Doctor's Surprise Twins | Written in the Charts | Rendezvous with My Resident | The Doctor's Twin Secrets | My Ex Boyfriend's Dad | Secret Baby for Dr. Dreamy | The Doctor's Secret | Baby Bump | Doctor Baby Daddy | Wi-Fi Wifey | Dirty, Bossy Doctor | Code Blue | Doctor Daddy Dilemma | Doctor's Orders | Dr. Wrong | Grumpy Doctor's Holiday Twins | Dr. Scandal Claus

Forbidden Temptations
Daddy's Best Friend | My Best Friend's Daddy | Daddy's Business Partner | Doctor Daddy | Secret Baby with Daddy's Best Friend | Knocked Up by Daddy's Best Friend | Pretend Wife to Daddy's Best Friend | SEAL Daddy | Fake Married to My Best Friend's Daddy | Accidental Daddy | The Grump's Girl Friday | The Vegas Accident | My Beastly Boss | My Millionaire Marine | The Wedding Dare | The Summer Getaway | The Love Edit | The Husband Lottery | Christmas in the Cabin | A Very Naughty Christmas | Make Me Whole | Take a Chance

Forbidden Promises
Maid Without Honour | The Wedding Witness | Honeymoon Hoax

CONNECT WITH SOFIE

Want to receive extended epilogues, sexy deleted scenes, freebies, and new release alerts?

For all things Sofia, join her VIP Hangout here.

Printed in Dunstable, United Kingdom